S0-FAH-728

"If I promise not to faint on you,
could I have just one last kiss?"

A chill of shock ran up her spine at her outrageous
words.

He froze, staring at her for several heartbeats as she tried
to convince herself that she hadn't really said it, that her
mind, fuzzy from champagne, had just imagined it.

Then she was in his arms, inside the cabin, the door
kicked closed behind him. He rained kisses across her
eyes, her cheeks, her mouth, down her pulsing throat. . . .

"Oh, thank you," she sighed, profoundly relieved until
she realized his hands still lingered inside her gaping
dress. She stiffened, but only for the briefest second—his
touch felt too undeniably delicious. . . .

RIVER TEMPTRESS

ELAINE CRAWFORD

DIAMOND BOOKS, NEW YORK

If you purchased this book without a cover you should be aware that this book is stolen property. It was reported as "unsold and destroyed" to the publisher and neither the author nor the publisher has received any payment for this "stripped book."

This book is a Diamond original edition, and has never been previously published.

RIVER TEMPTRESS

A Diamond Book / published by arrangement with the author

PRINTING HISTORY
Diamond edition / March 1993

All rights reserved.
Copyright © 1993 by Dianna Crawford.
This book may not be reproduced in whole or in part, by mimeograph or any other means, without permission.
For information address: The Berkley Publishing Group, 200 Madison Avenue, New York, NY 10016.

ISBN: 1-55773-867-X

Diamond Books are published by The Berkley Publishing Group, 200 Madison Avenue, New York, NY 10016.
The name "DIAMOND" and its logo are trademarks belonging to Charter Communications, Inc.

PRINTED IN THE UNITED STATES OF AMERICA

10 9 8 7 6 5 4 3 2 1

THIS BOOK IS DEDICATED TO

the child in all of us
and especially the imp
in all my girls:

Lisa, Susan, Rachel and Megan.
Julie and Valorie. Angie,
Caitlin, and little Em.

RIVER TEMPTRESS

Chapter
One

Oregon Territory, 1853

FROM HIGH ON the pilothouse deck, Georgie Pacquing saw him. Saw, heck! Who could miss him? The braggart strutted up the gangplank like some vain showboat actor, flaunting that lean, trim body in a silver-gray suit only an eastern tailor could've fitted so perfectly. With his stovepipe hat at that rakish tilt and his boots polished to a mirror shine, the man virtually exuded power and money . . . a little too much.

Georgie pulled a rag from the pocket of her dungarees and began wiping the engine grease from her hands while she continued to watch. A smug smile played across her lips. He couldn't fool her. The scoundrel was nothing but a gulling riverboat gambler. Although she'd been gone from the Mississippi for more than two years, she could still spot that cocky swagger in a rapids-shooting second.

Her gaze swept over several fool daughters of the local frontier folk who were vying for his attention. They crowded close, their behinds wagging worse than a pack of hound dogs'. And even the deaf could've heard their high-pitched titters, the way their caterwauling pierced through all the bumps and clatter of the merry crowd of boarding passengers on this balmy summer afternoon.

Taking up the rear of the little parade, a tiny Negro in a bright red coat led a dappled gray thoroughbred onto the steamboat *Willamette.*

The animal pranced aboard with a mane-tossing flare that matched its owner's.

The "southern gentleman" picture was complete.

Seemingly unaffected by all the adoring females, the arrogant impostor lifted his gaze and leisurely scanned the promenade deck. Probably looking for some likely suckers, Georgie thought with a snort.

He looked up higher, past the crew's quarters, to the top level, where his gaze skimmed past her as if she didn't exist.

She felt slighted . . . but only for a second. After all, from what he could see, she was nothing but some lowly keel boy. But she wouldn't have had it any other way. She'd never known such freedom before she'd arrived in Oregon and had been allowed to dress and work like her papa and her brother Cadie.

The man turned away to speak to the one with the horse while a fluttery-eyed female tugged at his sleeve.

"Hey, squirt!"

Georgie swung around to see old Hilly limping out the pilothouse door. "D'you find what caused that noise in the engine?"

"Yep." She made a point of twisting her face the way most lads did when they tried to look manly. Wouldn't do to have the gruff river pilot suspect she was a girl. "A coupla bolts needed tightenin', that's all."

"Then you best round up yer pa, boy. It's agittin' late, an' I wanna take this tub on upriver 'fer it's too dark to see. 'Sides," he said, peering down to the lower decks, "if'n we don't shove off soon, we're gonna be swamped.

'Pears like the whole blamed town's tryin' to ketch a easy ride to the doin's tomorry in Independence.''

Georgie tugged her floppy wide-brimmed hat farther down in an effort to hide her own irrepressible high spirits as well as any stray locks trying to escape the hidden coil of dark copper hair. ''Yeah. You'd think we were docked in a big city like New Orleans or St. Louie. But I guess now that Salem's Oregon's capital, it's really startin' to grow.''

The crusty-faced old grouch suddenly craned his neck and pointed downward. ''Would'ya look at that! That Kingston fella is gonna be ridin' our boat. He's the newcomer what outbid ever'body at the auction today. Plunked down seven hunnard dollars *cash money* fer McLean's racehorse. And would you believe that thoroughbred come with its own jockey? That must be some kinda animal.''

''I thought you couldn't trade in slaves here in the territory.''

''That was a sticker. They knew they couldn't put the little bugbear on the block, so the auctioneer let it slip out real slylike that his papers was in the same envelope with the stallion's.''

More interested in the new owner, Georgie eyed his ascent up the grand staircase to the promenade deck. ''Where'd you say Mr. Kingston was from?''

Hilly absently scratched his fleshy ribs. ''Don't know. All I heared is he was on his way to San Francisco but his ship couldn't make port 'cause a some storm. It sailed on up here, an' he took a notion to git off and have a look around. Some look! Now he owns the horse what's set to race Jake Stone's tomorry. This is gonna be the goldarnedest Fourth of July this territory's ever seen.

'Course, most ever'body's bettin' on Stone's Prince. We all seen that black streak run a time or two.''

Georgie looked down at the superbly-muscled animal being led toward the stern of the boat. "Well, if McLean had that gray thoroughbred shipped in to beat Jake's, it just might be somethin' to reckon with.''

The pilot gave a disdainful grunt and turned back to the wheelhouse. "Far's ever'one's concerned, that nag's chances is as dead as Kyle McLean, may the thievin' bastard burn in hell.'' He turned back. "Now, git on down and fetch yer pa, boy. Last I seen, the captain was over at Fiddler's celebratin' wi' that no-'count stern-wheeler pilot, Sooner Boone.''

"Fiddler's? Oh, no." Georgie clenched her fists. Papa was drinking again, and after he'd promised not to just last night. She sprinted for the steep stairway leading to the crew deck, then vaulted down two steps at a time. She had to find Papa and get him back without anyone noticing. Their life here in the West depended on it. She sailed down the next flight and careened out of the stairwell onto the passenger deck.

Strolling with his admirers, Mr. Kingston walked directly into her path.

She swerved to one side . . . just as he also bent in that direction to retrieve a wind-skittered handkerchief that one of the young ladies had dropped quite obviously.

The man's arm shot out, striking Georgie's waist.

She ricocheted off and landed several feet away in a bruising sprawl. "Judas priest!" she yelped.

"Watch your language," scolded one of the bevy, her hands set on a waist so tightly corseted it looked almost freakish above her cumbersome hoopskirt.

"And apologize to the gentleman *at once*," ordered another with a haughty sniff.

"Bilge water!" Georgie pulled her hat down more securely before rubbing the pain from a spot on her hip. "He knocked into me."

"The kid's right."

The man's smooth baritone voice drew Georgie's attention up to a face that caught her totally by surprise. He was perfect—features strong and masculine but with just a touch of refinement. The subtle outline of his cheekbones framed by dark sideburns, the straight nose, the no-nonsense chin—all bespoke a man who could easily take the moment, any moment. But then she looked up into the bluest eyes . . . and perfection stopped. Absolutely nothing of the man's character could be fathomed, no hint of an emotion. Not the slightest clue to his soul peeked through—if, indeed, the gulling gambler had one.

"What's the matter, kid? You hurt?"

Georgie felt dumber than a stump. She'd been gawking up at the most intriguingly handsome man she'd ever seen while she lay flopping on the deck like a fish. And she'd been rubbing her butt to boot. She scrambled to get up before he could catch her face turning red.

"Here, let me help you." He reached down to her as if he thought she was some whine-bag sissy.

She slapped his hand out of the way. "I don't need no help from some ol' fancy pants." After springing to her feet, she took off at a dead run.

"Young man!" one of the girls snapped as Georgie dodged away through a steady stream of passengers. "The captain's certainly going to hear about you!"

The captain's certainly going to hear about you. The waspish words echoed in Georgie's ears as she bounded down the gangplank and trotted past the warehouse toward Fiddler's Saloon at the far end of the wharf. It was glaringly clear that the uppity twit had been trying to get Kingston to pay her special mind—another pitiful attempt at netting what the ignorant girl thought was a splendid catch. Just like the other two. But of course the only thing any of those backwoods belles was going to catch was a draft up her skirts if she was ninny enough to let the bounder take her for a moonlight tumble. And from the looks of things, he'd be sure to get at least one of them. Unless . . .

Georgie slowed to a stop and let her boldly expressive Pacquing mouth slide mischievously into a grin. "Unless I step in and save them from the rake. Wouldn't it be fun to see their chins hit the ground as I waltz him out from under their noses? And I could do it, too, easy as floating downstream." After all, she hadn't spent most of her life aboard a big Mississippi side-wheeler for nothing. She'd seen every wile known to Eve used on an endless string of unsuspecting dolts. And hadn't her Mommy forced her to attend Miss Pritchard's Academy whenever there'd been extra money? With grudging reluctance, she'd eventually learned the part of the most proper Miss Lark Ellen Georgette Pacquing, accomplished in all the latest dances and able to pour tea with whalebone stiffness. She'd even learned how to flirt from behind a fan with the best of them.

"What's the matter with me?" she demanded as logic took the fore. "Why in tarnation would I want to spend the day dallying with some flimflammer?" She started again in a determined march toward the door of the squalid drinking shanty, now only a few yards away.

"But wouldn't it be fun to pluck that peacock's tail feathers?" Her steps faltered. "Make up for the way those scalawags gulled poor Papa after Mommy died." She sent the wide flare of her auburn brows soaring. If it hadn't been for those low-life gamblers, they would still have their own fancy steamboat on the Ol' Muddy instead of that grubby little stern-wheeler over on the Columbia. They wouldn't have had to make tracks out of there to escape the creditors. Wouldn't be out here alone, away from the rest of the family and their friends.

Until this last month, when her father had been asked to temporarily captain the *Willamette* on the Willamette tributary, and she'd once again felt the thrill of running a big river queen, Georgie had managed to bury the shame of losing their own side-wheeler, the *Ellie Sue*, along with her father's good name. But now an opportunity to make one of those thieves squirm a little reared its vengeful head. And who knew what else might present itself if she dressed up and started cat-and-mousing with him?

"Forget it," she muttered. One day's sport was in no way worth the possibility of having her sex discovered by the "good" ladies along the river. If they learned the truth, the old biddies wouldn't give up till they badgered her easygoing papa into trapping Georgie into a girl's life again.

A couple of laughing rowdies banged out of the saloon, then drifted in her direction.

With hands jammed in her pockets, Georgie gave them a wide berth as she passed by and stepped onto the loosely planked boardwalk in front of the crude building.

Even before she pushed her way through the swinging doors, she heard the slur in her papa's clipped Cajun cadence and the telltale buoyancy in his voice. An uneasy chill crawled up her spine.

Louie Pacquing lounged at the bar of the smoke-filled room with several others, too involved in the conversation to notice her entrance. Lazily propped on one elbow, he held aloft a small glass brimming with amber liquid.

"An' I say dis, huh? Da gray nag, it could grow wings, and Jake Stone's horse, he still take him. I see dat Prince run agains' some braggin' colonel's hunter last fall at Fort Vancouver. And Prince, huh? He take off so fast, it look like de udder he runnin' back asswards."

One of the rivermen guffawed like a braying donkey while the others chuckled at her father's story.

Louie's face crinkled gaily as he displayed every tooth in a rowdy grin that sent his thick black mustache soaring. He raised the drink to his lips and downed it.

The sight twisted Georgie's belly into a knot, and she stopped a few feet short of the clustered merrymakers.

"And I—" When Louie spotted his daughter, his lively expression collapsed and his snappy dark eyes lost their sparkle, but an instant later all returned with force. "Georgie!"

She made a haphazard attempt at returning his smile. "Hilly says it's time to go."

"Oh, right, right." He adjusted his captain's cap and ambled toward her while looking back over his shoulder. "Reckon I see you boys dere tomorrow." Then, amid a barrage of enthusiastic replies, he dropped his arm around Georgie and walked her out to the deserted wharf.

Nearing the crowd moving onto the huge moored boat, Georgie could smell the whiskey on her father's breath. She wrinkled her nose with distaste. "Papa, you promised."

He squeezed her shoulder and singsonged, "'Ey, I know. And I be keepin' dat promise, too, *chère*. After tomorrow not anudder drop pass dese lips. But dis be da Fourt a July, liddle one. A man, he gotta celebrate, huh? Gotta be patriotic." He glanced her way and took a long breath. "But you know dat Cadie a mine. He stubborn, just like his oder brudders. So, we let dis be our liddle secret, no?''

Georgie pulled away and eyed him.

He gave her his most pleading smile, the one that always melted her resolve.

''Oh, all right. But you know, if Cadie finds out, he won't leave, even if he does have his own paddle-wheeler waiting for him back in Natchez.''

Wagging his head, Louie shrugged. ''I know. 'Ey, all my boys, dey take after dey *maman*, no? God res' her soul. But she could be a hard woman sometime. But dat can be good, huh? Rou and Dulac, dey aready have dey own boats 'fore my Ellen is took from me.'' He flashed a hapless smile. ''Lucky ting for us, no?''

Georgie looked away quickly and started walking again, not wanting him to see any hint of pity in her eyes. ''Yeah. And it's been fun. Starting over out here with all the other pioneers, everything kinda loose and free. And the rivers are a whole lot more exciting, 'specially the Columbia. Wish we were back there now.''

Louie cuffed the top of Georgie's hat. ''My liddle tomboy, no? You sure love shootin' da rapids up on Da Dalles, don't you, huh?''

''You bet. Mostly when I'm at the wheel. Be glad when we can leave the Willamette River and this lumbering tub and get back to our own little boat.''

Louie's gravelly voice weakened, a longing coming through. ''I kinda like da feel a standin' high up on a pilothouse deck again. Captainin' a boatful a people 'stead a just a stack a logs, no?''

''We'll get it back, Papa. In time.''

''I don' know,'' he sighed. ''Widout you *maman* . . .'' He took her hand and pulled her closer, and for the first time Georgie noticed how much her father had aged in the past three years. "'Ey, did I ever tell you 'bout da first time I ever see her, huh? She be sittin' in a swing, lookin' so beautiful. In a light green dress, soft, like a summer day. I was walkin' up da road from Natchez, goin' to see ol' man Robeline 'bout a load a cotton he promise. An' dere she sat, all alone. Da sunlight, it peek trough da leaves a dat big old oak. Yeah . . . look like someone sprinkle new pennies all down her copper hair. And my Ellen, she smiled up at me. I never forget, huh? She dis sensible daughter a dat Yankee storekeeper. Ah, dat man, he don' even know how to smile. And me, I be dis happy-go-lucky Cajun river rat, huh? Still don' know how I ever talk her into runnin' away wit me. But she did." He nodded absently. "She did."

Georgie found herself caressing his stubbly cheek. "Mommy always said you could talk the birds out of the trees."

"Dat's why I insist we call you Lark when you was born wid her same copper hair. My sweet liddle Lark Ellen."

His eyes glazed with tears so wrenching, Georgie felt her own throat clog.

"Told her you was da purdiest liddle songbird I ever did talk outta her, huh? But you know you *maman*, she say it a frivolous name and insist on addin' Georgette, after my sister. . . . But you *beautiful* hair," he whispered, thumbing the limp brim of her felt hat. "You ought a be proud of it, 'stead a keepin' it hid all da time. You *maman*, she want—"

"I know, Papa. In fact, I was just thinking about getting all dressed up for the big day tomorrow."

"I'd like dat. Maybe you only have my Ellen's hair an' her long legs, huh?" Suddenly the sadness in his dark eyes turned to a watery twinkle, and he smiled. "But all da rest a dem good looks you get from you Cajun papa. But da way you carry youself when you all decked out, dat's when I see her most in you. . . ."

Watching his fragile joy begin to diminish again, Georgie took his hand and started pulling him toward the festive throng at the dock. "Then it's settled," she said before slipping into her most syrupy southern drawl. "Tomorra I'll turn mahself into the most *gorgeous* lil ol' heart-stopper y'all ever did lay eyes on."

Yes, Georgie thought, I'll do it. Excitement trilled through her, and she smiled. Tomorrow.

Chapter Two

PIERCE KINGSTON RUSHED out of his cabin aboard the *Willamette*. He rammed a second diamond stud through the starched white cuff of his brown striped shirt, then strode quickly down the hall and out onto the promenade deck. How could he have overslept today of all days? There was too much to do, too many preparations to make.

Walking toward the head of the grand staircase, he felt the twinge of a hangover and took a couple of deep breaths. The cool morning air helped almost immediately. Although he rarely had more than a glass or two of wine—in his profession, a muddled brain could easily wipe him out—last night in all the excitement, he couldn't stop folks from shoving drinks at him. And what the hell. It had felt good to have his company sought after, for a change.

And what a welcome change it was after years of being treated as if no amount of bathing would wash away his shame and no degree of accomplishment or amount of money could buy it away. But last night was a foretaste of how his life might be again. The way it had been before he learned the truth. And before that old witch saw to it that everyone else from New Orleans to St. Louis also knew.

But no more. That was all behind him now.

Shaking the hated feelings from his mind for what he hoped was the last time, he again recalled the reason for his overwhelming popularity, and a chuckle bounced out as he started down the flight of stairs. The riverboat had been virtually overrun with exuberant people intent on making him welcome *before* the big race, since they were all absolutely certain he wouldn't be celebrating afterward. Their overconfidence in the local favorite would only make the odds better, which hadn't dampened his own spirits one bit either. Because, if that little horse trainer was right, this was going to be one lucky day . . . for both of them.

Reaching the main deck, Pierce stopped long enough to tilt his low-crowned hat over one eyebrow before smoothing the fit of his tan linen waistcoat and checking the shine on his brown boots. Who would've thought last week, when the schooner had been forced to bypass San Francisco on its way to Portland, that he'd stumble onto such an incredible opportunity? And in the backwaters of this wilderness, of all places. Yes, Pierce, my boy, he told himself silently, today is going to be your lucky day.

"Mornin', Mr. Kingston," came a high-pitched trill.

He swung around to see one of the young ladies from the afternoon before closing in on him with her parents. "Good morning." Jennifer? Mary Lou? Damnation! Which one was she?

Wrapping an arm around the girl's waist, her amply padded mother smiled up at Pierce while giving the skinny lass a hug. "My, my, what a pleasant coincidence. We was just talkin' about you. Jenny, here, and me was just tellin' her daddy that we don't care if the whole of Oregon is bettin' on Jake Stone's horse. I got some egg money set aside, and me and Jenny's gonna put it all on yours, Mr. Kingston. Even if we have to march into that awful saloon and place the bet ourselves. Ain't that right, Jen?''

The freckle-faced girl's deep-set blue eyes avoided his and found her feet, her cheeks reddening to a mottled blush that matched the roses on her bonnet. ''Mama, *stop*. What*ever* will Mr. Kingston think?''

Her mother's expression turned conspiratorial as she held Pierce in her sights. ''Why, honey cakes, he'll just know we got a real eye for fine breedin'.''

The very phrase, ''fine breeding,'' set Pierce on edge, especially since she'd directed it at him. He forced a smile past stiff lips. ''Absolutely. A horse like mine wouldn't even know how to lose.''

''We'll see,'' came a congenial but smug reply from the rawboned father, an older male version of the freckled girl. He stretched out a callused hand in a friendly welcome. ''Don't think we been properly intro- duced. Name's Nate Swenson. I run a mill just downriver from Salem.''

Relaxing, Pierce matched Swenson's grip with a hearty handshake. ''Glad to meet you.'' He then swung his attention to a meadow across the river teeming with belly-high grass, then beyond to a forest of the tallest trees he'd ever seen. ''I just arrived a couple of days ago. But from what I can see, Oregon has the promise of a rich future.''

''Yeah. While all them gold-crazed fools is scratchin' an' fightin' over some colored dust down Californy way, we already got what they hope it'll buy.''

The man couldn't be more right. Damn, but it felt good to be here now with a handsome profit from his latest investments tucked in his breast pocket and a horse fully capable of multiplying his small fortune, turning his

dreams into reality. And for the first time since his secret
had been laid open and spread on the winds of gossip, he
felt an inkling of his respectability returning. It had been
years since any mother had sought him for her daughter.
"I do agree, Mr. Swenson. We're the lucky ones."

The man's narrow face cracked into a smile. "We was
just takin' a stroll around the decks before goin' in to
breakfast. Would you care to join us?"

The girl shot him a hopeful look.

His own gaze swept past her to the almost-as-eager
older couple. If only she appealed to him in the slightest.
"What a pleasant invitation. But, alas, I have business to
attend to. I was just on my way down to see about my
new acquisition."

Jennifer's mouth drooped at the corners. "Oh, what a
shame."

He couldn't help but pity the girl. Plain as she was,
beaux would be hard to come by. "But I'll be looking
forward to seeing you folks at the festivities. I understand
the horse race is drawing quite a crowd."

"Just about ever'body in the territory," crowed Mrs.
Swenson.

"Yes," Jennifer agreed with renewed enthusiasm.
"There's gonna be log-rollin' contests an' tree climbin'
an' a greased-hog chase an' pie judgin' an ever'thing.
Just like a fair. Better."

"Sounds like fun. But if I don't want to miss out, I'd
better take care of my business." With a nod, Pierce
tipped his hat and left them behind, striding off toward
the stern of the big boat. This would probably be the only
chance he and the Negro jockey would have to talk.
Before long, throngs of people would be crawling all
over the riverboat just as they had last night when it
arrived in the small settlement.

Independence. Even the name sounded lucky for a Fourth of July race.

But as he wove his way aft past bulging gunnysacks, bales, and barrels, that same old anxiety started gnawing at his gut again. It slowed him to a stop. Who was he to think Lady Luck would deal him a winning hand with this much on the table? Yet here he was, letting his hopes run away with him like some greenhorn fool.

Why not? He shot a glance at the river, clean and swift—nothing like the slow, muddy waterways back East. Yes, he had left all the muck and mire behind. Out here a man could stand as tall and straight as his accomplishments. His eyes wandered up the reddish bark of a massive cedar edging the bank. This would be his day. He'd take the gamble, cover every bet he could, make a bundle off the race. Then, with his winnings and that champion thoroughbred, he'd start a fine horse farm in this rich, verdant valley. He could already imagine the long stretches of whitewashed fence. A columned mansion standing at the end of a shaded lane, grand as any he'd ever seen in the South. Finer, even, than his father's. At the thought, a flash of rage bolted through him.

No! Absolutely no more dwelling on the past. He exhaled sharply, clearing all trace of the man from his brain.

Starting aft again, he returned to his pleasant musing. After he built the house, he'd find himself a lovely belle, the most gorgeous this new land had to offer. With her on his arm, he'd host such galas the countryside would be buzzing about them for months afterward.

He'd send for his mother.

If his horse won the race.

No, *when*. After all, how many thoroughbreds came with their own private trainer?

A whiff of frying bacon caused Pierce's stomach to grind. He hadn't realized how hungry he was. Dink, the tiny horse trainer was sure to be, too.

Dink.

What a twist of fate. To think he'd actually become a slave owner. What would his mother think? Or his Quaker friends in Pennsylvania? And after all the money he'd sent them to help finance the Underground Railroad.

But for better or worse Dink was his responsibility—at least for now.

A tantalizing aroma came from the cookhouse perched between decks on its storeroom.

Pierce started up the stairs. He'd knocked at galley doors more times than he could count back in the days when he'd made his first real money aboard the river queens. A little coin in the chef's palm and he'd never had to wait his turn in a salon filled with other travelers.

With two coffee mugs balanced on plates heaped with eggs, bacon, and biscuits, Pierce found Dink in a roped-off area within the shadow of the two giant side-wheels.

The slave's kinky head bobbed up and down just above the magnificent gray's back as he ran a big brush over the sleek coat. He broke into a brilliant smile as soon as he saw Pierce. "Massah Kingston. How's y'all doin' dis mo'nin, massah?"

The man's subservience bit into Pierce like a whip to an old wound. "I would prefer that you call me Mister. Mr. Kingston. Or even Pierce. Whatever." He handed a plate to the slave. "Take some time out and eat your breakfast. Sorry it's late."

Dink's thin brows soared, and he bounced onto his toes as he stared at the heaped plate. "Dis all fo' me?"

"I told the cook to give you extra."

"Dese biscuits, dey's got buttah an' jam on 'em, an' dey's cream in da coffee."

"Oh, I didn't think. I told him to fix both plates the same."

"Ain't no call to fret, sah. I's plumb tickled. You bringin' me all dem good fixin's las' night. An' now dis mo'nin'." His gaze locked on to the plate again. Picking up his fork, he attacked his food with gusto.

Feeling more pity than pleasure for the diminutive man, Pierce pulled out his handkerchief and dusted off a nearby crate, then sat down and motioned for Dink to join him. "Have a seat."

The slave's eyes darted to the long slatted box and back to him. "Sah, I cain't do dat. T'ain't mah place."

"Sit!" The harshness in Pierce's voice surprised him. But Dink's servility was wearing thin. Even the Negro's name sounded demeaning, and Pierce hadn't been able to bring himself to use it yet. "Sorry. Please, sit down. We need to talk."

Dink almost tiptoed as he sidled up and eased himself down, obviously uncomfortable as he balanced his plate on his lap.

Pierce noted that the slave's drab gray attire was rumpled, as if he'd slept in it. "Besides that red coat you had on yesterday, are those the only clothes you have?"

With a biscuit poised halfway to his mouth, Dink turned to Pierce. "Oh, no, sah, don't y'all be worrin' 'bout dat. Pegasus an' me, we'll both be sportin' fine colors fo' da race today. Massah McLean see to it dat we be lookin' proud as a Fo'th a July flag."

"Speaking of this Mr. McLean, I got the distinct impression last night that he wasn't at all well liked."

"Waal, sah, I don' know dat much 'bout him. He

brung me an' Pegasus out heah from Mar'lan' just a couple months back. But dat man, he sho had big plans.'' The Negro wagged his head. ''He say he gonna be the importantest man in dese parts soon. Say he ain't lettin' no dirt farmer brag on havin' da fas'est hoss aroun'.''

''I take it either McLean didn't have any heirs or there were a lot of debtors waiting with their hands out, since his estate was being auctioned off.'' Waiting for a reply, Pierce picked up his mug and took a sip.

Dink looked away. ''Not zactly. Massah McLean, he be cheatin' an' trickin' folks outta dey land. An' when he gots found out, he try to git away an' got hisself kilt.''

Pierce grinned. ''You don't say.''

The slave shot him a surprised look.

Pierce realized how crass he'd sounded and quickly added, ''Not that I'd wish anyone dead, but now I understand why everyone is so set on Jake Stone's horse winning. Not only is Stone well liked, but folks are figuring if McLean got his comeuppance, so will his horse. That's why I was able to get Pegasus so cheap. Hell, you alone are worth twice what I paid for both of you.''

''Yassah, that was a real shamin' thing, that mahv-'lous animal an' me goin' for such a low sum. I couldn't hardly hol' mah head up.''

Pierce stared at Dink, amazed, as the trainer shoveled in some scrambled eggs. It had never occurred to him that a slave would take pride in the amount he would bring on the auction block.

A few feet away, the stallion nickered, and Pierce took another long, appraising look at the animal. And again, as he had the day before, he couldn't imagine a more perfectly proportioned horse. Last night when everyone was spouting that same tired myth about a gray not being able to run worth spit, the talk had only served to elate him. He'd already made a point of getting the facts. Just before Pegasus was put on the block, he'd managed to get Dink aside long enough to slip the slave a gold eagle in exchange for some crucial numbers. And he'd hardly been able to believe his ears when he heard that the animal's best time for the mile was a minute and forty-four seconds flat. If the horse ran even close to that today, it'd be sure to win.

But he needed to hear Dink say it one more time. He turned back to the jockey-trainer. "You yourself witnessed Pegasus being clocked at one minute forty-four?"

Dink gulped down a mouthful of food. "Yassah. I's ridin' him at da time. My massah, he be real sad when he has ta sell him. But las' year was real bad fo' tobaccy, an' he jist got hisself a fancy new wife. Needed some quick money. Couldn't wait fo' racin' season."

"So you think Pegasus will beat Stone's Prince?"

"Ain't got nary a doubt, sah. Don' mattah what bloodline dat utter hoss come from or what a natural-bo'n runner he be. Mine has been trained fo' onliest one thing since da day he come outta his mama. Dat's ta carry me a winnah acrost dat finishin' line. We's built up his muscles to do jist dat. Now, folks 'roun' here'll tell you Massah McLean bought him for a saddle hoss, but dat ain't so. He only rode 'im out into the countryside a couple a times, so's folks'd think dat. Jist to raise da odds."

"Your Mr. McLean seems to have been a very clever fellow."

Dink's big eyes sparked. "Not clevah 'nough." The beginnings of a laugh squeaked out, but he muffled it with his hand.

Pierce's eggs looked cold. He took several bites, giving the trainer a chance to do the same before he asked any more questions. But once he and the slave had finished eating, he continued where they'd left off. "Do you know anything about the other horse's training?"

Dink set his plate aside and stood. Shrugging, he grinned. "It don' matter. The man what owns him uses him for a mount. An' from what I hear, da man's big as a tree. Dat means da hoss done be built up fo' carryin' 'stead a runnin'."

"So you're certain Pegasus will win."

"Lessen he trips in a chuckhole. An' I'll be walkin' ever' step a da racecourse dis mornin' to make sure dat don' happen."

Pierce could hardly believe his luck. Every time the man spoke, it was like being dealt another ace. But just to make absolutely sure . . .

Pierce rose to his feet, reached into the inside pocket of his waistcoat, and drew out a thick sheaf of bank notes. He counted out five one-hundred-dollar bills and handed them to his slave.

Dink just stared, his mouth slack. He didn't even close his hand over them.

"It's yours, win or lose. A little something for after the race. When you start your new life . . . as a free man."

Dink gasped. "What dat you say?"

"Think I'll take the rest of my money," Pierce drawled, stretching the moment as he stuffed the remainder back in his pocket, "and bet it on Pegasus. If you'd like, I'll place a wager for you, too."

"Did y'all say I's gonna be free?"

Pierce's eyes began to water as he rested a hand on the man's thin shoulder. Even winning the race wouldn't outdo this moment. "That's right."

"Then, here." Dink shoved the bank notes back at Pierce. "Bet it all! I's gonna be free *an'* rich!"

That was what he wanted to hear. If Dink was willing, *eager*, to bet the whole of his brand-new future on Pegasus, Pierce could do no less.

Then suddenly Dink's joyous expression collapsed. "Y'all's jist funnin' me, ain't ya?"

He took Dink by the other shoulder and gave him the sincerest look he could muster. "Believe me, I would never be so cruel."

"But I don' understan'. I's worth a pile a money. Why would y'all do such a thing?"

"Don't get me to thinking," Pierce said, releasing Dink. He paused deliberately, but a grin crept through as he stalled long enough to adjust the tilt of his rakishly shaped hat. "Or I may come to my senses."

The sharp crack of gunshots sliced the air.

He turned portside and glanced out between the paddles of the giant wheel. "Sounds like the celebrating is already getting started. Think I'll stroll on into town. Check out the odds." Cocking a brow, he thumped the slanted dip of the stiff brim. "And maybe a pretty face or two."

"From what I seed, they ain't nothin' 'roun' here but plain an' simple farm gals. Nothin' like dem fancy-dressed ladies what grows back home in Mar'lan'."

Visions of fetching young Louisiana belles flirting behind their lace fans accelerated Pierce's heartbeat. He had seen them strolling past the ornate iron scrollwork that adorned the windows and gates of New Orleans, their hooped gowns of every imaginable color swaying from side to side with each graceful step. So lovely . . . so forbidden.

Pierce's grin began to slip. He propped it up again. "Even in this rustic wilderness, there's bound to be one or two fair damsels who'd turn a man's head."

Chapter
Three

PIERCE SAW HER coming his way, this airy confection in pink and white. She fairly floated toward him beneath the lacy shade of a white parasol trimmed with roses to match those trailing down her voluminous tulle skirt. She so stunned the men crowded on the hotel's boardwalk that they stopped talking, and some literally jumped off to make room for the wide sweep of her hoops. Pierce couldn't have conjured up a more delectable sight.

"The race has been set for three o'clock," the Nordic-looking giant standing next to him said. "Will that be acceptable to you, Mr. Kingston?"

Turning away from her before he got a good look at her face took all of Pierce's willpower. He jerked a quick nod at Jake Stone. "Yes. Sounds fine." Then he cut his glance back to the lady who was now only yards away and closing on him. He could see her eyes, incredibly alive with a hint of mischief beneath an audacious arch of brows. And the color of those eyes! The richest deep copper, only a couple of shades darker than the light auburn hair piled above in curls. Pierce's heart started pounding like some fool schoolboy's.

"What's everybody staring at?" Stone asked as he turned toward her.

The beauty flashed a smile so broad, so stunning, it

rivaled her eyes. "Jake," she sang as she stopped before Pierce and the other horse owner, who was plainly dressed. She held out a sheerly gloved hand. "I haven't seen y'all in quite a spell."

Taking her hand, Stone stared at her as if he didn't recognize her. Unbelievable. How could anyone not recall this vision?

"Don't y'all remember?" she cajoled in a lyrical southern accent. "Trader Clerou's funeral? I was the one in the black dress. And at the jeweler's in Oregon City"—those gorgeous eyes drifted to Pierce and meandered up him—"I helped this forgetful man pick out a ring for his new bride."

"Oh, yeah. I, uh . . ." Stone still seemed at a loss.

Her gaze abandoned Pierce and returned to the other. "I trust the ring found favor with her?"

Stone grinned and slowly shook his head. "You *are* a surprise. A pure surprise."

She stepped closer to Stone, tilting her head upward. Damned if she wasn't even more enticing with her hair ribbons dancing among the cascading ringlets. "I told y'all I'd be here to watch your black streak beat Mr. McLean's."

A chuckle rumbled up from the man's massive chest. "You sure did. And as I recall, you said you'd be getting yourself all decked out, if that's what it took to see him win."

Pierce cleared his throat, a blatant bid to be noticed, but what the hell.

She and his adversary both turned to him.

"I'm forgetting my manners," Stone said. "This here's Mr. Kingston, the man who bought McLean's horse."

"Oh, my. The competition." Her delicately gloved

hand flew to her breast, enticing his gaze to creamy swells begging to burst from their prison of ruffled lace and satin roses. "I do hope we haven't offended you, Mr. Kingston."

"And this here's Captain Pacquing's daughter, Miss—"

"Lark," she offered, extending that lovely hand in Pierce's direction. "*Miss* Lark Ellen. I do believe my papa mentioned that you boarded our little boat at Salem."

Lark. No name could've fit her better. Not only did she sound as lovely as a songbird, but she seemed quite capable of a frolicsome caper or two. Keeping his eyes on hers, he lifted her hand and lightly brushed it with his lips.

She didn't demur in the slightest but returned his stare with equal boldness. An invitation or a challenge?

He welcomed either. Yes, sir, this was certainly going to be his day. He continued holding her hand while he spoke. "To meet you, dear lady, is a supreme pleasure." Then that incidental piece of information slammed into him: The southern darling's father captained a paddle-wheeler! "Pacquing, I don't believe I've heard the name. By any chance, did he ever have a steamboat on the Mississippi?"

Her gaze faltered for the merest second—just long enough to betray her reluctance to answer, unnerving Pierce even more. "Why, yes," she finally drawled. "But it's been quite a spell."

She was so gorgeous, so overwhelmingly charming. The thought that he might have worked her father's boat, that Captain Pacquing might know of him, sent an icy chill down his spine. But he had to ask. "I've traveled a time or two from New Orleans to St. Louis. What was the name of your father's steamboat?''

Her smile diminished slightly. "The *Ellie Sue*."

"The *Ellie Sue*," he repeated on a sigh of relief he hoped she didn't notice. "No, I don't believe I've heard of it."

Her smile splashed forth again in all its glory. "Oh, what a shame. But I do hope you're enjoyin' your stay with us now."

Stone intruded. "Mr. Kingston, I need to get back to my wife." He pointed past a dry goods store and down the dirt thoroughfare clogged with hundreds of milling people and numerous booths draped with patriotic bunting. "Let me tell you where we'll meet for the race. It'll start on the river road where this street crosses it. About a half mile down, a path has been cleared for the horses to circle around a barn. Then they'll come back and finish where they started. It's all marked with flags."

"Sounds good. My horse and I'll be there waiting for you."

Stone glanced at Lark and grinned as if they shared some great secret. "Well, suppose I better be going."

Pierce eased into a smile of his own. Three o'clock would arrive soon enough to wipe that look off his opponent's face.

As the blond hulk turned to leave, Lark reached out and caught his arm. "Jake honey, could y'all tell me where my papa is? I seem to have misplaced him."

The man's beamlike shoulders shook with suppressed laughter. He just couldn't seem to contain his overconfident glee. "Why, Miss Lark," he said in a strangled voice while attempting to keep a straight face. "I believe I saw him just a couple minutes ago when I was in the saloon placing my bet with the bartender." He sent a glance Pierce's way. "Only had to give three-to-one odds, too."

Lark looked toward the swinging doors at the end of the porch. "Well, if Papa is in talking to some men, I'm sure he wouldn't want to be disturbed by li'l ol' me. Guess I'll just wander around by mahself a bit." She released Stone's arm. "See y'all at race time. I'll be lookin' forward to meetin' your wife then."

"Sure thing." Swinging away, he walked down the steps.

She was alone? Unbelievable. "Miss Lark." Pierce drew her lush eyes back to him. Giving her a sincere look, he lifted her hand and leisurely thumbed the lacy glove's edging.

She did not pull away. Instead those wildly sensuous lips curled into the beginnings of another smile. "Yes?"

Pierce's heart literally skipped a beat, and worse, he didn't care. "I find it unbelievable that one as enchanting as you is without an escort. If I might be so bold, I'd deem it an honor to place myself at your service." Again she didn't resist when he tucked her pink bell-sleeved arm into the crook of his.

"Such gallantry in this rustic wilderness."

"I was just on my way to the livery barn. My horse and jockey are waiting for me there. Please, do join me."

"Oh, yes, that does sound like fun." Her fingers tightened around his arm as he led her down the steps. "I do so admire lookin' at a magnificent stud, runnin' my hands down along his sleek planes . . . even if he is goin' to lose."

Or rather, Pierce thought, letting her run her hands down *his* sleek planes. He began to harden at the mere thought. He shot an impatient glance skyward to a sun that hadn't even reached its zenith. Three o'clock was hours away. How would he ever hold out till this blasted race business was over with?

As they walked the short distance to Dooley's Livery Stable, everyone they passed gawked at the delectable maiden at his side. And, oddly, no one called out to her by name. Not a single beau happened along to try to take her away from him. She seemed as much a surprise to the stream of people coming from the wharf as she'd been to him. Skirting a number of wagons parked in front of the full corral, Pierce began to feel as though he'd captured the grand prize of the day even before the games had begun. His luck kept improving.

"My heavens, what a splendid steed," Lark cried as they entered through the wide doors of the barn. Tugging Pierce along, she swept into the cool shadows of the lofty building, past stalls of horses, to where Dink stood in the center plaiting Pegasus's pure white tail with red and blue ribbons.

Startled, the animal arched his neck upward, displaying a hint of his distant Arabian ancestry.

"Now, aren't you the proud one?" She reached up and twirled her fingers around one of the streamers flowing from the thoroughbred's mane braids. Then, swift as a bird in flight, she swung back to Pierce. Eyes all ashine, she began to twirl her parasol. "I can see why y'all bid on this stallion. You'll look ever' bit the lord of the manor sittin' astride him. Such a handsome pair y'all will make." She danced back a step or two and sent an impish glance from Pierce to the horse. Then suddenly her face crumbled into a look of despair. "Oh, dear, I do hope losin' today won't shame him too much. Break his spirit and all." Her dazzling smile reappeared just as quickly as it had vanished.

Pierce returned her grin gladly as his eyes drifted

down to the two lush mounds that strained against her low-cut pink bodice with every little rapid breath she took. Let her have her fun. A little teasing only added to his own anticipation. "If you'll excuse me for just a moment, I need to talk to the jockey."

"But of course." She turned to Dink, her eyes softening to pools of deep amber, and smiled at the slave with a gentle sincerity that took Pierce aback. "Good luck to you this afternoon. I'll be lookin' forward to watchin' you." Then, her skirts floating a scant inch from the ground, she strolled back toward the entrance as Pierce shook his head, pondering this unexpected compassion in her character.

But before Pierce concluded anything, Dink broke into a knowing, tooth-displaying grin and raised his brows.

Pierce matched the trainer's expression and shrugged while placing a silencing finger to his mouth. It took a moment before he felt he'd garnered enough control over his voice to relay the race information, especially since the jockey wouldn't stop snickering and rolling his eyes over Pierce's unbelievably voluptuous catch.

Three shots rang out in rapid succession.

Lark, a silhouette in the light of the doorway, whirled to face Pierce. "The log-rollin' race is about to start. Y'all almost finished here? I don't want to miss it. I do love watchin' big strong men battlin' one another."

Stunned by her uninhibited words and reckless tone—but just for a second—Pierce turned to Dink. "I'll meet you up on the river road at race time." Turning on his heel, he ate up the distance separating him from Lark.

"Mr. Kingston," Dink called after him in an exaggerated drawl, "if'n y'all gets waylaid, don' worry. I'll start *dis* race widout yous."

* * *

Pierce had never been to a log race before. To his amazement it took place not on the ground but in a sawmill pond next to the river. He guided Lark to one of the few unoccupied spots on the bank. Then, as she closed her parasol, he moved to stand behind her, the better to take in her delectable neck if the event proved boring.

Several men, each carrying a long stick, leapt from a small dock onto individual floating logs about eight feet long. Feverishly they poled away from the pier on unwieldy timber that threatened to roll them under at any second.

Lark looked back at him over her shoulder. "Have y'all ever seen a race like this one before?"

"No." This close, her perfumed scent intrigued him far more than some stupid contest, but he managed the pretense of an interest. "What's the object?"

"To get to the other side of the pond," she said with an excitement in her voice he couldn't fathom.

After all, how fast could a man go on a log? And considering her wanton remark before they'd left the barn, he'd half expected the men to be out there without their shirts on. But they weren't. Oh, well. He'd just spend his time considering exactly how many square inches of her neck, back, and shoulders were bared, waiting to be kissed.

She stiffened.

Could she feel his eyes on her? Even so, why would she be offended? Her every word, every smile, had been an invitation.

"Get him, Teddy!" A surprisingly unladylike yell burst from Lark as she jumped up and down.

Pierce jerked his head up to witness a wild brawl taking place in the middle of the pond.

The men hopped back and forth along their logs, swinging their poles in a free-for-all. Logs rammed into one another with loud shuddering thuds. The water now churned, causing more havoc.

All around the pond, the crowd began yelling. Other names rang out as people shouted encouragement to their favorites. Pierce even heard someone laying odds on one of the men.

"Teddy! Hit him!" Lark cried again while viciously swinging her closed parasol.

Which one of those running, dodging men, had caused her to forget her upbringing? Pierce, feeling an uncommon twinge of jealousy, cast a glance from man to man.

One got knocked into the water.

A woman close to Pierce sighed. "That's it for Jay."

"Teddy! Look out!" Lark lunged forward.

A short sturdy fellow whacked a gangly lad across the back, sending him into the pond in a flopping splash.

Amid the cheers for the other man, Lark slowly turned and looked back at Pierce with a shrinking grin. And if he wasn't mistaken, her cheeks had pinkened considerably. No doubt she'd just realized what she'd done. "Poor Teddy," she murmured. "He never does win." Even her southern accent seemed to have lost some of its syrupy drawl.

Pierce came close to frowning. Just exactly who was she, anyway?

Within seconds only one man remained afloat. That quickly it was over. A cheer went up for him. Then the crowd began to disperse.

Georgie couldn't believe how she'd undone herself. Why in tarnation had she gone and started yelling?

Showing herself for a fool? She'd had him hooked good, had been reeling him in pretty as you please. But now? He'd surely know she was a fake, a fraud. In defeat, she exhaled. All right, so she'd have to face her accuser. But, by jingo, she'd do it with style. She pasted a stiff grin on her face and swung around.

The man actually returned an easy smile. And even if the blamed thing didn't reach his unreadable blue eyes, it gave her hope. "Shall we be getting back?" He readjusted the tilt of his spotless tan hat, then took her arm. "Or would you like to offer your condolences to your friend?"

Was it possible he hadn't noticed that she'd lost her dignity as well as her accent? Who knew? Fraud that he surely was, maybe he'd been too busy playing his own part to notice her lapse. "No," she drawled, picking up her cue. "I'm sure Teddy'd prefer to lick his wounds in private."

"You know, I was beginning to wonder if you knew anyone here or if you'd just dropped out of the sky. Because I find it darned near impossible for anyone who looks like you to go anywhere unnoticed."

"I trust that's a compliment," she said, tossing out her most disarming smile. "But the truth is . . ."

He slowed as she deliberately paused in mid-sentence. She'd definitely piqued his curiosity.

". . . this month is the first time we've plied this river. We're usually over on the Columbia."

"I see." He picked up the pace again, guiding her across some water grass to the main road. "I'm getting hungry. I saw a booth earlier where ladies were selling pies. And I asked them to save me a berry one. Would you like to split it?"

"Split a whole pie? Such gluttony. Miss Pritchard would fairly roll over in her grave."

"And who, might I ask, is Miss Pritchard?"

"No one y'all'd be interested in. Just the most stiff-laced old maid the good Lord had the humor to put on this here earth. She was my instructress at her young ladies' academy in St. Louis."

"Oh. Then you were sent away to school, too. I spent ten long years at Baldwin's Academy for Boys just outside Philadelphia. In fact that's when I developed my taste for homemade pie."

A likely tale. What kind of fool did he take her for? If the upstart had ever actually been to boarding school, he'd know one was lucky if a mere dribble of honey ever hit a biscuit. She peered up at him with an arched brow that would've made her teacher proud.

A chuckle rumbled out of Kingston. "After going without pie all those years, I swore I'd never let another one slip by me." He squeezed her hand clutching his arm. "So, what do you say, Miss Pacquing? You ready to thumb your nose at ol' Baldwin and Miss Pritchard?"

Georgie laughed. "Why not?" Her spirits soared again. This slick fish was as hooked as ever. He still had every intention of trying to bed her before this day was done.

A few minutes later, with blackberry pie swimming in fresh cream and mugs of coffee in their clutches, they sat on the grass beneath one of the frail-limbed dogwoods that shaded an unpainted church. Other couples lounged all about. The young swains, many of whom wore identical flat-crowned straw hats decorated with patriotic-striped bands, and their sweethearts, with colorful calico or gingham swirling about them, partook of their dull dinners. But not Georgie and Kingston. Spooning in the

treat, they both ate with unholy grins on their faces.
Granted, the pie was scrumptious, but Georgie also knew
with absolute certainty what added anticipation lay
hidden beneath each facade. She also knew her smug
expression would still be there long after his had died.

Beaming, she made a toasting gesture with her spoon
before raising another bite to her mouth.

He did likewise.

What she wouldn't have given to tell him he'd just
toasted his own downfall. When he's lost the race, along
with all the money he's bet, *and* the most willing belle
he's ever encountered, Georgie mused, he'll feel at least
a little of what he and his fellow riverboat gullers have
been dealing out to poor unsuspecting souls for years.
Once again she saw her papa's red-rimmed eyes on that
woeful day. Heard the weary hopelessness in his voice
when he told her to pack. They didn't own their river
queen, the *Ellie Sue*, anymore.

Oh, yes. She would do it. Wait until that sublime
moment, then turn up her nose and walk away. A twinge
of uneasiness that she refused to accept as guilt skittered
down her spine. She had set out to avenge her father, and
she would . . . no matter how handsome her victim
was. Or how she loved the way his shiny black hair
swept away from his temples and the way it caused little
feathered curls to cling to his hat, or that cute habit he
had of keeping the brim at a tilt . . . or the restful effect
his voice had on her, even when she knew his evil
thoughts. Yes, she would enjoy every minute of his
downfall, by golly. Even if her corset was killing her.

While watching Kingston shovel in his pie with gusto,
Georgie sat up as tall as possible to ease the strangling
pinch of the hated undergarment. She reached into the
small pink reticule tied to her sash, drew out a lace-

trimmed hanky, and dabbed her lips. "I'm afraid that's all I can eat." She picked up her coffee and washed down the last of the pesky berry seeds.

"That's too bad," he offered with an insincere frown while eyeing the remaining pie in the pan sitting between them. "But I'll do my best to take up your slack."

Georgie laughed in spite of herself. The man did have a way about him. She had to give him that.

The same snippy threesome she'd seen chasing after Kingston the day before strolled by. Although they walked exceptionally erect and with their noses pointed straight ahead, Georgie saw them dart quick little glances in Kingston's direction.

She experienced a rush of triumph. "Why, look who just passed by," she crooned low. "Those three young ladies who were buzzin' 'round you yesterday."

If anything else had dared to try to escape her big flapping mouth, the sudden clog in her throat would have stopped it. How could she have been so stupid? Now he would put two and two together. He'd remember her as the loudmouthed kid from the day before. The blood drained from her face.

Looking up from his plate, Kingston found the threesome. While Georgie held her breath, he stared after them until they were swallowed by the noisy throng. No hint of an expression marred his dashing good looks. His attention then traveled to his cup. He picked it up and took a sip of coffee, as if she'd said nothing damning.

She relaxed, letting the trapped air trail out of her lungs.

Kingston pulled out his watch, and glanced at it. As he replaced it, his eyes roved up her with agonizing slowness until they reached her face, and still they didn't settle on any one spot. "It's almost one. We don't have too much longer to wait."

Something in his overly quiet tone told her that at the very least he knew their meeting hadn't been by chance. Keeping up her end of the banter would be much harder now. "For the race?"

His wandering gaze finally stopped at her eyes. "That too."

Dams and ditches!

Georgie made sure they spent the next couple of hours smack dab in the middle of things—the dust from stomping boots and all. She rooted for foot racers she didn't know, she put herself and Kingston through the punishment of a screeching, squealing hog-calling contest and even insisted they submit their necks to the strain of watching tree climbers clamber up stripped pines.

And during the entire time not a single complaint came out of the man's mouth. She was beginning to think she'd misread him. And if she hadn't known better, she'd have sworn he actually enjoyed all this countrified entertainment. In fact, the closer to three it got, the more her confidence returned. So much so that when they passed a booth with souvenir hats, she couldn't resist coaxing him into one more harebrained whim, especially since he seemed to fancy his own hat so much.

She pulled him toward the counter. "Mr. Kingston, y'all simply must get yourself one of these straw hats. Why, with your horse decked out in the colors of the day, y'all can do no less."

The man actually ducked his head and grinned like some dumb kid. "Naw. I'd look silly."

"Oh, but you'd look no such thing. You'd be cute as a bug's ear." Georgie turned to the elderly vendor inside the booth. "Don't y'all think so?"

The man shifted uneasily from one baggy-panted leg to the other, but he looked up at Kingston with the sincerity of a preacher. "Be just the thing to set the gals' hearts aflutter."

"It's tempting," Kingston said, moving away, "but I think I'll just stick with the one I have."

Georgie pulled him back. "If you won't buy one, then I will. Y'all wouldn't refuse a gift from a lady, would you?"

"I might take it. But I won't wear it."

"We'll see." She turned to the vendor. "How much?"

"Fifty cents."

As she rummaged through her reticule, Kingston pulled some coins from his pocket. "If you insist on buying one, I'll pay for the danged thing."

She pushed his hand aside and handed a half-dollar to the salesman. "No, please. When I see it sittin' on your head, I want the pleasure of knowin' I bought it for you." She lifted one off the stack of hats, then looked up at Kingston and smiled for the millionth time that day. Her cheek muscles ached, but this smile was worth it. She *would* get him to wear the ridiculous straw thing. And he was right. He'd look like a buffoon even if he did give it a cocky tilt.

Shaking his head, Kingston cupped her elbow and led her away. "We'd better get going. It's almost three."

The rest of the crowd must have also noticed the time, because the entire throng poured down the road toward the starting point. Excited chatter bombarded Georgie from every side, punctuated with the names of the horses and their owners. Since no one spoke directly to Pierce Kingston, Georgie assumed the vast majority didn't know that the man himself was among them.

But they soon would. And he'd be wearing the straw hat.

Georgie rose up on her toes and spoke close to Kingston's ear, so he could hear her above the mounting roar. "I have a proposition for y'all."

Kingston stopped dead, stared at her for several seconds, his stunned expression slowly relaxing into a lopsided grin. Then suddenly he veered off the road with her in tow and pulled her behind a big fir. Cupping her chin, he let his sky blue eyes bore into her. "I know I'll be interested in any proposition that's on your winsome little mind. But can't it wait until after the race? Just a few more minutes?"

He truly was a marvel. He actually thought she wanted to bed him here and now. "I'm sorry," she said, "but this particular proposition simply can't wait. I want to propose a bet."

"A bet?" The words seemed to just fall from his mouth.

"Yes. If your horse loses, I want y'all to wear this hat I bought you."

"And?"

"And what?"

"What's my prize if Pegasus wins?"

Oh, dear, she hadn't thought it out that far. "If you win," she ventured, slapping the hat on her head, "*I'll* wear the silly thing."

"Aha!" He took a step back, undoubtedly enjoying her latest blunder. "So you agree about the hat."

She opened her mouth, hoping something would come out.

Kingston beat her to it. "Tell you what, my sweet little river lark. I'll wear that idiot's basket if my horse loses.

But if *you* lose, you must agree to have a champagne supper with me. In a spot of my choosing. Agreed?''

Georgie's heart tripped over itself. Supper with him? Alone? In some isolated place? ''I don't know. I really need to find my papa. He must be worryin' about me somethin' fierce by now.''

''Where's that free-spirited girl from this morning?''

Where indeed? Not to mention the southern belle. She'd even forgotten her accent. But he hadn't seemed to notice. She looked from the straw hat to him. Judas Priest, but she wanted to see it on him. And Jake Stone's horse was going to win anyway. Everyone said so. And everyone couldn't be wrong. She hooked the country straw over the tip of her parasol and stretched out her free hand. ''You've got a bet.''

Ignoring her gesture, he stepped dangerously close. Before she could retreat, he slipped an arm around her waist, drawing her even nearer. ''I know a much better way to seal our little wager.''

Chapter
Four

PIERCE STARED DOWN in surprise as he lowered his
mouth to Lark's.

Her eyes had sprung wide, and she went rigid, all her
clever coquettishness gone.

Was it possible she'd never before been kissed? The
thought stopped him from recklessly vanquishing her full
lips. But he couldn't resist at least one light brush across
them before he released her.

As he left their tempting softness, her lashes fluttered
and her cheeks glowed red. She looked away. "We'd
better hurry," she said, her words no more than a breathy
whisper. Whirling around, she started back to the road.

Pierce chuckled to himself as he hurried to catch up.
The teasing imp was an absolute innocent.

His amusement had lost its edge, however, by the time
he reached her side and took her arm. His plans for after
the race could quite easily be thwarted. Then, seeing her
disconcerted expression as they forged a path through the
crowd, his desire for this capricious belle deepened. With
patience, he would be the first. And, he hoped, the last.

A moment later Lark led the way to the crossroad
where Dink sat astride the thoroughbred surrounded by a
throng of onlookers. Beside the rider stood Jake Stone
talking to a skinny kid mounted on the sleekest black

racehorse Pierce had ever seen. After one look at the powerfully muscled animal, he could easily see why the local citizens were so confident. Could see why he'd been able to get three-to-one odds for the fifty-five hundred he'd wagered. Pierce's hand went uneasily to the greatly diminished lump of bank notes in his breast pocket—his last five hundred dollars. What had possessed him to take such a risk on something as unpredictable as a horse race?

Lark moved ahead of him into the circle and searched the crowd, panic etching her eyes—far more panic than a brief kiss should have invoked. Perhaps he'd been wrong about everything. Why didn't anyone except Jake Stone know her? Was this race, this woman, all part of some devious game . . . with him playing the part of the fool?

Georgie knew that her papa was somewhere in the horde. And he undoubtedly saw her, since every face was turned her way, eagerly awaiting the big moment. If only he'd step forward, come to collect her.

Big Jake Stone pulled his timepiece from his pocket, glanced at it, and then, grinning, drew a young woman to his side and strode toward them. He gave Georgie a quick wink, then peered down at the one he escorted with the loving eyes of someone obviously enthralled. "Miss Lark, I'd like to introduce you to my bride. And Rachel honey, this is the girl I told you about. You know, the one who helped me pick out your ring."

The delicately featured amber-haired lady, with pale blue eyes fringed with silver, looked from her husband to Georgie. Then, bursting into a smile, Mrs. Stone offered her hand. "How do you do? Jake's told me so much about you."

Returning the friendly and obviously sincere greeting,

Georgie remembered how the big lummox of a mountain man had gone all soft as he'd tried to describe his beloved new wife's eyes when he and Georgie had searched for a ring that would do them justice. "Yes," she drawled. "And Jake spent a goodly amount of time recitin' all your charms. You seem to have completely bewitched him."

Mrs. Stone laughed and lifted an adoring gaze to Jake. "I've truly done my best."

Obviously embarrassed, Jake shifted his weight as he glanced from Rachel to Georgie. He cleared his throat and turned to Pierce. "And, Rachel, this is Mr. Kingston, the man who bought McLean's horse."

Raising the lady's hand to his lips, Pierce appeared as calm and charming as ever.

Georgie found herself more irritated than she cared to admit, considering the fact that those same lips had sent every trace of her composure to the winds just a moment ago.

"It's three o'clock," Jake said, replacing his pocket watch. "Are you set?"

After Pierce looked up to his jockey, who grinned and gave a quick nod, he turned back to Jake with those blasted steady eyes. "Yes."

"Get the horses up to the mark," Jake called out, pulling a pistol from his belt. He waved it at several people still clustered on the racecourse. "Clear the road!"

Tails high, nostrils flaring, the animals strained at their reins as they pranced in an excited side step to a line raked across the road. The stylish gray, sporting fancy ribbons, with the professional jockey in flashy red, white, and blue silks, looked almost silly beside Jake's un-adorned, no-nonsense black streak. The farm kid who'd taken the proven animal across the finish line many times before—always with lengths to spare—held his stallion in check.

Jake stepped to the side, gun raised to the sky.

Pierce grabbed Georgie's hand and held tight, the only sign of his nervousness. . . . Or was he just making sure she'd be there to pay up if he won?

The pistol exploded.

The horses leapt forward, and the crowd roared.

Pierce pulled Georgie with him till they reached the side of the starting line.

Feeling the tension still in his hand, Georgie looked up and saw a muscle bunched in his jaw as he stared after the horses rapidly diminishing in a cloud of dust. Following his gaze, she noted with profound relief that the black thoroughbred already led by at least a couple of lengths. She could've kicked herself for spending these last minutes since Pierce had kissed her in agony. Of course Jake's horse would win, and she'd soon be rid of this man who was beginning to send her heart into the craziest flip-flops every time she looked at him. If she stayed with him much longer she didn't even want to guess what else her unruly body might succumb to.

Glancing down at the straw hat speared on her closed parasol, she had to stifle a laugh as she pictured it on this debonair ''gentleman.'' A smile tickled the corners of her mouth, and she ventured another look at her perfectly attired companion.

Her smile died as her glance fell upon his lips. It seemed impossible that they could look that firm, almost hard. Yet when they'd touched hers, they'd been soft, tender, so warm, so . . . Georgie's heart leapt again, and she felt a strange yet thrilling tingle in her nether region.

Suddenly she saw that Pierce returned her stare!

He'd been watching her gawk up at him with moon eyes, her tongue tracing her lips.

His mouth drew into a knowing grin as he gave her hand a quick squeeze.

She could have died! She quickly veered her attention to the dust settling on the now empty stretch of road that curved out of sight a couple hundred yards ahead. Jake's horse had better still be out front when they showed up again, or she might just have to answer for a day's worth of outrageous flirting.

Thank heavens! That beautiful black streak was thundering toward her, still in the lead—but with the gray close on its tail.

As the enthusiastic crowd rooted Prince on, his young rider hunched low over the animal's neck and slapped frantically with a riding crop.

Suddenly, as if by magic, the gray drew alongside Prince without the black jockey so much as flicking his whip, then steadily moved ahead with exhilarating grace and speed. Seconds later Pegasus galloped across the finish line a full three lengths ahead of Stone's Prince.

Pierce broke into a wild whoop. He swept off his hat and sent it sailing through the air while Georgie and the other spectators fell into a stunned silence. Then, still hanging on to her, he rushed to where the gray stallion had come to a halt. "You did it!" he shouted up to his jockey. Releasing Georgie, Pierce pulled the grinning winner from the saddle and gave him a joyous hug before setting him down.

"Ah tol' you!" cried his slave, his dark eyes dancing. "Ah tol' you!"

One arm tight around the jockey's shoulders, Pierce caught Georgie around the waist with his free hand and drew her into his celebratory embrace. He hugged her so tight he nearly cut off what little air she'd been managing beneath her stays.

Grim-faced, Jake stepped up and held out his hand. "Congratulations, Kingston."

Georgie hoped the poor man hadn't bet more than he could afford. She gave him a halfhearted smile as Pierce released the slave and thrust forth his hand.

"Thank you. My pleasure," he said, pumping the big homesteader's hand.

More people crowded close, jostling Georgie, squashing against her hooped skirts, sending them bouncing in every direction until she felt like a cork on a stormy sea.

Without warning, Pierce scooped her up and set her and those bothersome skirts atop the gray stallion. "There, my beauty. You'll decorate Pegasus far better than any rose garland ever could." Then with an unabashed grin, he snatched the straw hat from off her parasol and slapped it on his head.

Well, he *was* wearing the stupid thing, just as she'd wanted. But why? And instead of looking ridiculous, he looked more dashing that ever. Judas Priest! Nothing was turning out the way she'd expected.

Pierce looked up at Georgie with the smuggest grin while he gathered the horse's reins. "Well, guess it's time I collected the rest of my winnings."

"Yassah," agreed the slave, whose grin matched Pierce's.

As they sliced a path through the crowd and headed toward the center of the frontier village, Georgie should've felt like a queen, riding high above on the victor. But the stallion she rode had been brought here by Kyle McLean. And she was sure those about her felt that the villain had reached up from his grave and caused the honest folk to lose again.

No one smiled as the crowd glared up at her, and she began to feel like the legendary Lady Godiva, a naked prize being led to her fate—a fate she had brought down upon her own head. She no doubt deserved some sort of punishment, but not too much. Nothing he'd said had swayed her from the belief that he was one of those riverboat gamblers. And besides, she thought, wincing at the pain the jouncing ride inflicted upon her ribs and waist, surely the agony of wearing this whalebone atrocity should be punishment enough. She shouldn't also have to confess that she really wasn't the willing belle she'd led Pierce to believe. Frantically she scanned the field of faces for her papa. For once, it was her turn to need him. But where was he? Dams and ditches!

Upon reaching the unadorned two-story hotel, Pierce handed the reins to the jockey. "Take Pegasus and the lady on down to the livery stable while I go in and collect."

Before Georgie could call after him, he dodged past the people lining the steps and ran through the saloon doors. Dressed as a young lady, she couldn't go in herself, but she could've had him ask the whereabouts of her father.

The crowd lost interest in her and drifted away toward other entertainment as Pierce's jockey hauled her to the big livery barn. As she entered the cool shade of the high-raftered building, a sudden wave of relief washed over Georgie. She wouldn't have to face Pierce's accusations after all, any more than she would anyone else's. Except for Jake and his wife, not one person had discovered her true identity all day, and now she was literally being handed the chance to escape. And, she

thought, stretching upward to ease the digging of her
corset, a chance to get out of this cursed instrument of
torture.

The slave led Pegasus into a stall at the far end of the
barn before stopping. Then, instead of helping her down,
he pulled a carrot from a burlap bag hooked over a post.

The horse whinnied.

The little man removed the animal's bit and, ignoring
Georgie, fed Pegasus . . . one dillydallying bite at a
time.

And she needed to get out of here. *Now.* "Excuse
me," she drawled, demanding his attention. "Would
y'all please help me down?"

"Ah couldn' do that, ma'am."

"Why the devil not?" she retorted, forgetting herself.

He looked nervously behind him, then back in her
direction, but not quite at her. "Well, fer starters, mah
hands, they's all dirty."

"So? Wipe 'em on a rag."

His eyes darted away. "Ain't got one handy."

"Oh, for Pete's sake. I don't give a plug nickel for this
dress. Just get me down." She didn't have time for all his
excuses.

The slave turned away and fetched another carrot.
"Ah still cain't do it. Mr. Kingston wouldn't hol' with
it." He shook his head as he held the treat up to Pegasus.
"No sah, not a'tall."

She looked from him to the ground, a good six feet
below. If she'd been in her dungarees it would have been
easy. But . . . "Turn your back," she told the jockey.
"I'm getting myself down." Rolling onto her belly, she
accidentally trapped one side of her hooped crinoline
beneath her, sending the opposite side skyward. And the
blasted thing took her skirts with it. Knowing only a

skimpy pair of drawers covered her behind, she tried to shove the hoops down, but they just sprang up elsewhere. Giving up, she slid off the horse as quickly as possible, but the dratted gown didn't follow. Her feet touched ground, but her skirts were over her head . . . and caught on the saddle!

"Can ah turn aroun' now?" the slave asked.

"No! Stay there! My dress is hooked on a buckle." She grabbed the sides of the snagged hoop and, jumping up and down, tried to release it. It didn't even begin to budge. Her only hope was to remount. Trapped within her skirts, she couldn't see the stirrup. Feeling around blindly, she found it up by her waist. She'd have a devil of a time getting her foot in it. Latching on to her suspended crinoline for balance, she flung a leg high.

Suddenly, sure hands circled her waist and lifted her up and away, freeing her skirts . . . which *dropped down over her rescuer's head.*

Georgie gasped and pulled away as he fought to get out from under her petticoats.

Finally, grinning like a fox in a chicken coop, Pierce emerged and straightened to his full height while running his fingers through his mussed hair. "Where's my hat?" The words tumbled out on a humiliating chuckle as he glanced her way.

If only the ground would have swallowed her up.

He looked down and searched the stall.

As she stumbled backward, her foot bumped into something. The blasted hat! Would this ordeal never end? With as much dignity as she could muster, she lifted her skirts and stepped to one side, exposing the odious straw thing.

"There it is," the jockey crowed. He pointed with one hand while hiding his snickering mouth with the other.

She had to get out of here before she screamed. She started for the stall gate.

While swooping the hat up to his head, Pierce caught hold of her wrist. "Please. I know how embarrassing this must be for you. But please don't let one silly little mishap ruin the most perfect day of my life."

"But I couldn't possibly—"

He reached out and pressed his fingers against her lips. His normally unreadable eyes looked at her with mind-stealing tenderness, holding her for several heartbeats. "It never happened. . . . Now," he added in a buoyant voice as he folded her arm within his, "my man, here, and I have a business matter to take care of. And I'd be honored to have you witness it."

He escorted Georgie out of the stall to a barrel next to the back wall. As the slave joined them, Pierce withdrew some legal papers, a pencil stub, and a bulging canvas bag from inside his coat. He laid them on the barrelhead, then sorted through the pages. "Here it is," he said, placing one paper on top—the slave's ownership document.

With a trembling hand, the Negro reached out and touched it. "Don' look near powerful enough to chain a man for life, do it?"

The sorrow in his eyes caught Georgie off guard, tore at her chest. It took a moment before she recovered enough to look up at Pierce.

His eyes glistened as if he, too, was near tears as she waited for him to speak. He swallowed, took a ragged breath, and picked up the paper. "It gives your name here as Dink of Darlington Horse Farm. Is that the name your mother gave you?"

"No, sah. She call me Davy."

"Then David it is." He crossed out Dink and wrote

the new name. "Now, for a last name. A freed man usually takes his owner's. Would you prefer Darlington or McLean?"

"You're really gonna do it," Davy choked out, a big tear rolling down his cheek, "ain'tcha?"

Pierce opened his mouth as if to speak, but swallowed instead, then nodded.

"Wahl, then, if'n y'all don' mind, ah kinda taken a likin' to Kingston. David Kingston. Has a real nice ring to it for a free man, don' it?"

Georgie couldn't believe her ears. Was Pierce planning to actually free him? Her attention swung back to Pierce.

Without answering, he picked up the pencil and started writing.

Georgie couldn't stop her eyes from brimming with tears, although she'd always prided herself in not being a blubberer. "Yes," she said, answering Davy's question for Pierce. "I think it's a fine name. A name to be proud of."

"Well, it's yours now," Pierce said in a raspy whisper, handing him the pencil. "Make an X there." His mellow baritone came out stronger that time. "Then give the pencil to Miss Lark so she can witness it."

While signing, Georgie almost forgot how to spell her name when Pierce reached into the canvas bag and drew out a handful of coins, along with a huge wad of bank notes. *And the sack still bulged.*

He started separating the money into two stacks. "I received three-to-one odds on the five hundred I gave you." He shoved the smaller pile to Davy whose eyes were round as moons. "There's the five hundred." He then pointed to another, larger pile. "And here's your winnings of fifteen hundred."

Davy reached for it, but stopped short, his hands quivering inches above the fortune, his cheeks now drenched with tears. "Ah's really gonna be free an' rich?"

Pierce clapped a hand on his thin shoulder. "This might look like a lot to you now. But if you're not very careful, it'll be gone before you know it. Keep it hidden, but not all in one place, and don't tell anyone you have it. Even if you are legally free, there are people who will take advantage of you, treat you bad just because you're not lily-white." His last words were filled with raw hostility.

The little man's eyes narrowed. "Ah know dat, an' ever since you say you's gonna do it, ah be thinkin' on goin' down to Mexico. Don't got no family no mo', an' ah hears a black man wi' money can live good as anyone there. Maybe ah get me mah own land. Raise mah own hosses."

"If that's what you want, I'll help you to get passage on a ship when we get back to Portland. Now pick up your money, and let's go get that bottle of champagne I ordered for you."

Georgie had never seen or heard of anything so kind or generous. This was no gulling gambler. There was no way this fine gentleman could ever prey on the innocent or the weak. And after she'd flaunted herself before him like a shameless hussy!

Finding herself squeezing her lacy parasol too tight, she loosened her grip, and an uplifting possibility surfaced. If Pierce was really a true gentleman, perhaps flirting was just one of many amusing distractions to him, one he wouldn't presume to act upon. Just maybe she wasn't in as much trouble as she'd thought.

"And as for you and me, Miss Lark." His voice

flowing warm like syrup, Pierce took her hand. "I asked the cook at the hotel to prepare us a very special picnic basket. By now it should be waiting for us at the back door."

"Back door?" Out of everyone's sight? Her lungs rammed against whalebone. She needed more air.

"I hope you don't mind if we avoid the crowds. I'm not the most popular man in town at the moment. And the woods behind the hotel look perfect for what I have in mind."

Chapter
Five

THIS HAD BEEN the craziest day. What had started out as a little vengeful toying with a supposedly unconscionable gambler was turning into Georgie's first real outing *and* with the most handsome gentleman a girl could imagine—one she found more irresistible with every passing moment.

As they'd whiled away the afternoon recounting the exciting and sometimes hilarious holiday games, she'd come to love the throaty sound of his laughter. She'd especially loved the exhilaration in his voice as he relived the horse race, particularly when he told her how beautiful she'd looked sitting atop the dappled gray stallion with her tulle skirt billowing about her, trailing roses and lace.

Although her common sense argued that her overwhelming attraction was probably due to the generous amount of champagne she'd consumed, her titillated heart refused to agree. She found it darned near impossible to take her eyes off him as he lounged on a blue-checked tablecloth shaded by a canopy of spruce and hemlock boughs. He had removed his tan waistcoat and tossed it aside, giving her an even better view of his virile contours beneath the thin pin-striped shirt.

While they finished their meal of honey-cured ham,

sweet potatoes, and the delightful wine, she was still astounded that she'd misjudged Pierce so profoundly. No slickster gambler would have done for the Negro what she'd witnessed. Pierce Kingston truly was the most wonderful man she'd ever met in her eighteen—well, *almost* eighteen—years. And here she sat, an absolute fraud!

"You've hardly touched your food," Pierce said, that silly straw hat pushed back, giving his face a dear open friendliness much like her papa's. "If it's not to your taste, I'll go get you something else."

"Oh, no, it's really delicious. It's just that I'm a bit uncomfortable," she said, trying to sit even straighter in her binding undergarments.

"Corset starting to bite?"

My, but he was getting familiar! But then, what could she expect? "A little."

"That can be easily remedied with a little loosening."

"Believe me, I've thought of it. But if I loosen the corset, I won't be able to rebutton the gown. It's cut for a twenty-inch waist."

"I thought the magic number was eighteen inches."

"When my mother wasn't looking," she said, a bit of her devilment returning, "I bribed the seamstress."

Pierce burst out laughing.

Georgie held her sides and joined him, despite the binding stays.

"You know," he said on a lingering chuckle as he scooted close, much *too* close, for the first time, "it's just the two of us. What's a couple of undone buttons? Let me help you loosen those strings. I'd much rather you enjoyed yourself in comfort."

Georgie was sorely tempted. Sorely. But the tone of his voice told her that he wanted to help her with far more than just her corset. "I think, instead, you'd better have another glass of champagne."

His mouth dropped open, then slid into a slack grin as he shook his head. "Dear Lark. Don't you know that's supposed to be my line?"

She felt her face flush for what must have been the tenth time today. "What I meant was you might need something else to occupy you, maybe cool you down a bit."

"You'd be surprised how wonderful warm can be." His words, so close to her ear again, poured over her.

Forget warm, hot was more what she felt. Glancing at the half-empty bottle, she wanted to blame it, but couldn't. She'd been weaned on rich red wine. Drinking this pale bubbly stuff seemed almost like drinking water. No, this man-woman business was proving much harder to handle than she'd thought—and chock-full of surprising new sensations, especially when the man was Pierce Kingston, the most . . .

Suddenly it dawned on her that she knew next to nothing about this one who was coming dangerously close to stealing her heart, and anything else he might ask for. She moved away on the pretext of pouring herself some more champagne. "I don't believe you mentioned where you're from."

"You mean originally?"

"Yes."

Georgie detected a hesitation before he answered. "My mother was from Jamaica."

"Oh, really? I don't hear the islands in your voice."

"She leave Ja-mai-ca, mon," he said in a West Indian accent, then finished the sentence with a southern drawl, "to go live in N'awlins 'fore I was born. And speaking of accents, you seem to have lost yours."

"Oh, that." Caught again in her deception! Her throat tightened. Oh, what the heck. "It goes with the dress."

That marvelously infectious chuckle rumbled out of him with the ease of water spilling down a fall of rocks.

Thank heavens. Her little game didn't seem to bother him. At least, what he knew so far. "Since I've spent most of my life traveling up and down the Mississippi with a Yankee mama and a Cajun papa," she continued, hoping to whitewash her subterfuge even more, "I have a whole slew of accents to pick from. But you . . . you sound eastern."

"Remember? I told you about my school days in Philadelphia. My instructors took particular pleasure in educating Louisiana out of me." He snorted, then grinned, his teeth just short of sparkling along with those eyes that had turned a deeper hue of blue in the forest shade. "But I shouldn't complain. My eastern accent comes in quite handy, especially when I'm trying to work a deal."

Work a deal? A sick feeling twisted her stomach. He *was* the flimflammer she'd first taken him for. His charity today had been an exception. He'd just gotten caught up in all the excitement. How could she have allowed herself to be duped so easily and, worse, so willingly? "What kind of deals?"

Before the race Pierce had thought Lark an intriguing, if outrageous, tease. And in the past, a bottle of wine had always made a young damsel even more flirtatious, more willing to cast caution aside. But it seemed to have had the opposite effect on her. Not that he wasn't still attracted—even more so. During the leisurely meal, a warm, interesting, and amusing young lady had emerged from the toying seductress. The afternoon had drifted away on happy chatter and laughter as they'd rehashed the events they'd watched.

Unlike other young belles whose thoughts always seemed centered on their like or dislike of another girl's bonnet, Lark had not only discussed the rowdy fun, but in the retelling, had made it seem even more hilarious, especially the greased-pig chase. She was proving to be not only the pampered belle he'd always dreamed would decorate his arm and warm his bed, but more, much more. This woman, he knew instinctively, could be a real friend, someone he could trust with anything. Except, of course, that one thing.

"What kind of deals?" she asked again, an unaccountable crispness in her tone.

"Brokering cotton mostly. Some sugarcane and rum."

"I don't recall Papa ever shipping for any Kingstons. Where's your family's plantation?"

He had no doubt she would recognize the name of Langetree Plantation if he mentioned it, and then the questions would start. "My father died when I was sixteen, and as it turned out, I was left with nothing. So, like many others you've probably met on your steamboat, I made my living dealing cards and gambling."

"I see." Those copper-brown eyes narrowed slightly. She obviously didn't find riverboat gamblers nearly as dashing and romantic as most young lasses did.

"Yes. But I've always wanted a stable future, so whenever I'd save a few hundred from my earnings, I would invest it with a couple of brokers I met in my travels. I was doing really quite well financially, but I kept hearing about the opportunities out here. So here I am. And now that I've acquired that magnificent stallion, the idea of starting a stud farm here in Oregon looks very tempting. Especially since I met you."

Pierce took Lark's stemmed goblet from her hand. As he slowly lifted it to his mouth and drank, he watched to see if his last words had erased his mention of being a gambler, if the intimacy of his sharing her glass would woo her to him again.

Her eyes softened into shimmering bronze pools, and the slightest smile curled the corners of those lush lips, prompting him to continue. "Do you know of any good land for sale?"

"Oh, that's the one thing Oregon has plenty of." She leaned forward and retrieved her goblet, displaying a generous amount of cleavage.

Pierce hoped the movement was deliberate, for it severely tested his control.

"But if you're really serious . . ." she said, sipping from the place where his lips had touched the rim.

He wished he were that cup. Wish, hell. Give him a few more minutes. She swallowed, and his gaze again wandered downward to the two creamy swells rising from the yards of gathered lace and ribbon roses.

". . . you should talk Davy into staying and working for you," she continued as he forced his eyes back up to hers. "He has to be an expert, the way Pegasus performed for him today."

"Davy's good, all right. But I couldn't ask him to give up his dream of freedom for mine."

"But if your dream is really to stay here in Oregon and start a horse farm—"

"The notion is becoming more irresistible all the time." Pierce left her boldly expressive yet delicate face to survey the cool, grassy glen in which they sat. Surrounding them, ferns and bright-leaved dogwoods flourished in the dappled light sifting through the boughs of ancient firs. A paradise. A cool green paradise compared to the sultry, swampy countryside of Louisiana. "Yes, it's perfect. All of it. And my mother, I'm sure, would love it here, too, if I could persuade her to come."

"Your mother?"

"Yes. I haven't liked the way she's been living since my father . . ." Noticing the sharpness in his voice, he shrugged, hoping to soften it.

"But I thought you were doing quite well."

"I was. I am. But she's a stubborn lady. She wouldn't let me do for her. But if I could get her to come here, everything would be different. She could have a whole new life."

"I know how you feel. Coming here gave Papa a fresh start, too. And who knows?" she said in a singsong voice, her ringlets bobbing as she cocked her head to one side. "Maybe your mama and my papa would become friends. I'll bet she's very pretty."

"More than pretty. She has an ageless elegance about her. Something she was born with. Like you."

Lark's luminous eyes darted away, and she caught her lower lip between her teeth.

Surely a compliment that true shouldn't have undone her. But for some unfathomable reason it had, intriguing Pierce even further. He stretched out beside her, resting his head on his hands. He wanted to study her at a new angle, watch the way the rays of the late afternoon sun set her hair afire. "I had planned to go to California, get in on the gold rush, but everything around here's just too perfect to go off and leave."

Her gaze flitted away again, but just for a second. "Then you're really going to stay here and raise horses?"

"Yup. Maybe a few kids, too, if I'm lucky."

"I—uh . . ." She took another sip. "I come from a fairly large family. I have several brothers. Two of them are still working on the Mississippi. And Cadie's running our stern-wheeler, the *Dream Ellen*, over on the Columbia while Papa and I are in charge of the *Willamette*."

"I can hardly imagine a flower as delicate as you firing up the steam engines or tossing one of those thick coils of rope to a dockworker."

A mischievous glint skittered across her eyes. "Looks can be deceiving."

"They certainly can." He returned her stare until it faltered, and she attempted to sit up even straighter. Pierce decided that maybe he'd better back off a little. "And where's your mother? Is she here enjoying the festivities with your father today?"

Lark turned away. "No, she passed on three years ago. Before we came to Oregon."

Pierce sat up. Poor child. He couldn't imagine losing his own mother, the one person in the world who'd completely cared about him, no matter what. "I'm sorry. My sincerest condolences."

She laid her hand on his arm. "I'm sure you felt the same loss when your father died."

Maybe for a minute, he allowed silently. But certainly not after he learned the truth. "We were never all that close."

"Oh, I'm sorry. Perhaps, then, your loss is even greater than mine. Papa and I have a lot of fun together. I want you to meet him. I'm sure you'll like each other . . . but not just yet." Her gaze softened into a welcome so warm, so enchanting, he felt himself being drawn into it, falling headlong . . . to the strains of a haunting waltz.

Suddenly Lark's wide brows flew upward. "Music.

The dance must've begun.'' Her fluid lips spread marvelously wide.

''My lady wishes to dance?''

''It would be fun.''

Pierce could think of something far more interesting, but for now a dance would have to suffice. He rose to his feet, then helped her up. Reluctant to release her, he was tempted to pull her into his arms, press her tight against his body, and not let her go until he'd satisfied his hunger. Instead, he dropped her hands and picked up the remnants of their meal.

In the fading light of dusk, they neared the edge of the forest to see a sparsely wooded clearing across the road where all the celebrants had converged. Numerous lanterns hung from the dogwoods and firs that were scattered among squares of whirling dancers. On a high platform to the rear, several musicians feverishly plucked or sawed out a Virginia reel while a gaunt fellow sang the calls.

The lively tune ended and another waltz began.

The idea of sharing the treasure on his arm with anyone else didn't appeal to Pierce in the least. He stopped, unwilling to leave the seclusion of their forest. Turning to Lark, he set down the basket and bowed. ''Would the lady care to dance?''

She looked about her, confused for the barest second, before picking up one side of her skirt and stepping into his arms. The copper in her eyes caught the light of a distant lantern as she gazed up at him. ''Why, yes, the lady would.''

Within the growing darkness, they waltzed between silhouetted trees on a carpet of tender grass, her billowing skirts creating a rose-scented breeze. Pierce yearned to pull her ever closer as they glided among the shadows.

He could not take his eyes off this enchantress, this vision who had appeared out of nowhere. He only hoped she did truly exist, that she really was the daughter of a Cajun riverboat captain, not merely a dream he'd conjured up. He prayed he wouldn't awaken in the morning and find himself back in Louisiana, back to all that he hoped he'd left behind. Worse yet, what if Captain Pacquing recognized him? Knew about him?

Damn, he had to stop resurrecting the past, spoiling this moment, this time with her, this new life.

Too soon the waltz ended, and "Turkey in the Straw" began, but Pierce could not bear to take his hand from her waist. Instead, he whirled Lark into his own version of a waltz to the lively tune.

After a fast spin, she burst out laughing, adding her own music as she merrily romped with him through the spirited dance.

He loved her for it—every hair on her head, every curve of that expressively beautiful face, every word out of her mouth. And again he let himself envision spending the rest of his life with her, finding exciting new ways each day to make her laugh.

As they, along with the music, careened to a stop, Lark gave him a plucky grin. "That . . . was . . . fun," she tossed out between rushed breaths, her tempting breasts straining against her ruffled bodice. Seemingly unaware of the effect their rapid rise and fall had on him, she reached up to her collapsing hairdo and shoved at a loose pin.

"Why don''t you let your hair down?" His own words came out jerky. "A few more dances like the last one and it'll fall anyway." Besides, he wanted to see it swirling about her. He could already feel his fingers running through its silkiness.

Her smile faded. A stillness enveloped her, and her eyes seemed larger, smoky. "Yes, I probably should." The words came out low, slow, as she raised her hands to her head.

All sound, all sight, blurred away as he moved closer. "Let me."

She said nothing as she dropped her hands, but her eyes never left his face as he reached into her hair.

Pierce had bedded any number of women, some who'd known about him and some who hadn't, but never in his twenty-seven years had he felt such an intimacy as he did now. Every nerve in his body thrummed as, with shaky hands, he drew out the pins one by one and watched waves of glorious auburn hair spill over her shoulders and down her back.

Out of the night a slow waltz drifted into Pierce's consciousness, and he realized how far away from the music they'd danced, how very alone they were. How rapidly she had begun to pant again, how ripe her slightly parted lips were. After slipping the hairpins into his pocket, his hands found their way into her hair. He leaned down, and her lashes fell shut as he found her mouth. Slowly he sampled its sweet warmth.

She moaned and reached up, wrapping her arms around his neck as she leaned into him.

His heart lurched. He traced her lips with his tongue. Through the thin fabric of his shirt, he felt a tremble course through her body. Her racing heartbeat matched his.

She pressed closer, seeking more, her breath coming in shallow gasps.

Her sounds pushed him past the bounds of restraint. His tongue plunged into her mouth with devouring urgency, deepening his kiss. One hand abandoned her tresses and crushed her to him.

A long sigh escaped her . . . and she sank in his arms like a rag doll.

Shocked, Pierce tore his mouth from hers and viewed the limp girl, her head lolled to one side. *She'd fainted!* "The corset! That damned corset!" he railed. Overwhelming disappointment and frustration ground at him as he scooped her up. He had no choice but to return her to the ship where she could be freed from the strangling thing and allowed to recover. "Dammit, there ought to be a law."

Chapter
Six

GEORGIE FLOATED UP through a thick, buzzing fog to become aware that someone was carrying her up a flight of stairs. She raised her lashes to a dim blur that gradually cleared to a star-filled night. She then focused on the deeply shadowed face of the one who held her. Pierce. Pierce Kingston. "What happened? Where am I?"

At the landing, he slowed. "You swooned."

"Really? I don't swoon."

His head dipped closer. "It must have been the power of my charms. Which stateroom is yours?"

"What?" Lark looked about and realized they were on the promenade deck of the *Willamette*. But the entire expanse lay in darkness—not a single lantern had been lit. Then she remembered the celebration. Everyone, including the crew, must still be there.

"Which way to your stateroom?" he repeated.

"My stateroom? I can't— We can't—"

"Shh, don't be frightened. I would never take advantage of you. I only want to see you safely to your cabin."

"It's up on the texas deck."

"I might've known it'd be at the top." He adjusted her weight in his arms and lengthened his stride. "But I guess it's for the best. I've got a while lot of energy that needs using up."

"Oh, I hadn't thought. You carried me all the way back to the wharf. You must be exhausted. Please, let me down. I'm sure I'm fine now."

"No, it's all right. I don't mind."

"Really, I don't want you to think I'm some wilting pansy."

"Believe me, no one will ever take you for one," he said without slowing his pace.

"Please. I can't let you do this. Put me down."

With a sigh he stopped. "If you're sure . . . " Carefully he lowered her feet to the deck.

Her knees buckled.

He scooped her up again. "Looks like you're stuck with me a little while longer." Holding her tighter than before, he didn't sound as if he minded in the least.

"This is so embarrassing." But even while she said it, she wound her arms around his neck and laid her head on his shoulder. She took a long whiff of his cologne, made more enticing by the faint musky scent that was his alone.

As she snuggled closer, she felt more than heard him groan, and a dizzying tingle spread from her head downward, even to the tips of her fingers and toes. As the exquisite sensation began to subside to a perplexing tickle in her womanly region, she blamed the light-headedness on her recent faint. But the rest? Oh, my. What a silly child she'd been her whole life, to think the most exciting thing to explore was an uncharted river. Nothing could compare to this—to him. And when he'd kissed her in the woods, really kissed her, every nerve, every muscle in her body, even her breasts, had strained for more. And a racking sweet ache had assaulted her core with such force—no wonder she'd swooned. What girl wouldn't have?

She looked up at those lips, barely discernible in the starlight, and wondered if he would ever kiss her with such passion again. Probably not, since she'd fainted from the last one. But that was probably mostly the corset's fault. Damn the thing, anyway. She would never put on one of the blasted contraptions again as long as she lived. . . . What was she thinking? Of course she would. A gentleman like Pierce expected his lady to be properly dressed.

Who was she kidding? She was no lady. She was a river-rat tomboy. And by tomorrow he would no doubt find that out. Unless . . . Unless what?

Too soon he'd climbed the next, steeper flight and carried her across the wide, vacant deck to the row of officers' cabins clustered in the center. Coming to a stop, he lowered his mouth dangerously close to her ear. "Which is my lady Lark's?"

The brush of his whispered breath sent a lightning bolt up her spine. This, she thought, must be what it feels like to be in love. She made a real effort not to croak her answer. "The one at the bow end."

In a wisp of a second they were there, and he lowered her to her feet. This time, thank heaven, her legs held. Pierce supported her with one arm, however, while she fumbled in the reticule chained to her sash until she found her key. With fluttery fingers she scratched around, trying to locate the lock in the dark.

After a moment Pierce covered her hand with his and guided the key home, turning it until the lock clicked. He opened the door into pitch blackness.

Georgie desperately did not want to leave him, to go inside and end this most wonderful of days. But what

else could she do after he'd carried her all the way up
there? After she'd wrecked their evening because of
some stupid female weakness. "Thank you so much for
everything. I don't know when I've had a better time.
I'm just sorry I ruined your perfect day. I hope you can
forgive me."

His fingers cupped her chin, raising it to him, while his
other hand toyed with the hair fringing her cheek.

Oh, yes! everything in her cried. Please kiss me!

"Don't you know by now that *you* are the perfection
that gave me this day?" His breath caught on a shudder.

Hers slid out on a sigh.

"And now I'd better leave you while I still can." His
hands fell from her, and he stepped away.

Panic seized Georgie. She caught his departing arm.
"Wait!"

He turned back. "Yes?"

"If I promise not to faint on you, could I have just one
last kiss?" A chill of shock ran up her spine at her
outrageous words.

He froze, staring at her for several heartbeats as she
tried to convince herself that she hadn't really said it, that
her mind, fuzzy from champagne, had just imagined it.

Then she was in his arms, inside the cabin, the door
kicked closed behind him. He rained kisses across her
eyes, her cheeks, her mouth, down her pulsing throat.

Her heart pounded, and hot blood raged through her
till she thought she'd sizzle from the sheer thrill. She
thrust her hands into his hair, knocking the hat from his
head as she let her hungering lips do their own impassioned exploring, laying claim to his own throbbing
temple, the curve of his cheek, a fringe of thick lashes.

He slid his hand down her neck, down over a bare

swell, and into her bodice. His fingers brushed the tip of her breast.

She gasped as sparks shot from there in all directions.

Suddenly he tore himself away from her and grabbed her shoulders. "Are you all right?"

The strangeness of the question cooled her enough to discern that she did feel light-headed again. "I don't know."

"Turn around. I'm getting you out of this damned corset." Within seconds he'd swept her hair aside, unbuttoned her gown, untied her petticoats, and ripped out the strings of the hated garment. He pulled it from around her and flung it away.

"Oh, thank you," she sighed, profoundly relieved until she realized his hands still lingered inside her gaping dress and that he was trailing kisses down her spine. She stiffened, but only for the briefest second—his touch felt too undeniably delicious.

Beneath her bodice, his hands found their way around her sides to cup her breasts, and more startling sensations so overwhelmed her that her legs again lost their strength. She leaned back into him for support.

He whispered something she couldn't hear above the fire roaring in her head as his thumbs teased her crests. She was on the verge of exploding into ecstasy when, to her utter dismay, he abandoned her and stepped back. "Those hoops have to go, too." He shoved all her undergarments down over her hips until they pooled at her feet, then swung her and her barely clinging gown into his arms again and stepped across the heap of clothing.

Acutely aware of his strength and his gentleness as he held her aloft, Georgie had never felt so utterly feminine in her life. She tried to kiss his neck, but his starched collar prevented it. "You could use a little loosening up, too," she murmured, undoing his top button.

A chuckle rolled out of him. "More than you know." He slid her carelessly draped figure down his lean frame and across a bulge in his breeches.

Another thrill curled through her as she realized she was the cause of his very particular discomfort—she'd heard plenty about it from the lads on the docks.

Georgie had little time to muse over her newfound power as his mouth claimed hers in a vanquishing kiss. His hands matched the fervor in his lips as they moved up and down her bare back.

But her greedy body still cried for more. Pulling him closer, she met his invading tongue with hers in a quicksilver duel.

Suddenly he wrenched away and clutched her shoulders. "My God, I want you." He whispered the words with such deep feeling that she couldn't possibly deny him.

She reached for him again.

He caught her arms and lowered them to her sides. "I've never wanted anyone so much in my life." He slid the gown off her shoulders and on down. "You're everything I ever dreamed of. More."

Standing nude before him, with his pleasuring hands caressing the smoothness of her curves, she felt no shame—he'd just said she was the dream of his life. This man, more wondrous than words could express, wanted her alone. Even in broad daylight she wouldn't have felt shy with him. In fact, she felt cheated because she couldn't see the adoration she was sure shone from his eyes. He truly cared.

Desiring to reciprocate, to touch his skin, to own him

as he did her, she hurriedly, jerkily, undid his shirt and unbuckled his belt.

His hands ceased moving, and his breath stopped when she started on his trouser buttons. At her shoulders, his fingers dug in, and she had no doubt the same hot madness assaulted him.

She ripped his shirt from his waistband and flung it aside, then pressed her molten flesh against the sinewy firmness of his chest. She rubbed her cheek across him until she brushed his flat nipple. Having an uncontrollable desire to taste it, she ran the tip of her tongue around the puckering flesh.

This time Pierce sucked in a sharp gasp. Hastily he stripped off his shirt and moved her to the bed.

She expected him to be right behind her, but instead she heard a loud thud, then another, and knew he'd discarded his boots and was shucking his breeches. She tossed away her own stockings and slippers, then lay down.

The bed sank with his weight.

She reached out, and he came to her, all of him, spreading over all of her. She reveled in every toned inch of rippling muscle and that hard, pressing, secret part, which she knew instinctively would answer her need. A need she had never even known existed until this night—this glorious night when she would learn what it truly meant to be a woman . . . his woman.

Rolling onto his side, he ran a hand slowly up her tender belly, over her ribs . . . higher. "My lovely Lark, you're far more perfect than I could've imagined. . . . Perfect." The breath from the low, husky words feathered over her yearning breasts as he descended upon it and took one crest into his mouth.

A wild blaze streaked from it downward, jolting her

depths into a pulsating, craving sheath of fire only he could quench. She grabbed his arms and hung on as her body melted, wet inside and out. She didn't know how much more she could take of this ravenous agony without screaming.

While pleasuring one eager tip with his mouth, he further inflamed her by teasing the other with his thumb. He slid his other hand down her belly toward a vortex of sharply throbbing hunger.

Pierce felt her arch against his seeking hand as her mewling whimper grew into a moan of anticipation—a mating call that sent blood racing down to engorge him past the point of pain. He tried desperately to go slowly, prepare her to receive him, but her quivering thigh moved against his pulsing manhood, driving him to the edge. And her hand also fluttered dangerously close.

Rolling on top of her, he took her mouth with his as he guided his length past her velvety entrance, then lowered himself slowly into her hot, sleek flesh, which surged with life as it closed around him.

She arched upward to take him deeper, tempting him to invade her with the force his own body demanded. But his desire to make her first moments as painless as possible overrode his own need. Ignoring the impatience in her thrusting hips, her digging fingers, her ravaging mouth, he slowly descended until he reached her maidenhead. There he lingered long enough to lace his fingers through her hair and capture her restless head . . . to quiet his love for one last tender kiss before he took her innocence.

With his mouth still moving gently across her soft swollen lips, he thrust swift and deep.

She gasped. Her body stiffened.

Buried within her, Pierce eased down his weight,

blanketing her, hoping to absorb some of the hurt. He gently kissed her lashes, her nose, her lips, felt the heat of her breath across his face as it came in feathery pants. "I'm so sorry. But don't be afraid. There won't be any more pain. Only pleasure. For the rest of our lives."

She began to relax, and her hands started wandering over his back again with returning fervor. Her tongue found that tender spot at the base of his neck and teased it, sending even more power to his already overstressed manhood.

He withdrew, then returned as gently as his excited body would allow. Trembling from his constraint, he didn't know how much longer he'd be able to hold himself in check.

She surprised him with a thrust of her own, taking him all the way in.

Swiftly he retreated again to her very edge. Then, all caution lost on the sound of her sigh, he plunged in, then again, and again.

She met him with her own frenzied need, digging her nails into his back as his chest again and again met the hardening tips of her breasts until, with a last shuddering thrust, he poured all his love, all his desire, into her in wave after wave of exploding ecstasy.

A small scream escaped her lips, and her clinging, panting body went limp. Only her hands continued to make love to him, weaving circles across his own heaving, sweat-slick back. After a long time, she sighed, "Oh, my," in the softest trill against his cheek.

A tingle of excitement skittered across his heart. He wanted to take his lovely river lark into his arms and crush her to him, but knew it would immediately ignite him again, and he didn't want to rush her. Reluctantly he withdrew and instantly regretted the loss.

"Oh, my," came again, but stronger this time.

Rolling to her side, he pulled her to him and buried his face in a swirl of her hair, a glorious abundance that from this moment on would always remind him of the delicate aroma of roses . . . and this precious moment. He breathed deeply until he nearly burst from the love he felt for her.

"Thank you," came her emotion-filled voice. "Thank you so much."

"What?" His joy tumbled out on a chuckle as he swung her on top of him, spilling her and her luxuriant locks over him. "Anytime, my love, anytime."

At a rapping on the door, Pierce was unwillingly roused from a deep blissful sleep. Who could that be in the middle of the night? He started to call out, but a hand clamped itself over his mouth. Whose? Then he remembered. *Lark's.*

Chapter
Seven

GEORGIE HELD HER breath, all vestiges of sleep gone, as Papa knocked again with his old familiar combination of taps. She listened for the click of the door latch, her heart hammering from the horrifying thought of being caught with a man in her bed.

Please, God, she silently prayed, don't let Papa come in.

Pierce's hand covered the one she held over his mouth and pulled it away. But, thank heaven, he remained quiet.

After what seemed like an eternity, she heard her father turn, and the sound of his footsteps slowly receding. She let out a whoosh of breath. Saved for the moment. "Get up," she hissed and shoved at the form next to her. "You've got to get out of here before Papa comes back."

Instead of obeying, he rolled toward her and stroked the hair flowing over her shoulders. "Don't worry. "He's probably gone off to bed."

"No, he hasn't." She gave her whispered words as much emphasis as possible. "I would've heard his door shut. He's still wandering around out there. He'll come back. I know he will." She pushed again, this time using her feet in an effort to eject him from her bed.

"All right." He sat up and swung his feet to the floor. "But next time—"

"*Next time?* Are you crazy? I can't take a chance like this again. Papa would . . . Get your clothes on and get out. Now."

"I'll have to light a lamp to find 'em."

"You can't do that. He'll see it."

"But I don't—"

"Do it!" Georgie shoved at his back again, and he finally lumbered to his feet. She watched his darkness-shrouded figure take a couple of slow steps, then stop.

"If I bolt the door, I don't see any reason why I can't just sneak out first thing in the morning."

"You don't?" This man simply wasn't grasping the gravity of the situation.

"After all the celebrating, everyone's going to sleep late in the morning," he went on. "And I'll be careful. No one'll see me leave."

Georgie gritted her teeth to keep from shrieking as she rose up on her knees. She pulled a blanket up to shield herself, though she knew he couldn't see more than her silhouette. "If you don't do as I say, I'm going to scream the roof off this place."

"All right," he grumbled.

She heard more than saw him stumbling about, rustling her heaped petticoats as he stepped on them, bumping a boot. He was taking forever. She bounded off the bed, blanket in tow. "Here," she said, locating some fabric with her foot. "I think I found your shirt." She bent over to fetch it. Coming up, she banged the top of her head hard against his chin. She yelped.

He grunted, then caught her to him. "Are you hurt?"

His deep musky warmth enveloped her, assaulting her with a thousand remembered sensations. She hastily thrust herself away from him. Wrapping the blanket around her with one hand, she shoved his shirt at him with the other. "Put it on. You've got to hurry."

Swinging away, she heard him chuckling as she felt about until she'd found and collected more of his attire. "Have you got your shirt on?"

"I'm still buttoning it."

"Forget the buttons. Here are your pants." She pressed them into his hands.

He laughed again, low, as if he knew some secret joke while he pulled them on.

She shoved his stockings and boots at him.

"Don't you think folks'll think it odd, me walking downstairs to my cabin half undone? 'Specially if my trousers fall down."

"This is serious." Georgie pushed him back to sit on the bed. "If Papa ever found out, I don't know what I'd do. I'd just die—I know I would."

"Sweetheart, you're making this out to be much worse than it is. Once I talk to him, I'm sure he'll—"

"*No. You can't!* If he even thought we might have—" She spun away and bent over, swiftly sweeping her hands across the floor, looking for his vest.

"But, Lark, I thought—"

"Where *is* your waistcoat?"

"It's not here. I left it back in the woods with the picnic basket." He stood up and caught her as she straightened. "Lark darling, you've done nothing to be ashamed of. Calm down."

She jerked away. "Keep your hands to yourself. They've already done enough for one night." Before he could catch her again, she dashed to the door and flung it open, letting in a measure of dim light.

"I can't leave you in this state. Please believe me, everything's going to be fine. I want to marry you."

"Go!"

He stepped up to her.

She snugged the blanket tighter around her bosom.

Smiling down at her, he cupped her chin. "I'll be back in the morning."

"No, you can't. *Papa* . . . I won't be here."

"Oh, yes you will." His lips descended upon hers, that mouth that had taught her so much, made her feel so much. And, heaven help her, her lips had no choice but to respond, to mold themselves to his and again begin to move, to taste, entwine, to become one with him. Her traitorous arms found his neck, pulled at him as he folded himself around her.

Laughter drifted up from the deck below, and a door slammed, bringing Georgie to her senses. She tore herself away and collided with the doorjamb behind her.

In the faint starlight she saw Pierce's eyes leave her face. His breath caught as his gaze slid down her form.

Bilge water! Her fool hands had dropped the blanket. Struck dumb, she flung her arms across her chest.

In an instant Pierce retrieved the cover and wrapped it around her, then gently pushed her inside the cabin. "Sweet dreams, my love."

Still speechless, she reached for the door to close it.

He stopped her. "I have to say just one more thing before I go."

Despite herself, she lifted her gaze to his, so luminous in the elusive light. "Yes?"

"You're even more beautiful than I'd imagined. Even more perfect."

Watching him disappear into the night, she clutched

the blanket tighter in a desperate effort to fill her suddenly overwhelmingly empty arms.

A gem, Pierce thought as he descended to the promenade deck, fastening the last of his buttons. The girl was like a diamond of many facets, and she sparkled from each and every one of them. He'd even enjoyed being thrown out by the Papa's-little-girl side of her. And here, in faraway Oregon, there would be none of the outrage, none of the accusations. This time he would be free to claim this loveliest of belles.

Reaching the bottom step, Pierce turned toward the corridor that led to his cabin.

"Hey, you!" The shout came from behind, echoing from the dimly lit salon across from the stairwell. Pierce turned around to see someone standing in its wide doorway—an older man wearing an officer's cap.

Lark's father.

The man must have seen him leaving her cabin. Pierce had a wild impulse to run, or at least check his buttons. But instead he walked toward Captain Pacquing, knowing just how a man must feel on his way to the guillotine. "Are you speaking to me?"

"You dat Kingston fella, eh?" The Cajun-accented words sounded like a challenge as Lark's father waited, lounging against the doorjamb, arms folded across his chest.

The captain undoubtedly knew of him—the circumstances of his birth, his mixed heritage. Pierce stopped a few feet short of him. "Yes," he replied on a defeated sigh.

"You da one what take ever'body's money today. You must be pretty rich man now, eh?"

The question caught Pierce off guard. "I . . . uh, did quite well."

"An' I don' see you playin' cards later. Dat wasn' friendly, you hidin' out, not givin' folks a chance to win back some a dey money." His voice sounded thick with whiskey, and red tinged his dark brown eyes.

"I'm sorry if I offended anyone. But as you must know, I'd made other plans."

Pacquing's wide unruly brows crinkled in a puzzled frown. The man acted as if he hadn't even seen Pierce and Lark together.

"Weren't you at the race?" Pierce said.

"I was in da middle of a hand. I miss it. But if you really sorry for not bein' a gentleman, I give you chance to make up for it now."

Lark's father knew absolutely nothing. Pierce smiled with genuine warmth at the shorter man. "Believe me, I don't want you thinking I'm anything less than a gentleman. Tell me what I can do to redeem myself."

At the sound of eight bells, Georgie drifted awake on a lazy stretch, and every bare inch of her tingled with scrumptious satisfaction. Remembering why she'd awakened in resplendent nakedness for the first time in her life, she smiled with glorious delight. She knew she should feel terrible, should conjure up at least a smidgen of remorse, but she'd never felt so good in her entire life.

Hugging her pillow to her, she rolled onto her side, wishing it were Pierce's chest pressed firmly to her yearning breasts. She tried to gaze into his imaginary face, but instead discovered a billowing heap of petticoats and, a few feet away, her discarded gown. My goodness, but she'd been brazen. She'd even helped him undress. Heat rushed to her face. Yet he'd acted as if he loved her. He *did* love her. She just knew it. Hadn't he asked her to marry him? She should've said yes then and there. She'd die if she lost him, she loved him so much.

The realization hummed through her like a song. "I really do." She brushed a cheek against the coolness of her pillowcase and wished it were his shoulder. Noticing a tenderness, she ran her hand across the sensitive flesh. "His whiskers. From all the kissing." Her heart jumped, and shivers of excitement careened through her belly at the memory of his mouth touching, tasting every inch of her face. Her lips . . . She brushed their swollen fullness with her fingers. Somehow, some way, she had to have Pierce in her bed again tonight and every night from now on.

"But how?" Georgie sat up, clutching her pillow to her. How was she going to sneak him past Papa? A sudden giggle erupted at the picture of her and her lover skulking hand in hand through the dark passageways and stealing kisses behind all the crates and bales.

Her amusement died as her most pressing problem intruded—how to keep Papa from giving away her secret to Pierce and how to keep the crew quiet once she appeared this morning as Lark.

The urgency of her mission prodded her into action. She jumped out of bed. After leaping over her petticoats, she dropped down beside her trunk, threw up the lid, and started digging past Georgie's work clothes. She simply had to get into one of her long ignored day gowns, arrange her hair into some semblance of fashion, and get up to the pilothouse. She had to do some fast talking before Pierce came looking for her.

And he would come, wouldn't he? Struck with uncertainty, she turned toward the door . . . and spotted his Fourth of July straw hat sitting in the corner next to the entrance. Her doubts vanished. Of course he'd come. He loved her. He never would've worn that silly hat if he didn't.

Her attention moved from the hat to several sheets of folded paper stuck under the door. A letter! Rising from her knees, she hurried to retrieve it. She knew it must be from Pierce. "My first love letter."

She swept it up, then adjusted the shutters at the small window to shed more light before shaking the paper open.

"My dearest daughter," the missive began in her father's scrawl.

Instant disappointment weighted her chest. Then, just as quickly, she squelched it, scolding herself for being a silly ninny and for starting to moon over Pierce like a mewling sissy.

She snapped the letter before her again. Papa had never slipped a note under her door before. Oh, dear. Her fingers tightened, wrinkling the edge of the pages. He must've seen Pierce leaving her room last night. She looked up at the ceiling. Please, God, don't let it say that. Closing her eyes, she took a deep breath, then opened them to his first words.

I'm so sorry. Please try not to hate your poor old papa. I love you so much, my little bird. I did not mean for things to go so far. I guess my boys, they are right. I just ain't got no sense when I start to drink. I been awake all night trying to figure a way out. But it is no good. I have to leave. I be gone before you wake up.

Gone? Georgie couldn't believe her eyes. She scanned the last sentence again. What could have happened? With fevered urgency, she continued to read.

Everyone said Jake Stone's horse would win. A sure thing. I think this is my big chance to get you some of the pretty girl things you been missing out on. I take the money from the boat safe—$535. I bet $500. When I lose, I know I have to replace it or go to jail. So I get in a poker game to win it back. I am not so lucky. Then I draw this sure hand. Three aces. I need to raise the bet, but I no have enough. I bet the Dream Ellen. *God help me, this bastard, he has a straight. I had to give this man, Samuel Stokes, my IOU for our little stern-wheeler. I don't know how, but I think maybe he cheat me.*

Georgie's mouth dropped open. "Papa! How could you?" The *Dream Ellen* was their home. Their living. What were they supposed to do now? Hoping his last words were all a lie, a bad joke, she read on.

When I come back here, some men are playing cards in the salon. I think maybe the angels will smile down on me this time. But I lose the Dream Ellen *again. Jasper Blackwell has my second IOU. This one, he has the evil eye. I think he kill me if he finds out about the other IOU.*

"Oh, my God. How could I have left him to the mercy of those cheating, murdering gamblers? It's not like I didn't know he'd be drinking."

I know I am crazy useless old man. But please try to understand that I was just trying to make it all right again. That is why when I see Mr. Kingston, the cause of all my troubles in the first place, I think finally my luck, she is going to change. To make sure this one

*don't cheat, I shuffle the deck, and we cut for high
card. But somehow he must have palmed that queen.
He now has IOU number three for our boat.*

Pierce? Impossible. He wouldn't do a thing like that!
Hot bile rose from Georgie's churning stomach. But the
story was all right there. He had left her bed, spouting
marriage, to go and take advantage of her poor befuddled
father. *How could he?*

Georgie's knees began to wobble. She stumbled back
to her bed and dropped down. Tears sprang into her eyes.
Savagely she swiped them away. "*How could he?*" A
deadly rage gripped her. "Lying, cheating, no-account
gambler." She glared at the vile hat across the room and
snatched up the letter again. What else had the swagger-
ing polecat done to her papa?

*I know I am a coward, but I can't look you or Cadie
in the face again. And I must escape before these men
find me out. I want you to go back to the Mississippi
with Cadie when he leaves next week. And please try
to forgive this fool of a papa for being gulled by a
bunch of gamblers again. I love you, my little Lark
bird.*

George let the letter fall to her lap and this time didn't
stop the tears from rolling. Her papa was gone. He'd left
her. Alone. What would she say to the owner of the
Willamette? He would be returning on Saturday. He'd
trusted them, had given Papa a second chance to captain
a big river queen again, even if it was for just six weeks.
And Cadie. What would she tell him? She shrugged her
slumping shoulders. Could she tell him that instead of
keeping an eye on Papa, as she was supposed to, she'd

been playing the whore for some silver-tongued snake of a gambler. And now not one but three men would show up in Portland waving Papa's IOUs under Cadie's nose to claim their little logging boat.

Georgie swallowed hard. "What am I to do?" Somehow she had to return the money to the safe. But as for their own boat, she just didn't know.

Chapter
Eight

FOR THE SECOND time in one night someone pounded on Pierce's door, awakening him.

Opening his eyes, he noticed it was morning. "Hold on!" He reached up and grabbed his trousers, which were dangling from the bunk above. "I'll be there in a minute."

While shoving his foot into one pant leg, he grinned, remembering his last hurried dressing. He wished he were still in Lark's bed, making love to her in the rosy light of morn. Tossing on his shirt, he walked to the door of the narrow white-walled cabin and opened it.

A kid stood there, his floppy hat pulled low over his brow, obscuring all but his grimacing mouth.

"Yes? May I help you?" he asked while buttoning up. The boy tilted his face upward, and despite the surly expression, displayed an incredible likeness to Lark.

"Hey, Georgie!" someone called from the fore end of the hall. "Have you seen your pa? Hilly wants to know what time we're pullin' out."

The kid jerked his head in the crewman's direction. "Tell him I'll be up in a minute." He swung back to Pierce.

"So," Pierce ventured in an affable tone, "you must

be a younger brother of Lark's. Have you seen her up and about yet?''

The boy's face scrunched up as if he didn't understand anything.

Maybe he wasn't real bright. In fact, wasn't this the mouthy kid who had slammed into him just before they left Salem?

Georgie's features relaxed slightly. ''I need to talk to you. Can I come in a minute?''

''Sure.'' Pierce stepped back, letting the youngster into the cramped room. He would have offered the boy a seat, but the cabin had no chair, only a stack of three bunks. ''Is there a problem?'' He picked up his boots.

The kid shot him a defiant look and snorted. ''You might say that. Papa's gone, and it's your fault.''

''What are you talking about?'' he asked, thrusting his foot into one of the boots.

''It's all right here in his letter.'' The lad pulled it halfway out of a pocket in his loose-fitting dungarees, then shoved it back down. ''It says how you cheated him out of his boat.''

''It doesn't say that. It couldn't.'' Pierce jerked on his second boot and moved past the belligerent boy to the doorway. He couldn't believe how badly his encounters with Lark's family went. First the father and now the brother. ''Let's go find Lark and the captain,'' he said, tucking in his shirt. ''I'm sure this can be all worked out.''

''Yeah. I'm sure you're real good at that.''

Pierce clenched his fists. He had an almost uncontrollable urge to thump in the kid's head. He stiffly led the way into the corridor and waited until the lad came out. ''As I said, let's talk to your father and—''

"You don't listen real good, do you? I said he's gone. Run off."

That scrawny neck would be so easy to ring. But, brat that he was, he was still Lark's brother. Pierce took a slow, calming breath, then spoke in quiet, even tones. "I'm sure your sister knows where he is."

"My sister?" Georgie's eyes grew wide, and he angrily yanked his hat farther down over his ears. "She's, uh . . . she's just as gone as Papa is."

Pierce grabbed the boy's skinny arm and pulled him close. "What do you mean, gone?"

"*Oww!*" He wrenched away, rubbing the place where Pierce had clutched.

"I said, where is she?"

The boy stared up at him, with eyes narrowed menacingly, then abruptly looked away. "She went with Papa."

Pierce's chest tightened. He couldn't believe it. How could Lark desert him after what they'd shared last night? He's asked her to marry him, for God's sake. Her father must've known about him after all, and taken her away. No. That made no sense. The captain had seemed interested in nothing but gambling.

He reached into his pocket and touched Pacquing's IOU. If the man hadn't run off so fast last night, Pierce would've made him take it back then and there. Such a generous gesture would surely have softened up Lark's father enough for him to agree to Pierce's suit. But now they were both gone. And this mouthy whelp blamed him! "All right, kid. Tell me everything. And don't leave out a word."

Pierce could hardly believe his ears as, bit by stammering bit, the boy, Georgie, revealed the enormity of the hole his father had dug for himself. The lame-brained fool'd had no choice but to disappear. But why in the world had he dragged Lark off with him?

As Georgie finished the sordid tale, his voice faded away to nothing. He stuffed his hands into his pockets and shrugged. And for the first time Pierce noticed how spindly his shoulders were. Maybe the kid wasn't so bad after all. He'd been slapped with quite a lot this morning.

A picture flashed through Pierce's mind of that fateful day when he himself had stood in front of his headmaster's desk and listened while Principal Baldwin read the terrible letter from his father's wife. Pierce had been only two or three years older than this kid at the time. Compassion stirred him into clapping a hand on Georgie's shoulder. "I know this is hard, but—"

Georgie jerked away. "How could you possibly know? Someone like you? Nonetheless, I've come with a proposition for you. And if you care about Lark at all, you'll agree to it."

Pierce's heart pricked at the word "proposition." Just the day before, magical yesterday, she'd used that same word. "Well, spit it out."

Georgie's eyes, that same unusual shade of burnished copper, snapped up to his. "You replace the money Papa took from the safe. You can afford it, since you took some from just about everyone yesterday. If you do, I'll see that you get our stern-wheeler, the *Dream Ellen*, instead of one of those other cardsharps, even if your IOU is at the bottom of the list."

Pierce found it hard to believe that, with a mouth like his, the kid had lived this long. A flat no would have been easy to say, but he knew he couldn't do it. If he didn't replace the stolen money, the sheriff would be called in. His lovely Lark might be tossed into jail along with her worthless father. "For your sister I'll do it. Where's the safe? Can you get into it without anyone knowing?"

The boy swung away, rubbing his eyes with knotted fists. Then, nodding, he started at a fast pace toward the stairwell.

In the captain's untidy office, Pierce watched as the lad swiftly and efficiently opened the combination safe, and silently vowed never again to place his own savings in someone else's keeping.

After Georgie locked in the $535, he peeked outside the office, both ways, then beckoned impatiently.

At the door, Pierce's gaze drifted longingly to the other end of the officers' cabins. Just a few hours ago he'd been ensconced in the last one, making love to the one who could have been a part of his rightful future, fulfilling his deepest need. Why the hell had he let her throw him out?

"Psst!" Georgie, already at the head of the stairs, motioned frantically.

As if someone would actually guess what they'd been up to. Pierce himself had a hard time believing he'd let the lad talk him out of his money that quickly. Taking one last look at Lark's door, Pierce strode across the wide deck to the boy who waited in that god-awful felt hat.

Hat! Pierce shot a glance back to Lark's room. He'd left his lucky Fourth of July straw hat in there. Later, after the kid settled down, he'd tell him that Lark had borrowed it or something and get him to fetch it.

Descending behind Georgie, Pierce saw two men start up the stairs.

One, a gaunt-faced man with pop eyes, caught Georgie's arm. His wiry black brows soared as he leaned down.

"Well, if it ain't Louie's busy little whelp?" he said in a deep gruff voice.

"Let go of me." Georgie tried to break away, but the man held him fast.

"Sure. Soon as you tell us where your pa's hidin' out," his companion added, an unfriendly smile creasing his blotchy skin.

The middle-aged men both looked as if they'd been in more than their share of barroom brawls. But no matter how obnoxious Lark's kid brother might be, Pierce couldn't let them harm him. "The boy's with me."

The two men swung their attention to Pierce.

The one clutching Georgie looked Pierce up and down, undoubtedly taking his measure, then grudgingly released the boy. "The only interest we got in the squirt is his pa's whereabouts."

"Yeah," agreed the second, his voice sliding like an out-of-tune violin. "Me an' Mr. Blackwell here has just discovered we have somethin' in common. Ain't that right?" With a mop of graying curls spilling out beneath his hat, he directed a sneer of a grin at the other.

"That's right. Mr. Stokes here an' me seem to be holdin' markers from the boy's pa for the same boat."

"There must be some mistake," Georgie said with the sincerity of a choirboy as he glanced from one gambler to the other. "Papa's over at the smithy's getting an engine part welded. It may take a while. Why don't you go on over there and get the problem settled?"

"Yeah. Think we'll do just that," the pop-eyed one drawled, looking at the other man. He reached inside his black frock coat and rested his hand on the butt of a revolver. "You up to settling a few things, Mr. Stokes?"

The other's menacing grin widened. "Primed and ready, Mr. Blackwell. Primed and ready."

As the two wheeled around and started down the steps again, Pierce noticed Georgie's shoulders heave with a big sigh. He had to hand it to the kid—he was fast on his feet, and he didn't get rattled. Suspicion surfaced. What if Georgie had lied to him, too. Tricked him.

"Mr. Kingston! Thank the good Lord." Panic laced Davy's voice as he appeared at the bottom of the stairs waving a piece of paper.

Blackwell and Stokes stopped, blocking the tiny man's way, both obviously curious.

"Yes, Davy?" Pierce answered, looking over their heads from a step above.

"Pegasus! He gone!"

"*What?*" Pierce pushed past the others. "Where?"

"Don' know. Yesterday bein' such a big'en an' all, I slept late dis mornin'. When I goes to check on him, he be gone." He shoved the sheet of paper at Pierce. "Dis was stuck on a nail."

As Pierce took the note, the Pacquing kid crowded close, and he wondered again how this unmannerly upstart could possibly be related to his Lark. . . . Just thinking about her, he could have sworn he caught the faint whiff of her rose-scented hair. He gave his head a quick shake and looked at the message.

Mr. Kingston,

> *I have urgent need of a swift horse. I will leave him at the livery stable in Portland.*

Captain Louis Pacquing

As Pierce stood there, numbly trying to digest yet another misdeed of the Cajun scoundrel Lark loved so much, Georgie slammed past Blackwell, almost knocking the man off his feet.

"You little heathen!" Blackwell shook a bony fist after the kid. "When I catch that by-blow again, I'm gonna twist his ears off."

"What's the letter say?" Stokes asked, snatching it away to quickly scan the two lines. He then passed it to Blackwell. "No wonder the runt took off. The lying little bastard! Bet he was plannin' to trick us off this boat just long enough to leave us behind."

Blackwell snorted on a nod. Swiping a long string of dark hair from his eyes, he turned to Pierce. "Guess you won't be so quick to defend that trashy river pup when we snag him next time. Now I'm goin' on up to the pilothouse and tell 'em to get a head of steam up fast. Get this bucket on downriver, 'fore that thievin' Frenchie bastard beats us back to the Columbia and the *Dream Ellen*. Sneaky as he is, he'll probably light out on it and take your horse with him." A murderous glare caused his mud-brown eyes to bulge even farther as he swung his gaze from Pierce to Stokes and back. "You two comin' with me?"

Chapter Nine

IT HAD TAKEN three hours for the mechanic to find the problem in the starboard engine and get it running again. The man had accused someone of deliberately tampering with the pistons. And of course Pierce had no doubt about who the culprit had been—Georgie.

As Pierce stood at his cabin window, gazing past the half-closed shutter slats, he barely noticed the never-ending parade of strolling, chatting passengers or, beyond them, the tree-crowded shoreline they floated past. Instead, he mulled over every word, every detail, he'd learned in the past few hours. He had to think it through, make the right moves. For the first time in his life his future could be whatever he made of it. But what actions should he take? Yesterday's perfection had turned into a calamitous mess.

Sighing deeply, Pierce closed his eyes. How could someone as wonderful and cultivated as Lark have such a villain for a father? It seemed so damned unfair.

Louie Pacquing. Pierce shook his head. The man had a real knack for taking the life out of his long-awaited dreams. Taking the horse *and* his bewitching Oregon belle.

A light tapping sounded from the hall.

"What now?" Pierce muttered between gritted teeth as he went to answer the door.

When he opened it, the Pacquing kid slipped by him without permission.

Typical of his rude behavior.

"Sorry it took me so long to get here," Georgie said in a rushed whisper as if they'd had an appointment or something. He ran to the window and peeked out. "Between the crew looking for me, and Stokes and that evil-eyed Blackwell, I had a heck of a time gettin' here." He spun back around and scowled. "Shut the door!"

Without thinking, Pierce did as instructed, then wanted to kick himself for obeying the upstart. He leaned against the door, arms folded across his chest, and decided unequivocally that if anyone needed a good kick in the pants it was this ill-mannered squirt. If it hadn't been for his remarkable similarity to Lark, Pierce would never believe his lady and this urchin were remotely related. "What do you want now?"

Georgie clutched his hat on both sides of his head and, as if he thought a big wind was coming, pulled down hard before looking up at Pierce with those distrubingly beautiful eyes. "Nothin'. I just come to tell you nothin's changed. You replaced the passage money, so I'll see to it that the papers to the *Dream Ellen* are signed over to you. I ain't no cheater, like you gullin' gamblers."

God, how Pierce wished Georgie wasn't Lark's little brother. It took supreme control to keep from jerking him up and giving him a good paddling. "I'm more interested in finding your sister. *And my horse.*"

The kid swung back to the window. "Yeah. Me, too. I gotta warn Papa about those two men. Blackwell especially. He's real creepy-lookin'. Like he can see all the way through you."

"Oh, I'm sure your father already knows how much trouble he's in. Or else he'd still be here," Pierce couldn't resist adding.

Still peeking through the shutters as if half the crew and passengers were searching for him—and, knowing the kid, they probably were—Georgie only shrugged at the gibe. "I'm sure Papa's come to his senses by now and will be waiting back at our boat. When we dock in Oregon City, I know a shortcut to where the *Dream Ellen* is usually moored over on the Columbia. Now if you don't mind"—turning around, Georgie moved toward the bunks—"it's been a real busy morning. I'm going to climb up on top and take a little nap."

Pierce's mouth dropped open at the kid's audacity. Then he wondered why it amazed him in the least that Georgie had picked his cabin to hide in. This whole day had been full of surprises, not the least of which was the fact that he himself hadn't even considered *not* trying to save Lark. And even more amazing, Georgie also seemed to take it for granted. But then, as beautiful as his sister was, the boy was probably used to men fawning over her.

Georgie crawled into the narrow space between the ceiling and top bunk. Dropping down, she rolled onto her side and faced the wall in the hope that Pierce would ignore her. And as rude as she'd been, he probably would. *Good.* She despised the very idea of being in the same room with the lying cheat. Defiler of innocent girls.

But he had come to her defense earlier. And now she'd have to take a chance that he'd continue to protect her from Blackwell and Stokes. They were still out there turning the boat upside down looking for her. And they'd keep at it, too, until tomorrow night when the *Willamette* made its last stop above the falls at Oregon City. Fear clawed at her throat as the thought of what they must have planned for her—especially after she'd jammed those pistons to give Papa more time. Even as the crow flies, Oregon City lay a good forty miles to the north, and their stern-wheeler on the Columbia was another twenty. And Papa wasn't much of a rider.

The door handle clicked. Someone was trying to get in! Panicked, Georgie rolled over to face the entrance, then placed a hand over her pounding heart to still it as she saw Pierce step outside, closing the door behind him. She then heard the rattle of a key as he locked it. Thank heaven. He was keeping her safe from the other two while he was away.

Or he could be going to find them, she suddenly realized and sat up, banging her head on the ceiling. "Yikes!" She crashed back onto the pillow, rubbing the sore spot.

No, she decided, curling up again. He wouldn't do that. He was too nice.

No, he wasn't, she almost shouted as she thrust her legs out straight again. He was the same snake she'd taken him for the first time she laid eyes on him. He was just in a generous mood yesterday, being the big winner.

"Yeah," she muttered as guilt squiggled through her bound chest. "And I sure topped off the day for him, didn't I?" The tingle betrayed her by turning into one of desire that raced down to her pelvic region to become a quivering ache. She groaned and grabbed the pillow, ramming it hard against herself as she squeezed her legs together. This was terrible. All she could think about was climbing into bed with him again. She punched hard into the feathers, then again. She couldn't afford to let her mind drift like this. Too much was at stake.

By the time Georgie heard a key in the lock, she'd

spent several hours drifting off to sleep only to jerk
awake again—a thoroughly miserable time. She quickly
adjusted her hat over her coiled braid as she huddled
against the wall.

It was Pierce, thank goodness. He walked in, glanced
up at her without the slightest expression, then placed a
tray heaped with food on the wide shelf attached to the
opposite wall.

The aroma went straight to her stomach, knotting it
with hunger, and she realized she hadn't eaten since
yesterday's picnic.

Those sky blue eyes looked at her again. "Climb
down and get some food. After all you've been up to, I
imagine you've worked up a powerful appetite." Sarcasm rode on his words.

But Georgie didn't mind a smidgen, because Pierce
had on that silly straw hat. He was hooked. Smitten with
someone who didn't exist. All she had to do was reel him
in.

As she climbed down to the floor, her conscience
seized her again, but she slipped out of its grip with
amazing ease. After all, if it weren't for Pierce, she
could've hidden from all her pursuers, even the crew, in
her southern belle disguise. And, she rationalized as she
took another whiff of the food he'd provided, she
planned to tell no more lies than were absolutely necessary to see her papa safe again.

Pierce's back was turned to her as she moved the few
paces across the close room. He had taken off the hat and
was making space in one of his trunks for it. Heaven
forbid he should crush the precious thing!

She wanted to laugh at the fool, relishing the idea that
for once he was the one who'd been flimflammed. She
had no doubt he was mooning over his lady Lark, since

he continued to stroke the striped hatband for several seconds before safely tucking it into the trunk.

But then he straightened to that lean, manly height and ran his fingers through his crisp black hair. The muscles corded across those broad shoulders, and Georgie's palms tingled from the remembered smoothness and heat even now.

Her heart leapfrogged around in her chest.

He turned and caught her staring. "Eat up before the food gets cold."

Fortunately the bindings she always wore to flatten her breasts hid the thumping of her heart. She desperately wished she could strip off the strangling clothes and throw a pitcher of cold water over herself to douse the steady rise of her temperature. Tearing her attention away from those bluest of eyes, she looked down at the two bowls heaped with ham and beans and suddenly realized he intended to eat in here with her. Oh, dear.

Without another word he picked up one of the bowls and some crackers, then moved to the lower bunk and sat down.

Facing the narrow shelf, Georgie had the hardest time concentrating on her food. She forced herself to remember the despicable way Pierce had misused her papa. But all the while, the hair prickled at the back of her neck—a sure sign that he was watching her. And if anyone could discover the truth about her, it was Pierce Kingston. Hadn't he measured every inch of her with those arousing hands just last night?

"Kid."

Georgie jumped. The spoon dropped from her hand and clanged loudly against the bowl. Too scared to turn around, she picked up the utensil as casually as she could while trying to ignore the tightening in her throat. "Yeah?"

"Did Lark speak to you before she left? Did she leave a message for me?"

"No." Well, it wasn't a lie, exactly.

She heard the bed creak and knew Pierce had risen. Heard his footsteps as he came up so close behind her she caught a hint of his cologne.

He clamped a hand on her shoulder.

She froze to instant ice, waiting for the damning words.

He reached past her . . . and placed his empty bowl on the tray. He then picked up a cup of coffee and strode out the door, locking it behind him.

Her relief so profound, Georgie began to shake with such violence she barely made it to the lower bunk before collapsing. She'd been sure he had recognized her, this man who'd gone so far as to say he wanted to marry her. But then, she reminded herself, she'd so dazzled him with the illusion that he couldn't see past it. Couldn't see the real her.

But she hadn't seen the real him either. No matter how her traitorous body clamored for him, she could never forget that the real Pierce Kingston was a heel of the first water.

The tremors died to a soft trill, and she rolled over to get up. Her cheek pressed across the pillow where only hours before he'd lain, and his musky male scent tricked her body into an onslaught of yearnings, starting in her groin and reaching all the way to her fingertips.

Her breath coming in sharp spurts, she flung herself from the bed and scrambled up to the top bunk. When she had sprawled across it, she felt so exhausted she thought she could sleep for a week. "Yes, God," she whispered as she looked heavenward. "At least let me sleep until we get to Oregon City." She kicked the covers to the foot of the bed. It was one infernally hot night!

Georgie woke to the early morning light and some scuffling sounds. She rolled over . . . to the torturous view of that magnificent bare back. She almost drooled at the sight of the smoothly tanned skin bathed in the golden light of dawn, the corded muscles in his shoulders and arms flexing as he buttoned his trousers next to her bunk. They hugged his slim hips and a waist that tapered up to the winged muscles of his upper back.

Dang, she wished she'd wakened in time to see him before he'd put on his breeches.

With the harshest silent scolding she could muster, she swept her attention upward to his crop of silky black hair. Without her realizing it, one of her wayward hands reached out to touch him.

He swung around.

She snatched her hand back.

"I see you're awake now," he said, slipping into a starched white shirt. "All I can say is, I'll be damned glad to get rid of you. I never heard so much tossing and turning in my life. I hardly got any sleep at all."

"Well, your snoring isn't exactly a lullaby, either."

"I don't snore."

"Really?" Georgie quipped, keeping the lie going.

He challenged her with a long unblinking stare, then turned away. He ran a set of pearl studs through his cuffs, then picked up the straw hat now perched on his trunk. After tilting it at a precise angle, he turned back to her. "You know, I find it hard to believe that Lark would ride off into the night with your father *on my horse* without at least saying good-bye." He exhaled sharply. "The captain must've forced her to go with him. But why? Surely he knew he could make better time without her."

Yes, that was a logical conclusion. Her mind whirled as she searched for a believable answer. "I guess Papa figured he needed her. She's the one who takes care of him, keeps everything goin' right. And besides, all the trouble he got himself into is partly her fault. She should've been lookin' out for him instead of runnin' around with you all Fourth of July."

Pierce stabbed her with a sharp stare. "It's time your father took responsibility for himself." He stalked to the door and shoved the bolt aside. "I'll bring you some breakfast later. Maybe." He started out, then turned back, with a surprising grin and one brow quirked. "Has your sister ever talked to you about the way you sleep in your hat? That's really queer."

Before Georgie could think of an answer, he left.

"Well?" Georgie asked impatiently before Pierce had even closed the door behind him. "Have Stokes and Blackwell gotten off the boat?"

"Nope," he quipped with an irritating smirk on his face. "They're still positioned on either side of the gangplank, just the same as they have been at every other stop between Independence and here."

"Bilge water. I was sure they would've gotten tired of each other by the time we reached Oregon City. Unless . . . Maybe they've made a pact to share the *Dream Ellen*."

"Who knows? But one thing I know for sure—they haven't lost interest in you. They probably plan to hang on to you until your father signs over the boat. Now, isn't it a shame how suspicious some folks just naturally are?" Pierce was obviously enjoying himself.

"Don't worry. I'll see you get what's due you. I'll sneak down to the stern and slip over the side into the river. I can easily swim underwater until I'm way under the dock." Georgie opened the door a crack to see if the passageway was empty.

Luckily it was.

"Tell you what," she continued. "Why don't you go on up to the livery barn—you can't miss it after you get up the bank—and rent us a couple of horses? Take 'em out back. I'll be there waitin' for you. And hurry. Like I told you, I know a shortcut to our stern-wheeler. And I've got to get to Papa before Stokes and Blackwell do."

Pierce narrowed his eyes and clamped his jaw tight, a sure clue he didn't like being told what to do.

Pretending not to notice, Georgie peeked out again while she waited for an answer.

"All right," he said through drawn lips. "But don't make me wait."

At last she had finally dried out, Georgie noticed with relief while clinging to Pierce as they rode through the rapidly cooling night air on a long-legged bay gelding. When someone fell overboard by accident, it was bad enough. But to have to deliberately slide into that icy river . . .

Pierce, of course, had been able to disembark with no more than a comradely nod from Stokes and Blackwell, since they had no idea he also held a note from Papa. While she froze in the water, watching for the right moment to dive under, she'd watched Pierce walk onto the dock sporting that dumb straw hat and that cocky swagger of his. Then, later, when she sneaked out of the bushes to meet him, he arrived with only one mount. He gave her some feeble excuse about it looking suspicious for him to rent two horses. But she knew he just wanted to show her who was boss. Or he was just too cheap to get her one, even though he could easily have afforded it. When he pulled her up behind him, he also muttered something about not letting a drowned rat of a wolf pup ditch him in the dark.

That was all right. She'd gotten even. She'd pressed her dripping wet body flat against his.

But, Judas Priest, how her own arms, her own body, had tested her willpower. Already chilled, she'd turned to a mass of gooseflesh from the thrill of the warm sensual wall of his back moving against her with the rhythm of the horse's gait.

Even now the bound breasts beneath her shirt strained to be next to him. *And* his intoxicating scent.

She gritted her teeth. She *would* get these disturbing sensations under control. Soon. After all, she was only half Cajun. The other half was hard-nosed Yankee. And the time had come to draw on some of that staunch discipline.

"Hey, kid, which way do I turn?"

"Don't call me kid. The name's Georgie. Georgie Pacquing." Leaning past Pierce, she heard the steady roar of the mighty Columbia and knew they'd reached the road that ran alongside the river. Across it and slightly to the west twinkled the scattered lights of Fort Vancouver and its adjoining officers' row. "Go right. There's a dock about a hundred yards up."

Topping a small rise, Georgie spotted the dim glow of lantern light and its reflection in the calm water of a small cove. But she saw only one boat, although three were docked there most nights. She shot a plea heavenward that this one was the *Dream Ellen*.

Pierce eased the horse down the embankment.

"Diggity dog!" she shouted and gave Pierce's mid-section a squeeze before she thought. "It's our boat." Without waiting for Pierce to dismount, she slid off and ran onto the dock and up the gangplank.

"Who goes there?" demanded a rusty voice.

"It's me! Georgie!" Dodging past a stack of logs on the deck, she slammed through the galley door, a wide grin of relief splashed across her face. She quickly scanned the small plain room, and her smile collapsed. "Where's Papa? And Cadie?"

Abe Grohman, a used-up-looking older man who did odd jobs along the river, pulled up his sagging britches and stepped close. "What you doin' here at night by yourself?" The foul odor of whiskey wafted out on his words.

"Papa—have you seen him?" She grabbed his flabby arm and stared into his bleary eyes.

He glanced down at her clutching hand, then up again, irritation evident in his bewhiskered frown. "As far as I know, Louie's where he's supposed to be—on that fancy *Willamette*. And as fer that itchy-footed brother a yers—"

Ducking beneath the low lintel, Pierce strode in.

"Who's that?" Abe spat. He never took kindly to having his drinking time disturbed.

"The name's Kingston." Pierce's voice virtually rang with authority. "And who am I addressing?"

"Abe Grohman. I'm lookin' after things till Louie gits back."

"But where's Cadie?" Georgie asked.

"Gone."

"Where? For how long?"

"Fer good. We was droppin' off a load a timber out to the coast last week, an' some sea captain was lookin' fer replacements. Half his crew got gold fever and jumped ship in San Francisco. Cadie signed on. Figured to save hisself some a the fare back to New Orleans.''

"He's gone?'' Georgie couldn't believe it. "Without even sayin' good-bye?''

"He left you a letter.'' Looking around, he walked on unsteady legs to the cupboard above their little round-bellied stove. "Might be here.'' He rummaged around for a few seconds, then turned back. "No. Maybe he locked it up with yer important papers. I dunno where the key is, so I guess you'll have to wait fer Louie.''

Cadie and Papa both gone? Had the *Dream Ellen* been sitting here doing nothing for a week, when they needed every cent they could scrape together? "You been doin' any haulin' for Simmons this week?''

"Cadie didn't say nothin' 'bout workin' the boat till you got back. Jist said to see nothin' happened to it. I'm jist one man, you know. He said with all the money Louie'd make on the *Willamette*, you'd be rollin' in it, an' you'd have no problem a'tall payin' me for my trouble.''

"I, uh . . .''

"How much does Pacquing owe you?'' Pierce couldn't believe the words that came out of his own mouth. He was actually on the verge of getting the brat out of another mess. And from the way the kid swung those big Lark-eyes up at him, he could tell that Georgie was just as surprised as he was.

The drunken coot paused and glanced away for a second. Then, throwing back his shoulders, he attempted to straighten his stance, but his head still listed slightly to one side. "Fifteen dollars.''

"Why, you lyin' old thief,'' Georgie railed, taking a step toward him. "We do no such thing.''

The man shrugged a bony shoulder and gave the kid a quick grin. "You're right. I's jist roundin' it off. Fourteen dollars."

"A dollar a day's more'n your worth, just sittin' here doin' nothin'. I'll go get your pay." Georgie started for the door.

"Cadie took all the money out of the box."

"*What?*" Georgie swung back, his mouth open.

"Left me just enough coin to buy firewood so's I could get back here from Astoria."

Georgie clenched his measly little fists and got in the man's face. "More'n likely you took the money and drunk it up, you lazy bag a rags. Get your bony butt off my boat."

The old geezer surprised Pierce by stumbling backward. His mouth flapped a couple of times before anything came out. His gaze darted to Pierce. "You can ask anybody up an' down the river 'bout ol' Abe. I ain't no thief."

Pierce looked from the smelly man to Georgie and shook his head. Trouble must be the kid's middle name. Everywhere Georgie went he was up to his ears in it. Pierce reached into his pocket and withdrew some coins. Stepping close to the lantern attached to the wall, he found a ten-dollar gold piece and handed it to Grohman. "Probably be best if you left for a while."

Closing his hand tightly around the gold coin, Grohman grabbed a misshapen cap from a hook by the door. Dropping it on his head, he turned back to Georgie. "I'll be talkin' to yer pa 'bout how you sass yer elders."

"Yeah? Well, I'll be talkin' to him about you, too."

"Good night, Mr. Grohman," Pierce said with finality.

The man wheeled around and fled.

"And good riddance!" Georgie yelled as he slammed the door behind him. He swung back to Pierce. "He's nothin' but trash. I can't believe Cadie—"

"Shut up and make some coffee." Aside from the fact that Pierce had been really counting on catching up with his capricious belle, he'd had all he could take of the kid's scrapes for one day. "I need something hot to ward off the chill till the back of my coat dries out."

The kid's eyes widened into a dumb, guileless look, as if he hadn't deliberately rubbed his whole drenched body all over Pierce.

The door crashed open.

Now what? Pierce spun around to see two men charge into the cramped room.

"Mr. Stokes!" Georgie squeaked, backing into a table that filled the center of the small room.

Stokes and some stranger were pointing long-barreled revolvers at Pierce.

Stokes's grinning face looked more malevolent than usual in the shadowy light of the lone lantern. "Thought I'd drop by and collect what's mine. You don't have no objections, now, do you, Mr. Kingston?"

Pierce shot a glance at Georgie. The kid looked as if he'd swallowed an apple whole. "No, Mr. Stokes," he answered, palms out. "You seem to have things well in hand."

Stokes waved his gun at Georgie. "Go get the papers, wart. Then you an' yer guardian angel here can get the hell off my boat."

Chapter
Ten

PIERCE STALKED OUT of Portland's only livery barn and into the early morning light. Hauling Georgie along by the arm, he desperately wanted to slam his fist into something, and the kid's big mouth was incredibly tempting.

That bastard Pacquing had escaped him again.

The stable owner had just told Pierce that Pacquing had never come to return Pegasus, but he'd seen the captain at the Driftwater Saloon the night before. And this morning he'd heard that Louie had booked passage on a boat headed downriver to the coastal port of Astoria . . . taking a *fine*-looking gray stallion with him.

Pierce glanced down at Georgie's shabby excuse for a hat. Even it would've made a fine target. But damn it all to hell, the kid looked too much like Pierce's vision in pink. Besides, he still needed the brat to help him track down the horse and Lark, *if* she'd been fool enough to stay with her thief of a father.

"Keep up," he growled, stretching his strides as he hurried toward the wharf. He cared not a whit if Georgie had to run to keep from being dragged.

"I know Papa," the boy said, his words bouncing out

as he trotted along. "Mr. Weston must've just heard it all wrong. Papa wouldn't steal Pegasus."

"Just like he didn't steal the money out of the riverboat's safe?"

"He intended to put it back, and you know it."

"Yeah, like he intended to return my horse."

Georgie tried to jerk away.

Pierce tightened his grip. "Where can we catch the quickest paddle-wheeler out to Astoria? I've got to catch him before he reaches the Pacific and escapes on a seagoing vessel." He halted abruptly to eye the little squirt.

Georgie stumbled to a stop a couple of feet ahead.

Pierce yanked him around. "And don't you lie to me, or I'll tan you so good you won't be able to sit for a month."

The boy flinched. Then his eyes widened with the innocence of a newborn lamb. "Why would I lie to you?"

Further angered that such a poor excuse for a kid would have those burnished copper eyes, Pierce bent down, inches from the boy's face. "Which way?"

The following evening as a miserable fog rolled in off the Pacific, the *Columbia Belle* bumped to a stop against the dock near the river's mouth. Georgie stood toward the bow, waiting for the dockworkers to tie off the boat and for the crew to drop the gangplank. Tucked under her arm, she held a cloth bag stuffed with the one change of clothes she'd found on the *Dream Ellen*, along with everything else she could gather before Stokes threw them off.

And now Pierce, the tyrant, overshadowed her as he

scanned the long dreary wharf, searching each face. If that wasn't disheartening enough, the arrogant bastard still looked as infernally handsome, as neat and unwrinkled, as he had when he'd donned his dove gray suit two days before. But then, why shouldn't he? While visiting the riverboat's barber for a shave and a hair trim, he'd had his clothes brushed and pressed.

On the other hand, Georgie had never felt so ugly and bedraggled in her life.

Her tormentor grabbed her by the arm—the one that no doubt still bore the finger marks from all the other times he'd hauled her along. "Come on. There's a saloon over there. Since your father's so fond of them, we'll look there first."

Salty Joe's, a slapped-together shanty, leaned against the side of one of the giant warehouses across from the wharf. Georgie had been there a few times with Papa and Cadie and was fairly certain that Joe, the owner, would remember "little Georgie."

As Pierce reached for the latch of the rough-plank door, she pulled out of his grasp. "Let me do the talking. The bartender's a friend of Papa's. As mean as you look all the time, he probably wouldn't tell you anything." She flung open the door and shoved her way past the bully.

Too early yet for business to be booming, only two properly dressed customers sat at a table near the entrance to the shallow room, and a dockworker lounged at the bar that ran the length of the back wall.

The balding bartender turned from drying glasses and, thank goodness, recognized Georgie almost immediately. His big smile widened an already round face which matched his protruding apron-covered belly.

"Well, if it ain't Louie's kid. From the way your pa talked yesterday, he said you an' Cadie wouldn't be headin' out this way for another week or so."

"You saw him, then," Pierce piped up as they reached the bar, trying to take over as usual.

Georgie butted the side of his leg with her boot. "Papa forgot to take some important papers with him. I'm trying to catch up to him. Do you know where he's staying?"

Some of Joe's flab bulged onto the counter as he leaned against it and looked at Pierce. "Maybe your friend here would like a beer."

"Sure. And maybe some coffee for the kid," Pierce's words flowed mellow and relaxed now, as if he weren't the least bit hurried.

Georgie watched, her own patience dwindling as the bartender lumbered about filling their order.

When he returned, he set a foam-capped glass and a steaming mug before them, then took Pierce's money before finally answering her question. "You're too late. He's already gone. Ain't that right, Cal?" he called to the other man down the bar from Pierce.

"Yep. Sailed with the tide this morning. Took the *Pacific Queen* down Frisco way. And that was one fine-lookin' horse he had with him, too. Said he won it in a poker game.

"Yeah," Joe added. "He was in a real celebratin' mood. Bought drinks for the house."

Georgie felt herself begin to cave in, but seeing the muscles in Pierce's jaw bunch, she knew she couldn't. She tugged on his coattail in warning while leaning forward to get a better view of the dockworker. "Well, dang it, guess I'm gonna have to follow him on down to

San Francisco. He's gotta have those papers. Are there
any other ships in port right now?''

"The *California Lady*. Spent most of the day unload-
in' her. She should be headin' out again in two, three
days.''

Pierce opened his mouth as if to say something, but
picked up his glass instead and guzzled the entire
contents. He then slammed it down and wiped his mouth
with his coat sleeve, completely forgetting his highfalu-
tin manners. He glared down at Georgie. "Drink up.
We've got business to take care of.''

When she set the earthenware mug on the counter after
only one sip of the hot brew, Pierce snatched her by the
collar and propelled her toward the door. Once outside,
he abruptly stopped and looked in both directions.
"Which way to the nearest hotel?''

She wrenched herself free. She'd had all of his
bullying she was going to take. "Keep your blasted
hands to yourself.'' After all, he wasn't the only one with
reason to be upset.

He threw both up in the air. "Fine!'' The word
cracked out of him like a gunshot. "Now, which
way?''

"Down there,'' she returned with equal venom and
jabbed a finger to the west. "Down the wharf, then up
the hill.'' She took a breath to calm herself. "If we get
rooms on the third floor, we'll be able to see the whole
harbor when the fog lifts.''

He stretched those long legs into powerful strides.
"Rooms?'' his low voice reverberated. "Unless you've
found some money somewhere—as that father of yours
keeps doing—there'll be only one room and one bed.
Mine. You can sleep on the floor.''

She was really growing to hate him. "But you got me

my own room the last two nights. And besides, you said I make too much noise when I sleep.''

''Looks like it's just one more thing I'll have to get used to.'' He paused, and the hard set of his expression softened for a second. ''Because, as much as I'd like to, I can't bring myself to abandon you the way your father did.''

His pity upset Georgie far more than his usual arrogance. It seemed to make everything Papa had done even more disgraceful.

Reaching a road that led away from the riverfront, he stopped. ''This it?''

With the word ''abandon'' still ringing in her ears, Georgie didn't feel up to answering. She shot past him and up the hill toward the stores and shops of the small hamlet. Though it was still a couple of hours before dusk, lamps already glowed from the row of buildings on either side of the road, making warm patches in the fog. The sight should have consoled her, but it didn't. And she wondered if she'd ever feel comforted again, with this last piece of bad news to add to the rest. While she'd been taking Pierce's handouts for her every morsel, Papa had been buying drinks for a whole blasted saloon as if he didn't have a care in the world.

Upon reaching the hotel, Georgie had to take a second look. Since the last time she'd stayed there a few months back, an entirely new facade had replaced the plain old white front. Wood scrollwork and gold-trimmed pillars greeted her as she climbed up the broad steps to the leaded-glass doors. Sparkling from within was a crystal chandelier that held at least a hundred candles. Civilization certainly was catching up with Oregon.

Pierce reached for the handle, then paused. He stared down at her with those unfathomable eyes. "I accept the fact that you don't have any better clothes with you," he said in that all-knowing tone of his. "But I'm telling you unequivocally that you will not sit down to a meal in this fine hotel wearing that god-awful hat."

"What?" Georgie grabbed the edges of her wide brim and pulled it down even tighter.

"You heard me. The hat goes or you don't eat. Ever again."

"But I—"

"No buts. If I hadn't met your sister, I'd think no one had ever taught you any manners at all."

"I could always sit at another table. It wouldn't bother me one bit, you being a gambler and all."

She hadn't believed his expression could become any stonier, but it did. His lips tightened, and she knew he was barely controlling an urge to retaliate.

Well, at least he wouldn't want to eat with her now.

"And just how do you plan to pay your bill?" he asked in a baiting tone.

"You could give me the money in advance."

"Sure," he snorted derisively. "*The hat goes.*"

Georgie knew the inevitable moment had arrived. Pierce had left her alone in their hotel room to clean up for supper in the dining room—supper, that is, *if* she removed her hat like a little gentleman.

The hair would have to come off . . . all her thick, beautiful hair. If it was just the one meal, she could go hungry. But Pierce had been adamant. Hat off at the table or no food. Ever.

Doffing the hat, she hung it on a hook and double-checked the thrown bolt on the door. Grudgingly she uncoiled the light auburn braids and brought them over her shoulders. Her hair ended mere inches above her waist. It would take her years for it to grow back in. She sighed, remembering how much her father had always loved to look at it, especially after Mommy died, and Pierce had seemed enthralled as he ran his hands through it after he unpinned it the other night.

Catching herself, she stiffened. ''The rat deserves to lose his lovely Lark's hair.''

She pulled a pair of scissors from her canvas bag and walked to the oval looking glass hanging above a marble-topped commode . . . and started at her reflection. It wasn't his hair. It was hers.

She felt her courage slipping. Holding her breath, she open and closed the shears several times, listening to metal slide across metal, assuring herself that she did have the strength to perform this task. It really was the only practical thing to do. The only safe thing. She couldn't sleep in her hat every night, and she couldn't possibly expect to spend the next week or so on the breezy Pacific without it blowing off at least once.

Georgie grabbed one of her thick braids. Then, turning her back to the mirror and ignoring her shaky hand, she placed the shears at the base of her neck. She snipped hard several times before the braid finally came loose. Eyes closed, she tossed it in the direction of the bed, then quickly cut off the other one.

Turning slowly to face the mirror, she'd never felt so pillaged in her life. Nothing was left but a scraggly mess.

Her eyes spilled over with tears of self-pity as she trimmed the remaining straggles into an even cap. While she worked, the tears rolled down, catching on cuttings, causing her face to itch. Even if she had kept her long hair hidden most of the time, it had always been there, waiting for a time when she wanted it—like the Fourth of July. Now it would be years before she could be pretty again.

Laying the scissors on the commode, she swiped at the wetness blurring her vision and took a long look at herself. Beneath a fringe of bangs, her eyes seemed even larger than before. She reminded herself of a silly fairy-tale elf who wore a bell-trimmed hat and a flaring smock over a pair of tights. The comical sight made her trembling lips tilt into a half smile, and she began to feel a little less melancholy.

"Oh, for goodness' sake, Georgie," she scolded herself as she tried to slick down the hair. "It's not like it'll never grow again."

Sweeping the loose cuttings from her bangs into her hand, she walked to the window and then dropped them outside instead of putting them in the wastebasket. It wouldn't do to set Pierce to wondering. She turned back to the bed, and the sight of her two amputated braids sent another twist of pain through her.

Before she could sink deeper into lamentation, she promised herself she'd have them made into a hairpiece once everything returned to normal. That way she wouldn't have to wait so long to play the part of a lady—that is, if she ever dared to do so again. This last performance had turned into a disaster. But just in case, she snatched the braids up and stuffed them to the very bottom of her cinch sack, beneath her meager possessions.

"Out of sight, out of mind," she said, parroting the old saying as she tossed the bag into a corner. Then, with just one mournful backward glance, she rushed to the door.

Beside the entrance, her old brown hat caught her eye. The strongest instinct told her to put it on. She looked entirely too feminine without it. But she'd have to chance it. Or starve.

Georgie walked into the fair-sized dining room, noticing another new crystal chandelier dangling above the white linen–covered tables. She sighed. More niceties creeping in to crowd out her beloved frontier, this not quite tamed wilderness that had afforded her so much freedom.

Scanning the diners, she spotted Pierce sitting at a table in the far corner. She started toward him on uneasy legs. Dear God, she prayed, if he sees through the disguise, don't let him make a scene in front of other people.

As she passed under the brightly lit chandelier, he looked up. In an instant his eyes flared wide, and he lurched to his feet.

Georgie stopped dead in her tracks. *He knew.* An instinct to escape almost gave her feet flight before her pride took over. She wouldn't run from him or anyone else. Besides, this whole mess was mostly his fault anyway.

Pierce continued to stare at her like some dumb ox until she reached him. Then he dropped like a rock into his chair again.

Wishing desperately that she'd opted for the chicken's way out she warily took the seat across from him and waited for what seemed hours—but was probably only a few seconds—as he pinned her with one of his damnably unfathomable looks.

"I've already ordered, Georgie. The food should be

here any minute. And I've been thinking," he continued as he began to toy with his fork. "I guess I was a little hard on you back there. I could use a good night's rest. I'll be getting my own room. . . . Damn, but you do look like your sister!"

Chapter
Eleven

PIERCE LEFT THE captain's cabin in a foul mood. He'd just been informed he would lose his privacy for the next ten or twelve days, the time it would take to reach San Francisco. Coming up on deck, he found the sails unfurled and the small two-masted schooner already moving with the tide out to sea. Spotting Georgie's crumpled hat poking just above a stack of lashed-down lumber, Pierce headed toward him.

The kid pushed away from the railing and hurried over. "What did the Captain want? Has he heard something about Papa?"

"No, nothing like that. He said our belongings—what little I've been able to replace since everything I own is still back in Oregon City . . ." The thought sent his temples pulsing. "Another thing to thank your father for."

"Get to the point. What did the captain say?"

"We have to share a cabin. Seems he gave yours to some other men."

"No! He can't do that."

"My sentiments exactly. But nonetheless—"

"But we were here first. It's not fair."

"Did I hear the word 'fair' comin' outta Pacquing's

by-blow?'' The gravelly voice from behind them sounded ominously familiar.

Georgie spun around and gasped.

Turning, Pierce came face to face with the repulsive Jasper Blackwell, the man's protruding eyes dancing with malicious amusement. The foul-mouthed bastard undoubtedly was one of the passengers who'd dispossessed them.

Uncontrollable rage pumped into Pierce's muscles and took over. He yanked the skinny weasel up to within inches of his nose. ''You say one more word to the boy, good or bad, and I'll throw your scrawny ass overboard. The kid's not responsible for what his father does.'' Then, astonished by his violent protectiveness of Georgie, Pierce eased his grip and let Blackwell down.

The gangling man, whose eyes had doubled in size, stumbled back a step, then, regaining his composure, stiffened as he straightened his plain black coat. He then reached inside it and settled his hand on the butt of his holstered weapon. ''You needn't get in such a lather. If it wasn't for that sneaky Cajun pa of his, neither of us would be on this boat.''

''Mr. Kingston still has business with Papa—the matter of his horse,'' Georgie piped up. ''But you . . . Why aren't you back in Portland haggling over the *Dream Ellen* with Mr. Stokes?''

Pierce shot the kid a stern look. ''I'll do the talking here.'' He swung back to Blackwell, who was staring at Georgie with unmasked rancor. ''The lad has a point. What *are* you doing here?''

Though his eyes never left Georgie, Blackwell's sparse lips stretched into a one-sided grin.

Pierce's fingers began to tingle. If the man even pretended to make a move or say anything to the kid, he'd find himself over the side so fast that hog iron of his wouldn't even begin to clear leather.

Blackwell glanced back at Pierce, and his smile disappeared. "No sense fightin' Stokes over that run-down tub. He's got legal title, as you well know. But with you bein' in such a hurry to get to Astoria, I guess you didn't hear."

"Hear what?" Georgie said along with Pierce. It never did do any good to tell the kid to keep his mouth shut.

"Louie won a bundle a money in Portland. And guess what he was usin' for his ante?"

Pierce didn't say anything, and for once, neither did Georgie. The answer was too obvious.

"Yes, sir," Blackwell drawled, his bony chest puffing out. "Winnin' and that horse of yours just seem to go together, don't they? Anyway, thought I'd mosey on down Californy way, see about gettin' what's due me. And believe me," he said, slamming a fist into his palm, "the money won't near cover it." He slid his attention back to Georgie. Eyelids lowered, he nodded, not even trying to hide his enmity.

Pierce felt Georgie tightly clutch the sleeve of his frock coat. He hadn't liked the man from the start, and now he could easily understand why the lad feared him. There was a fiendishness about Blackwell that Pierce would just as soon deal with here and now.

But the swine prudently turned and walked away.

Pierce patted the kid's hand gripping his arm. "Don't let him scare you. His kind is more talk than anything else."

Georgie's fingers relaxed. Then, after a few seconds, he let go and latched on to the ship's rail. "I hope you're right."

"I am. By the time we reach San Francisco, he'll most likely be satisfied with money for his expenses and a little extra for his trouble."

The kid obviously wasn't convinced. A frown creased the bridge of his nose.

"Stop worrying. Even if he isn't, I'll be there to see that no harm comes to Lark or your father."

Georgie's eyes flashed. "You'd protect Papa after everything he's done? After what we just heard?"

"Look, I know I've been making a lot of noise—just like Blackwell—but the truth is, anyone who could raise and care for a daughter as lovely and charming as your sister can't be all that bad. And besides, I plan to ask him for Lark's hand, and I don't think he'd be all that willing to give her to me if I'd just throttled him."

"She's worth that much to you? Worth all the money he's cost you? All the trouble? Puttin' up with my big mouth?"

"In a few years you'll understand. When you grow up, you'll meet your own lovely belle, and she'll be everything you ever wanted. So beautiful you'll want to memorize her every move, her every sigh . . ." Looking at the distant horizon, Pierce could almost see Lark floating toward him across the sparkling sea as she'd done the first time he laid eyes on her. She drew close and the mischief in her eyes softened to the purest love. "She is the very essence of gentility, and her laughter sounds like music. . . . In her I see the hope of regaining all that the South stole from me. A lady to—"

"I'm gettin' real hungry," Georgie broke in. "Think I'll go on down to the galley and see if Cook will give me a biscuit or something." Spinning away, the kid took off for the passageway as if he'd been shot out of a gun.

Pierce chuckled to himself. "Guess I was getting too mushy for him." Just as well, he thought. Now I can really concentrate on remembering every velvety curve, her rose-scented hair . . .

The corset felt like a wide band of steel. It squeezed her chest tighter and tighter. But she had to endure the pain. And the loss. Georgie could live no more. For Pierce, she had to become Lark. She didn't know if she could do it, but for him she had to try.

She breathed in, and sharp bolts of pain ripped through her breasts. But she would endure. She must dress like a lady. Act like a lady. For Pierce.

He walked out of the forest toward her. Love shone from the crystal-blue eyes that roved over her face, her body.

Her heart battered passionately as she reached out to him, beckoning him to come to her, to release her from her shackles, to let her fly free with him, body and spirit.

He dropped down beside her and gathered her into his arms. "Lark, my beautiful Lark. Don't ever leave me again. Stay with me. Forever." His hands moved up her back, freeing her from the hated ties.

He'd truly come for her. She breathed deeply. But still there was an ache. Her breasts clamored to be taken by him. They peaked and thrust toward him.

"Love me." He pulled her against the muscled mass of his bare chest. "Now. Forever."

The intensity of his plea pierced through her. Both her nipples tingled and hardened.

Sensing her need, he eased her onto her back and took one crest into his mouth. He drew on it until an exquisite thrill spiraled down to ignite her gnawing emptiness— the very spot he now entered with a breath-stopping thrust.

"Georgie, Georgie," he whispered.

Her heart stopped. He knew her name, her secret.

He withdrew slowly, agonizingly.

He was leaving her! She held on to him.

No, she was mistaken. He again drove into her with such filling power she thought she'd explode from sheer ecstasy.

"Georgie," he repeated louder. He squeezed her shoulder. . . .

She opened her eyes and saw the silhouette of his head within inches of hers. Her fingers clenched something scratchy. Her blanket. She was lying on the upper bunk, and he stood beside it. Oh, God, he wasn't actually making love to her. The fiercest ache ravaged the place where she'd imagined him to be. It had only been a dream. She squeezed her legs together, trying to end it.

"Georgie. Wake up."

Perhaps all was not lost. Maybe he'd discovered her secret and loved her, wanted her, anyway. "Yes?" she breathed.

"Good," he said with more emphasis. "Something's been bothering me, keeping me awake."

"Yes?"

"No one has ever mentioned Lark, either in Portland or in Astoria. I don't believe she's with your father. What if she left him to go back to the *Willamette* and found that I was gone."

Trickles of guilt doused her disappointment. But with long days at sea before them, she couldn't chance a confession. At least not until they landed in San Francisco. She'd have to come up with a plausible lie. But what? "Well, uh . . . Lark wasn't at the dock when we arrived, so you can forget that dumb idea. Besides, no matter what you think, my papa wouldn't deliberately desert *any* of his children." Blast. She shouldn't have been so all-fired rude. But what difference could one more insulting remark make. No matter how much she wished she could be his Lark, when he found out the truth, he wouldn't want her—a lying, conniving hoyden of a girl. Besides, she hadn't even lasted a day pretending to be a lady.

"Then why hasn't anyone mentioned Lark? As striking as she is, I can't imagine anyone who saw her not making a comment."

Why wouldn't he stop tormenting her with these infernal questions? Didn't he know he was forcing her to lie to him again? "Well, silly. Do you really think Papa would take Lark into the saloon with him and wave her in front of a bunch of horny drunks like a red flag? She's with him, all right, or she would've gone back to our boat. Now leave me alone so I can go back to sleep."

He sighed, but his shadowy figure did drop out of sight.

The bunk creaked below, and she knew he'd lain on it with that lithe, absolutely glorious body. Stretched out across the sheet . . . instead of across her. She ground her rough woolen covers against herself, gouging at the starvation of her desire.

"You're right, I guess," came his husky voice from below. "We'll find her in San Francisco. I wonder if she knows I'm coming to save her, can feel me getting closer.''

Georgie let his words hang unanswered rather than tell yet another lie. But, God help her, she was caught betwixt and between. They had to get to her father and warn him before Blackwell tracked him down. She knew as surely as she knew he was on this ship that he planned to kill her father. The unholy evil in his eyes was unmistakable.

A terrifying thought surfaced, and she had to bury her face in her pillow to keep from crying out. Once Pierce learned all about her, he might become just as murderous as Blackwell.

She pulled at the buttoned-up collar of her shirt. She could already feel Pierce's hands at her throat. And who would blame him?

Time aboard ship dwindled slowly with Georgie trying to avoid both Pierce and the vile Jasper Blackwell. Evenings were easiest for her, since they always played cards with the other men. She was unaccustomed to having her breasts bound even at night, and she had become increasingly uncomfortable. Every day she counted the hours until she could bolt her door and feel safe enough to unwrap herself, wash, and truly relax.

During the daytime, she distanced herself from her predicament by hanging around the crew. She helped them mend sails and swab the decks. The pilot even let her take a turn at the helm every afternoon. More important, she always made a point of surrounding herself with them at mealtime.

And, thanks to Pierce's watchful eye, Blackwell never uttered another word to her during the rest of the trip. But the man's hateful leer stalked her whenever he was near. Unsettling her further was the evil, long-toothed grin that always accompanied it. But she refused to let him intimidate her. Not once did she give him the satisfaction of showing her fear.

Pierce, however, was something else entirely. No matter how many times she reminded herself it had been only minutes from the time he crawled out of her bed until he'd crawled into her father's pocket, his tempting presence threatened to undo her. It would have helped if just once a crewman had even hinted that he'd cheated. But, no, they treated him with the friendliest respect.

All things considered, she felt safest when she climbed up a mast to its crow's nest.

Perched high above her cares, she would remove her hat and let the breeze ruffle her short hair as she turned her face into it, receiving its soft caress. She would let her gaze wander aimlessly along the distant shoreline they paralleled, and pretty soon the exaggerated sway from so high up would lull her into a peaceful bliss.

Her thoughts would drift to the imagined scents and sounds and the vibrant colors of exotic lands on the other side of the vast Pacific. Then, unwilling to stop herself, she always allowed a daringly dashing, darkly handsome lover to emerge as her companion. And of course, she always dazzled him by wearing the most exquisite Oriental silks and brocades.

In her daydreams a waist-length mass of light auburn tresses still fell loose to swirl about her. His deep blue eyes would behold her, not with condemnation but with the same inviting warmth they'd held that wonderful afternoon the two of them had whiled away in their magical glen . . . and in the dreams that taunted her each and every night.

On their eleventh day at sea, Georgie sensed a definite changing of course. Standing upon her lofty platform, she saw the sails flap crazily in the sparkling afternoon sun, rattling the yardarm beneath her feet. She grabbed hold of the mast as the water grew increasingly choppy. Looking down to the deck, she saw the sailors scrambling about, loosening lines, adjusting the angles of the spars. She riveted her gaze to the shoreline and, within seconds, found a wide opening . . . the famous Golden Gate. A thrill shot through her. Just as quickly a prickle of foreboding replaced it.

Grabbing the mast for support, Georgie searched below until she sighted Mr. Blackwell near the bow. He leaned against the rail as if to help speed the ship on to port.

Suddenly Blackwell spun around and stared up at her with that same fiendish grin. At this distance he looked like a fleshless laughing skeleton with pop eyes. He raised a hand to her and clenched it into an ominous fist.

Georgie pretended, as usual, not to notice. Besides, she knew without a doubt that she'd find Papa long before Blackwell could. The man was nothing but a harness salesman. She, however, would know any number of the seamen waiting on the wharf for the return trip north on their logging schooners . . . sailors with nothing better to do than gossip about one another's comings and goings.

But Blackwell might get lucky.

Georgie quickly scanned the deck until she spotted Pierce on the bridge talking to the captain. He could make Blackwell go away if only he would. He had tenfold the money it would take to buy that Judas devil off.

She scrambled down the rungs, hating the idea of adding one more to the growing list of debts she owed Pierce. But as long as he still thought she was Lark's little brother, he would probably help, if just for her. He'd certainly mentioned Lark often enough. Her grace, her elegance, her fine manners.

Georgie felt her insides cave in at the thought of how she, the little brother, had been so outrageously rude to him. And in a few short hours Pierce would know who she really was. The charade would be over.

As she reached the deck, she again had to remind herself of her purpose. Papa. With halfhearted determination, she intercepted Pierce just as he strode down from the bridge.

Pierce glanced at her and then looked shoreward, his eyes sparkling with enthusiasm. "The captain says we'll make port before dusk." He started around a pile of lumber and toward the rail.

She turned and caught up with him. "Yeah, I know. And before we do, I need to talk to you."

The kid looked up from beneath that hat, treating Pierce to those deeply rich and long-lashed Lark-eyes. Again he had to tell himself that they weren't his beauty's but her brother's, the little imp. "Well, spit it out."

Georgie darted looks all around, then grabbed Pierce's shirtsleeve and pulled him toward the stern, out of hearing of two crewmen tying off some rigging. "I know you're kinda mad at Papa right now for taking your horse."

"For a start."

Appearing not to have noticed Pierce's barbed answer, Georgie looked out to sea and continued while twisting the end of his worn belt. "Well, I've been thinkin'. If Papa won a bundle, like Blackwell says, he'll be able to make good for all you've been out, and Blackwell, too. So I was wonderin', seein' as how you're so rich, if you'd just go ahead and pay the snake, say, three, four hundred dollars now. Get him out of our hair."

Pierce grinned as he looked down at the punched-in top of the boy's hat. Beneath it, that brain was always spinning, trying to figure some new way to save his worthless father. Georgie was one loyal kid—Pierce had to give him that.

The kid turned and looked up at Pierce, obviously waiting for an answer.

Pierce wished he could tell Georgie what the boy wanted to hear. "It's a good idea, and I've already approached Blackwell. He refused. He's determined to deal only with your father." Not wanting to worry the boy any more, Pierce chose not to add that when Blackwell turned Pierce down, he'd acted as if his vengeance was ensured, as if he knew something Pierce didn't and was savoring every jot and tittle of it.

All in all, between guarding Georgie against Blackwell's fomenting animosity and worrying about Lark, this had been a decidedly disturbing trip.

Pierce turned toward the gap in the California coast. Thank God the journey would soon be over. Very soon now he'd find Lark. And after what she must've gone through with her leaky vessel of a father, Pierce had no doubt he could easily win her hand, especially if he made a show of forgiving the old goat. Hell, if Pierce had to, he'd even forfeit Pegasus for her.

He grabbed the railing in a stranglehold. God help him, he would have this belle. The Lange woman wouldn't be here to stop him this time. Not her or any of her hired detectives.

Chapter
Twelve

RACING AHEAD OF the wispy evening fog, the schooner swooped into the breezy bay under full sail. To Georgie's amazement, literally hundreds of ships bobbed at anchor in the huge bay. On closer examination, she noticed that only a dozen or so were rigged with canvas, waiting offshore for a berth among the forest of masts crowding the docks. Then she remembered hearing stories about untold numbers of ships being abandoned in the first throes of gold fever.

Scanning the bows of the vessels, she searched in vain for the *Pacific Queen*.

"Strike the sails!" ordered the captain, all decked out in a dress uniform.

Anticipation, mingled with foreboding, thrummed through Georgie as she watched the crew scramble for the lines.

"Drop the anchor!"

With every crank of the capstan lowering the double-fluked iron anchor, Georgie felt that much closer to touching the shore of the burgeoning city—a rip-roaring, brawling boomtown, if all the sailors' talk was to be believed. As far as the advancing tendrils of mist would allow, she saw buildings covering every space, even up the steep hills behind the wharf.

Slinging her canvas bag over her shoulder, she edged toward the side where the dinghy would soon be lowered to take the passengers ashore.

Pierce, looking like a prosperous gentleman in his one good gray outfit, already waited there along with Blackwell and the other passenger, a sturdy Oregon logger who'd been thoroughly bitten by the gold bug. Noticing Pierce's lone carpetbag of items he'd purchased in Astoria, Georgie had no doubt he'd be searching out a tailor, and soon.

She glanced down at her own dingy and wrinkled brown coat, tan dungarees, and scuffed boots, then looked ashore again at the fine new hotels, the stores, and, high above, the grand mansions. She still looked as dowdy and ugly as ever. But that would change when she found Papa. He'd see she had money for new clothes. Maybe even some pretty dresses if, by some miracle, she and Pierce could find a way around her lies. *If* Papa still had the money he'd won.

Georgie's heart seemed to lose its grip. She darted a glance at Blackwell. Then, propelled by urgency, she moved to the crank and started lowering the dinghy herself, without waiting for permission.

Pierce stepped toward her, his grin turning to a scowl. He looked over his shoulder; then, turning back, he shrugged. With that persistent smile in place again, he walked over and gave her a hand. "Doesn't look like anyone minds."

Rusty, the youngest crewman, rowed Georgie and the other passengers ashore. As they neared, she studied the long embarcadero that seemed to go on forever, made even more impressive by the fact that San Francisco had barely existed a mere five years ago.

After guiding the dinghy through a deep canyon made by two sleek clippers sharing a wide slip, Rusty maneuvered the little boat against a ladder hanging down from the wharf.

Georgie jumped up and bounded over the others' feet. Grabbing a rung, she scrambled halfway up before remembering to thank the redheaded seaman. She stopped and turned. "Rusty, tell the other men how much I appreciated their kindness to me during the trip."

"We should be thanking you," Rusty said, calling up to her, "for pitching in and helping out like you did."

Pierce, a few rungs below Georgie, glanced up at her, a puzzled frown scrunching his eyebrows.

Georgie realized she'd sounded far too polite, far too grown up. Looking quickly away, she raced up the ladder before he had time to ponder it.

At the top, the noisy embarcadero smelled of fish and the more pleasing aroma of fresh-baked bread. Workmen, passengers, and loafers milled about. Above their hubbub, the hollow rumble of freight wagons crossing the timber wharf competed with the sharp cries from street pitchmen.

When Georgie and Pierce began to move among the crowd, she could distinguish the words of the nearest hawkers, who tried to interest folks in everything from the purchase of practical gold-prospecting equipment to the sampling of one of the hurdy-gurdy dance halls. The sign over every second or third building lining the waterfront advertised a saloon or bawdy house. One they passed boasted having the prettiest mademoiselles west of Paris.

Georgie had thought she was prepared for San Francisco, after all the talk she'd heard, but the unabashed sin being flaunted on every side appalled her.

An underfed Chinaman wearing loose-fitting cotton pants shuffled toward them in slipperlike shoes. Blocking Pierce's path, the little fellow bowed deeply several times, then looked up with an eager expression. "You buy virgin? Got beautifu' China gir'. You buy cheap."

Pierce's face took on that dead calm as he stared at the man. "How much?"

Georgie couldn't have been more stunned if Pierce had slapped her face. This was the man who'd talked of nothing but his lady Lark? And now he was ready to toss her over for the first available virgin? Fine. All the better. She didn't need him anymore anyway.

"Twenty dollar," the Chinaman said. "You pay now."

Georgie shouldered Pierce hard as she stalked by.

He grabbed her collar and pulled her back as he continued dickering. "I want to see the girl first. I'll pay you after we sign the papers."

Georgie looked up at Pierce unbelieving.

So did the Chinaman. "Papers? No. You buy virgin. One hour. Twenty dollar."

"Oh." A sheepish grin spread across Pierce's face. "You're not selling her, just her services." Shaking his head, he sidestepped the flesh peddler. "Sorry. I'm not interested in any used virgins today."

As the man wasted no time shuffling over to another prospect, Pierce's last words—"used virgins"—grated across Georgie's ears. Used virgins, indeed. That was exactly what he'd turned her into. She tried to jerk free of him, but Pierce's grasp held.

"It's not what you think. I just hate slavery. Come on," he said, releasing her.

"Yeah?" she sniped. "Well, we don't have the time to spare for that kind of benevolence."

Just ahead, a door banged open.

She jumped back, lest she be run over as rowdy, laughing customers spilled out singing the coarse words of a lively tune. Inside, someone played a piano with pounding force.

Pierce started for the entrance. "Looks like as good a place as any to start."

Peeking over the swinging doors, Georgie saw men draped all over women in shiny dresses that showed half of their legs. Aghast, she grabbed Pierce's coat sleeve, stopping him just as a big bruiser booted a smaller man out onto the boardwalk.

The evicted customer landed in a loose-jointed sprawl at their feet.

"And don't come back till you've sobered up," the thick-necked bouncer bellowed.

Someone bumped past Georgie. *Blackwell!* He must've been following them.

"What's the matter, kid? Ain't you man enough to go on in?" With that damnable leering grin, Blackwell pushed his way through the doors.

Pierce removed her grasping fingers from his coat sleeve. "What is it?"

Even if Blackwell hadn't just entered, the sight of the sniveling drunk lying in front of them, reeking of sour beer and sweat, should have curdled his stomach as it did hers.

But Pierce seemed oblivious.

"I'm not going in there. Besides, it would take us days to go from saloon to saloon trying to find someone who's seen Papa. I'm sure the *Pacific Queen* is still in port. Someone aboard will be able to tell us where he is. I'd be willing to bet money he's waiting for a ship going south, if he hasn't already taken one."

"If you *had* any money," Pierce gibed with a derisive snort. "But you're probably right. It would be beyond imagining to expose a delicate flower like Lark to this cesspit." He spread an all-encompassing hand. "Even your father would have enough sense to know that. Let's go. If we hurry, maybe we can find the ship before dark. He might be keeping Lark and Pegasus aboard until he can make other arrangements."

His last words turned her legs to lead. In addition to Pegasus, he'd be finding the truth about her. And, after that, there was no telling what he'd do. But, she thought, a chill racing up her spine, Blackwell had left no doubt about what he planned to do. She ran after Pierce.

The wind gusted, and Pierce chuckled as he watched Georgie hold that beat-up hat on his head with both hands while trotting to keep up. The kid absolutely had to have a new one. Glancing down at the shoddiness of the rest of the boy's clothing, Pierce decided that as soon as they found Lark, he'd buy her brother a whole new outfit, top to bottom.

"Yoo-hoo, handsome," came a sultry voice from above.

Pierce looked up and spotted a brassy-haired whore leaning out a second-story window, her full breasts threatening to pop out of a red silk peignoir.

She stretched out a hand and beckoned. "I got a real fine welcome waitin' here for y'all."

Without slowing a step, Pierce politely tipped his new black hat and traveled on. He grinned as he envisioned

Lark making him the same offer. How silken she would soon feel beneath his hands. His fingers tingled at the thought, and a charge of excitement coursed through his body.

As the rapid tapping of boots on the boardwalk reminded him that the kid was trotting alongside him, Pierce was suddenly dead sure that buying Georgie new clothes would *not* be the first thing he'd do after finding Lark. Nor would it be the tenth. Hell, the kid would be lucky to get a new outfit a year from now.

They reached the entrance to the next pier, and Pierce could barely make out the hulking silhouettes of ships moored on either side in the thickening fog and fading light.

Georgie broke into a run as if someone were chasing him. He raced toward the vessels, his canvas bag bouncing against his shoulder.

Pierce hurried after him to get close enough to read the ships' names.

Before he could catch up, Georgie returned and sprinted on by. "Neither of 'em is it," he called over his shoulder as he ran back onto the embarcadero. Dodging through the crowd, the kid ran past another warehouse and on to the next pier. He raced back, then went on to several more without success.

Returning to the end of a dock where Pierce waited in the growing darkness, Georgie tripped over a loose plank and tumbled into a sprawl on the wharf.

Pierce reached him before he could regain his feet and helped him up. "You're going to break your neck if you don't slow down. Take it easy. We'll find them."

"But," Georgie sputtered, out of breath, "we have to find the *Pacific Queen* now! High tide is within the hour."

"You know as well as I do the ship only arrived a day or two ago. It won't be leaving for some time."

"I know that," he spat back with an impatient scowl. "But Papa might've transferred to a ship that's sailing tonight. He could be on it right now, ready to leave for New Orleans."

"*New Orleans*?" Panic squeezed Pierce's own heart.

"Where else did you think he'd go?" Georgie swung away. "Come on."

The kid's urgency infused Pierce. He, too, broke into a zigzagging run through a crowd that had dwindled down to a scattering of meandering drunks. He had to find Lark *now*. He would never go back to Louisiana, not even for her.

"Hey, Georgie! That you?" a young lad called out. He sat on a stack of burlap sacks in a circle of light cast by a lantern post.

Georgie veered toward him. "Eddie!" Reaching the other boy, dressed in baggy clothing similar to his, Georgie stopped. "Thank God! A familiar face." He clutched the lad's hand. "Have you seen Papa? Captain Louie?"

Breathing hard, Pierce stopped beside Georgie.

"Yeah. But your pa never said nothin' 'bout you bein' here with him."

"I wasn't. I just sailed in on the *California Lady*. But I've gotta find him. *Now*."

The straw-headed lad looked up at Pierce. "Who's he? Ain't never seen you with him before."

Georgie shot a glance at Pierce before answering. "He's helpin' me. Where's Papa?"

"You're too late. Cap'n Louie left yesterday mornin'."

"Already?" Georgie wailed and slumped against the mountain of gunnysacks.

Pierce's legs also felt shaky. Lark was gone. Forever.

"Yeah," the lad said. "I tried to talk to him, but he paid me no mind. Just went right on by like I wasn't there. My brother said Louie was in a bad mood 'cause he lost a lotta money playin' cards down at the El Dorado. Said he even lost *himself* to some man lookin' for a steam engine expert."

Lurching away from the bags, Georgie grabbed the boy. "Stop your useless jawin', Eddie, and tell me which ship Papa took."

Jerking free, the lad regained his seat. "That's what I was tryin' to do. This man that Cap'n Louie was bettin' against found out he was a riverboat captain. The man is startin' a ferry business and won your pa's services for a year. And he—"

Hope scudded into Pierce again. "You mean Captain Pacquing is running a riverboat here?" He dropped his valise and lifted the lad off the sacks. "In the bay?"

Eddie's almost colorless eyes widened.

Pierce realized he was holding the boy aloft. He lowered Eddie to his feet and released him, only to have Georgie grab the lad and shake him.

"What's the name of the boat? Where's it docked?"

Eddie wrenched free, his eyes narrowing fiercely. "Lay one more hand on me, an' I ain't tellin' you nothin' else."

Georgie took a step back and spread his hands. "Sorry."

"That's better," the boy spat while tucking in his shirt. "Your pa left yesterday with this Mr. Mitchell on the *Wanda Call*, headed across the ocean to China. To Hong Kong."

"*Hong Kong*?" Georgie gasped.

Pierce's hopes also took a dive, but they didn't crash entirely. The British Crown colony did lie halfway around the world, but anyplace was preferable to New Orleans.

Then reality overtook him. He couldn't possibly be considering following Lark all the way to China—a woman he'd known for only one day? Pierce shook the nonsense from his head . . . but his desire for the gorgeous belle drew his gaze westward, past the muted ship lights in the foggy bay. No one would think he'd lost his mind if he said he was going after his racehorse. And he did want the prize stallion almost as much as the lady. They were both essential if he was to turn his most ardent dream into reality.

But had Pacquing taken the animal with him? Or Lark, for that matter? Pierce turned back to the boys.

Aside from his quivering chin, Georgie seemed frozen in place, his big eyes a brittle glitter.

Sensing the boy's pain, Pierce paused a second before swinging his attention to the other lad. "Thank you, Eddie, you've been—ooph."

Georgie slammed against Pierce, face burrowed into his chest, almost knocking him off-balance. Clutching at Pierce's coat, Georgie made no sound, but his body convulsed.

Poor kid. Pierce understood the boy's despair only too well, knew what it was like to have one's life ripped out from under him. And he liked the kid, big mouth and all. Georgie had spunk, and he was as loyal as a dog. In fact, Pierce would have liked to get to know him better. Would've too, if the kid hadn't made such a point of avoiding him during the last week or so. Pierce knew he should say something, but he wasn't accustomed to consoling anyone, especially a half-grown squirt. Stiffly, gingerly, he gave Georgie a few pats on the back.

"Think I'll go see if I can find my brother," Eddie said, his gaze darting off uncomfortably. He turned and fled.

"Wait!" Pierce called.

Ignoring him, the lad disappeared into the mist-shrouded darkness.

"Damn." Returning his attention to the clinging Georgie, Pierce gave a reassuring squeeze to one of his frail shoulders. The kid was far too young and spindly to be left behind by his father again. "Look, it's going to be all right. I'll put you on the next ship back to your brothers in Louisiana."

Head wagging against Pierce's chest, Georgie eased away. "No. I can't." He straightened and took a deep shuddering breath. "Blackwell won't give up. Can't you see how he's eaten up with the need for revenge? He wallows in it. He won't stop, so I can't."

"He's not going to follow your father all the way to China." Pierce darted a glance off to one side, aware that he was considering doing exactly that. "Nobody's that crazy."

Georgie, his jaw set at a stubborn tilt, stared up with moist yet determined eyes. "Yes, he will. And you know it."

As much as Pierce hated to admit it, Blackwell had seemed almost demented . . . as dementedly determined to destroy Pacquing as Simone Lange had been to destroy Pierce after she learned of his existence when she read her husband's will. Feeling a strange kinship to the boy, Pierce attempted a buoyant smile. "I suppose this means you're going to insist on coming with me to Hong Kong.''

Georgie blinked tears from those big bronze-colored eyes and grabbed Pierce's lapels, his small wet face becoming one big grin . . . just like Lark's. ''You mean it?''

Pierce gently dislodged the kid's hands. ''Yes. I guess so, unless . . . Your father just might have sent Lark on to New Orleans without him.''

The kid didn't say anything for several seconds. He just stared up with those heartbreaking drippy eyes. ''No. He'd never do that.''

''You're sure? Then I guess we're off again—right after I get us outfitted with some new clothes.''

''You needn't bother about me,'' Georgie spewed in a rush.

''That's up to you. But you're not coming another step with me looking like that. You need a bath, too. We could both use a good soaking. I wonder if there's a bathhouse nearby.''

''*Bathhouse*? I'm not going into any bathhouse and take my clothes off in front of a bunch of—of strangers.''

Challenged as usual by the kid's back talk, Pierce glared at Georgie until the kid shrank back.

Then, swiping the wetness from his eyes, Georgie straightened and returned Pierce's stare. ''From what I heard aboard ship, beds in this port are hard to come by. You should be worrying about that first. Heck, we can always order up baths in our rooms. If we get any.''

''Oh, don't worry about that. You'd be surprised how loud money talks. Almost as loud as bigoted gossip. Almost.''

''Bigoted gossip? What are you talking about?''

"Nothing. Forget it." Pierce couldn't believe his tongue had slipped so easily after just the mere mention of New Orleans. He grabbed Georgie's arm. "Come on. Let's go find the fanciest damned hotel in this miserable hole."

Chapter
Thirteen

"BUT I HATE going into those places." Balking, Georgie tried to escape Pierce's grip.

"Fine." He was through putting up with the kid's childishness—last night over a bath, and now this. He freed the lad and threw up his hands.

At the sudden release, Georgie stumbled off the boardwalk and into the muddy street before catching his balance.

"If you want to come to Hong Kong with me, you *will* get yourself fitted for some new clothes."

Georgie pulled that moth-eaten hat down farther and jammed his hands into his pockets. "I don't care what you said, you could've bought my clothes when you got yours. The socks and underwear you brought me fit fine."

Pierce refused to be badgered any more. Without a backward glance, he strode up the hill toward DiMario's Haberdashery, knowing without a doubt the stubborn imp would follow. After a visit to the harbormaster's office this morning, they'd learn that, of all the ships in port, only one was destined for the Orient, and the *Westerly* sailed on the evening tide.

By the time Pierce reached the door of the false-fronted men's clothier, he could hear Georgie's footsteps close behind him.

The kid grabbed his coat sleeve.

Irritated, Pierce glared down at the hand rumpling his new gray pinstripe.

"Sorry," Georgie said, quickly letting go and smoothing the fabric. "I'll go in with you. But I'm not going to take off my clothes in front of some long-fingered old men."

"*Long-fingered*?" Bursting out laughing, Pierce cuffed the top of the kid's hat. "I've never heard them called that. But there's nothing to worry about. The proprietor is married and has children."

"How would you know?"

"He and his family live in an apartment above the store. This morning I thought the roof would fall in from all the banging about up there."

"I'm still not dressing in front of anyone."

"Suit yourself. You can change in the stock room."

The bell above the door rang as Pierce strode into a shop overflowing with all of a man's fashion needs, down to his shoes. As always, he thoroughly enjoyed the aroma of freshly dyed wools and linens mingled with that of new leather.

The impeccably attired Italian who'd waited on him earlier came forward, smiling broadly, while adjusting his somber frock coat. "Mr. Kingston. I see you bring the *ragazzo* now. Is-a good. I have suits *perfetto* for heem all laid out."

Noticing the stubby hands the man waved about, keeping time with his words, Pierce almost laughed again at Georgie's description of men who preferred boys. "Let's have a look at them," he said, returning his attention to the tailor.

"Thees-a way."

Pierce nudged the reluctant lad ahead of him as they followed the man around a clothing rack and stopped at a table with several smaller ready-made coats and trousers piled atop some long underwear. After rifling through them, Pierce chose a couple of dark blue outfits with brass buttons. The cut was similar to those worn by seamen. He shoved them into Georgie's hands.

From behind them, the shopkeeper grabbed for Georgie's limp brown coat.

The kid jerked away and sent Pierce a rebellious glare.

"Is there someplace the boy can change in private? He's a little shy."

"Of course, of course." With a tired smile, the tailor opened the rear door and stepped aside.

Clutching the pile of clothes to him, Georgie scurried through and slammed it shut.

Chuckling at how quickly his brave little rooster could turn into a frightened chick, Pierce strode to the wall racks that held boots and shoes. Georgie's feet were exceptionally small. He hoped he could find some to fit.

While looking through them, Pierce remembered again the evening before. As disappointed as he'd been over failing to catch up to the capricious southern belle who haunted him day and night, he couldn't forget the despair of the clinging boy. He could still feel the sobs convulsing those frail shoulders, could still feel the heat of the little head burrowed against his chest. From now on, he would treat the kid better. Keep in mind that a very frightened boy hid behind those brave combative words.

By the time the boy sidled back into the room, Pierce had found two pairs of black lace-up shoes that might fit him. The trim lines of the jacket and trousers did wonders for the thin boy's appearance. If it hadn't been for that floppy hat, he would've looked like quite the little gentleman.

Pierce ripped the odious thing from the kid's head.

"Hey!" Georgie snatched for it, but Pierce held it aloft.

"Mr. DiMario, would you please dispose of this rag?"

"No!" Georgie jumped up, trying to reach the hat. "I need it."

Restraining the lad, Pierce handed it to the shopkeeper, who left the room holding it gingerly between two fingers.

Still hanging on to the kid, Pierce plucked a navy blue sailor's cap banded in white from a high shelf, then hauled him to a long mirror. Holding him before it, Pierce placed the jaunty cap over the thick crop of auburn hair. "Now. Tell me you don't look a hundred times better."

Georgie screwed up his face as usual. "What I look like is one of those spoiled-brat rich kids."

"Exactly. Instead of a ragamuffin. Now, I've found a couple pairs of small shoes. See if either of them fits." He directed Georgie to a stool near where he'd placed the footwear.

While pretending to be distracted by a display of cuff links and tie pins, Pierce stole glances at the boy.

Georgie's eyes were lowered as he bent over the shoes, and his long lashes feathered above a face in a rare state of repose. With the boldness of his lively eyes hidden, his features and his smooth tawny skin took on a fragility that even his flaring brows couldn't diminish. And the fingers working to tie the laces were as slender as a girl's. All of him so incredibly like Lark.

The boy forgotten, Pierce's thoughts drifted to his lovely belle. In a luxurious gown of the richest russet, she stood at his side in the wide entry hall of their home. She held a flirty black lace fan in one hand while she extended the other to a stream of elegantly dressed guests. . . . The swirl of her skirts, the throaty tinkle of her laughter as he waltzed her across the highly polished floor that reflected the sparkling light of the chandeliers almost as perfectly as the mirrored walls. Her beauty and grace returned to him from every side as he whirled her across the floor. And the love in her eyes was unmistakable. He saw the two of them galloping across dew-kissed hills, her hair flowing free in the wind, her face glowing with the thrill. She rode beside him on an elegant gray filly that was as perfect a match for Pegasus as Lark was for him.

He had to find her, make her his. With her beside him, he could erase all the pain. Forget the headmaster's accusing tone when the withered man informed him of his immediate dismissal . . . and the odious reasons why. Forget the defeat in his mother's eyes when she confirmed that not only had she not been married to his father—whose name was not Kingston but Lange—but that she had been his slave before he freed her after Pierce's birth.

She'd been deliberately bred to be light in color by a Jamaican slaver, then trained to be the perfect octoroon mistress. White by all outward appearance, but with the documented one-eighth Negro blood in her veins, she could legally be bought and sold the same as any full-blooded African just off the boat—and at ten times the price. Only the richest slave owners could afford such a luxury, and even fewer counted themselves wealthy enough to bestow freedom upon one such as she, as his father had the day Sheenee of Kingston gave birth to his son—one of his father's very few charitable acts toward her.

After years of thinking of himself as the legitimate heir to a prominent Louisiana businessman, Pierce had been reduced on that fateful day when he was sixteen to a "high-yellow" bastard, scorned by the southern gentry. Good enough to entertain, but not to be entertained. Good enough for a dalliance with a bored society matron, but absolutely unsuitable for her unmarried sister. Neither his education and accomplishments nor any amount of money he could ever acquire would change the fact that he was, in their eyes, tainted from birth.

"These fit." Georgie's gruff yet thin voice wrenched Pierce back to the present as the boy stared up at him with his sister's eyes.

Pierce shrugged off the emasculating memories and forced a smile. "Now you look fit to be Lark's brother. And, very soon," he added with the utmost determination, "my little brother-in-law."

The English clipper ship cut through the waves with far greater speed than the little schooner had. Under most conditions, Georgie would've been swept up in the thrill as the vessel cut through the soft warmth of the salty trade winds while she leaned against the rail, even the singing lines of the taut rigging and the multitude of ballooning sails couldn't allay her trepidation. Not even the colorful flags flying from the tops of the masts could not do that.

Any day now they would make port in Honolulu and most likely catch up with the *Wanda Call* before it sailed again. To make matters worse, from the moment she'd stepped aboard this ship in her fancy new clothes, half the scurrilous crew had leered at her as if she were one of those females she'd seen through the doors of that San Francisco saloon, or that one in the upstairs window who'd called down to Pierce. And the rutting black-guards thought she was a boy!

The sultry voice of the waterfront whore who'd beckoned to Pierce invaded Georgie's thoughts, along with the sight of her leaning out, most of her bosom falling out of her slinky red wrapper. Yet, to Georgie's joy, Pierce had scarcely glanced the strumpet's way, nor had he looked at any other woman they'd passed. His faithfulness to the flirtatious belle who'd so totally captured his fancy was unwavering. More and more, Georgie wished she could really be that young woman. Of course, when Pierce discovered the truth, the light that came to his eyes whenever he spoke Lark's name would be snuffed.

If only she wouldn't have to be there to see his face when it happened.

Georgie let her eyelids fall shut as she sighed.

She could've run away, escaped her inevitable downfall by signing on with one of the mail steamers going south. Too bad she'd discovered before they sailed that Blackwell hadn't boarded. Either the snake had not discovered Papa's destination or he had decided that further pursuit would be too costly. Instead, she was traveling halfway around the world with this man who filled her thoughts night and day, who made her insides feel as if she'd swallowed a flock of butterflies every time he looked into her eyes.

But there was no telling what he'd do when Papa spilled the beans. Yet, heaven help her, she'd have to see it through, be there to keep Pierce from doing something dreadful to Papa.

Pierce strode up beside her, looking as maddeningly

handsome as ever in a black cravat, crisp white shirt, and the gray pin-striped vest and trousers he'd purchased in San Francisco. If she hadn't known better, she'd have thought he was deliberately trying to drive her crazy as he ran fingers through his wind-ruffled hair.

For a moment she watched him, mesmerized. If he only knew how his every careless gesture sent jolts of yearning through her.

Toward the stern, three unsavory louts knelt on the deck, sewing a rip in a large expanse of canvas. Each man looked up at her with a suggestive grin. One, with missing front teeth, grabbed his crotch and winked.

Georgie's stomach bucked at the disgusting display. Abruptly she turned a snubbing back to the loathsome degenerates. Never in all her years along the rivers had she known of such crude behavior, such depravity. She wondered if these men had acquired their abominable traits in the notorious ports of the Orient. A shudder coursed through her as she speculated on what other barbarity might await her in Hong Kong if, by chance, Papa's ship left Hawaii before they arrived.

"G'day to ye, there, Mr. Kingston," called one of the creatures. "Out fer a Sunday stroll wi' yer li'l girly-boy?"

Pierce seemed not to have heard the cockney's slur as he looked out over the vast blue ocean sparked with silver . . . except for his knuckles, which had turned white from his grip on the railing.

Georgie grinned, wondering which riled him worse, the men's blatant lusting after his young charge or their assumption that Pierce, too, preferred young lads. Yes, she knew exactly where he'd like to place one of those sets of straining knuckles. But of course he couldn't. He was outnumbered twenty to one, and telling the captain could easily have made the situation even uglier.

"Land ho!" came a cry from aloft.

Excitement ignited Georgie. After nearly a month of staring out at an endlessly empty seascape dotted only by an occasional passing ship or a frolicking porpoise, they approached the first land west of California, the Hawaiian Islands—or the Sandwich Islands as the crewmen called them. Shading her eyes, she squinted up a tall mast at the sailor who was pointing ahead with an extended telescope. Holding down her sailor cap, Georgie grabbed Pierce's hand and pulled him with her toward the front.

The seamen, neglecting their chores, harangued them with whistles and catcalls.

Although he didn't slow his step, Pierce's fingers went rigid, and he dropped her hand like a hot skillet.

Reaching the bow, Georgie leaned out over the point where the sea cut away on either side. She strained her eyes, searching the horizon. "Do you see anything?" she yelled above the roar of slicing water.

"There!" Pierce pointed a little to the southwest.

Looking where he directed, Georgie spotted the peak of a mountain.

"And there," he added, drawing her attention more to the west. "And over there, too. Looks like three islands."

"We should be making port in a few hours."

Pierce leaned down slightly but still had to speak with force to be heard. "Last night the captain said we've had excellent sailing. He said we would easily reach Honolulu before the *Wanda Call* sets sail again. This time we won't be too late." Obviously forgetting himself in his excitement, he captured her hand again and gave it a squeeze.

She slid into the deepest grief as she viewed the joy in his eyes—joy that would very soon turn to hatred. Looking again at the mountainous islands, Georgie thought they loomed much closer now than they had just seconds ago.

The distance had been deceptive, and the *Westerly* didn't reach the small harbor tucked away on the far side of one of the isles until almost dusk—the longest afternoon of Pierce's life. The ship, after being tossed by incredibly high surf, gently settled into a smooth glide as it slipped within the shelter of a huge bar of sand just offshore of the port.

Hanging on to the rail, he reveled in the lushness of the island's greenery. It had a soothing effect on his eyes after weeks of enduring the glare of the sun's reflection off the water. And for late August, the air seemed much lighter, much more temperate than he'd expected for this latitude. Perhaps it really was the paradise the captain had touted it to be.

Georgie stood beside him, looking as unaccountably surly as he had all day.

The kid never ceased to be an enigma. But nothing the boy could say would dampen Pierce's spirits today. Before the sun sank into the sea this night, Lark would be in his arms again.

Only five other sailing vessels floated among a clutter of strange-looking native craft. And, lo and behold, painted on the hull of the first ship they passed were the most wonderful words Pierce had ever read . . . *Wanda Call*. His heart started pounding, and he very nearly let out a whoop. In a sudden flash of brilliance, he decided that his first daughter would be named Wanda to mark this momentous day.

"Well, there it is," Georgie said, lacking any enthusiasm at all.

Maybe the kid was coming down with something. "Are you feeling all right?"

Georgie lifted those deep copper eyes. They held an unfathomable sadness as he failed at a tight-lipped grin. "Sure. But you gotta promise me. No matter what, don't hit Papa. It's really not all his fault. If Mommy hadn't died, he'd . . . I'd . . . " The kid shrugged, and his voice trailed off.

"Don't worry. I'm not going to hurt him. I'm too happy to hurt anyone today. Now, come along. Let's go haul my trunk up on deck."

"Stop lagging behind," Pierce tossed over his shoulder to Georgie as he started up the gangplank of the *Wanda Call.*

Anxious as she was to see her papa again, to make sure he was all right, her own impending doom far outweighed any pleasure in the moment. In a halfhearted effort she forced herself into a faster gait.

"Request permission to come aboard," Pierce called to an officer directing the loading of a large crate.

"Put it down over there." The man motioned to a dockworker guiding the dangling cargo. Once the container settled onto the dock, the man turned to Pierce, who had reached the top of the gangplank. Vanity showed in the officer's chest-thrusting strut and even more in the graying sideburns bushing out from either side of his face. His small blue eyes obviously took Pierce's measure . . . and approved. He extended a hand. "Permission granted. What may I do to help you?"

They stepped aboard and while Pierce shook the

officer's hand, Georgie quickly glanced around, looking for her papa, but she wasn't surprised when she didn't see him. From recent experience, she suspected she'd find him in some palm-roofed saloon like the shanty they'd passed on their way from the *Westerly*.

"I'm looking for Louie Pacquing," Pierce said in a mellow but sure voice. "I understand that he is traveling with you to Hong Kong."

"Oh, yes. Pacquing. Mr. Mitchell's hired man. Well, I'm afraid he's not here. He left Mr. Mitchell high and dry, he did. Mr. Mitchell's out scouring the island right now, looking for a replacement. Perhaps you might know of someone who's adept at working on a steam engine?"

Relief crowded past Georgie's apprehension. She'd been given a reprieve, however temporary.

"Didn't Mr. Pacquing sail here with you?" Pierce asked, his tone edged with concern.

"That he did. But he deserted Mr. Mitchell and signed on with the *Flying Cloud*. A native boy brought Mr. Mitchell a note last night *after* she left port."

A note? Another blasted note? At least he was consistent, Georgie thought bitterly as the news of yet another of her father's shameless misadventures sank in. She peeked up at Pierce and noticed his chest expand with the deepest breath.

The muscles in his jaw worked. "And where," he grated, "was *that* ship headed?"

"Back to San Francisco. Mr. Pacquing said something in his letter about not being willing to travel so far from his children. I got the impression that he'd left Louisiana under some kind of a cloud, but had decided to go back and face up to it. A lot of good that's doing poor Mr. Mitchell, though, with a hold full of steamboat parts and no one to assemble them when we reach Hong Kong."

"You haven't mentioned a horse, a gray thorough-bred, or Pacquing's daughter, Lark." Pierce's words came out controlled but deadly. "They weren't with him, were they?"

Her heart threatened to burst through her bindings as Georgie took an instinctive step to one side.

"I'm sorry, sir, but I know nothing about a horse or a girl. Mr. Pacquing kept pretty much to himself. Moody sort, if you ask me."

Pierce wheeled around. He shoved Georgie aside and charged down the gangplank.

She looked from his rapidly retreating back to the ship's officer and smiled nervously. "Mr. Kingston's kinda upset right now, so I'll thank you for him." Turning to follow, Georgie tipped her cap. "I'd better go after him."

By the time she reached the entrance of the pier and turned down the wharf, Pierce had stalked past a mix of sailors and nearly nude native dockworkers. He made a beeline for the tavern they'd passed a few moments before—the Rum Cove.

She sprinted after him, but without the slightest notion of what to say that would make up for another fruitless trip. And the horse. She didn't even want to think about what had become of the magnificent steed. She caught Pierce's sleeve just as he reached the woven-reed swing-ing doors framed with bambo.

Veins bulging at his temples, he swung around and loomed over her, his body so tense it quivered. "Get out of my sight before I . . . " He cocked a fist.

Georgie backed out of range.

Lunging around, Pierce crashed through the doors.

Georgie stood in place, staring at them as they banged back and forth until they gradually settled to a stop.

Maybe it would be better to let him blow off some steam, she reasoned. She certainly wasn't in any hurry to face his wrath *or* the inevitable barrage of questions.

"I'll just go see if one of the ships in port is sailing for America," she said to herself. Turning away, she nodded. "Yeah." She would arrange passage and get their things aboard, make it easier for Pierce, keep busy. . . .

Reaching into her pocket, she jangled her few coins, sure they'd be enough to hire a couple of men to collect Pierce's trunk for her.

Georgie learned from a loitering seaman that the *Golden Duchess*, an American ship moored at the next pier, was scheduled to leave for California the next day. The captain, a fatherly-looking man with a stern voice but kind eyes, granted her the only available cabin at a fair price, even allowed her to bring their things aboard. But he'd insisted upon payment for passage before he retired for the night, since they would be sailing on the morning tide.

As she returned, past a row of warehouses, to the Rum Cove, dread plagued Georgie's every step. If she told Pierce the truth, that might ease his frustration somewhat, she argued. He might be so glad to have his Lark that he'd overlook her little deception. Might wrap his arms around her, forgive her, look lovingly into her eyes.

Don't be a fool, she told herself. She wasn't the lovely belle he was looking for, and a man as cultured as he would accept no less.

Reaching the doors, she gritted her teeth and slipped through them into a large, crowded room filled with smoke, music, and loud talk.

Georgie's eyes widened at the sight of three bare-breasted, brown-skinned maidens dancing on a small stage in the far corner. Their hips swayed to the exotic rhythm of strange-sounding reeds and drums. Several other women, also clothed only in long grass skirts and the drapery of their sleek black hair, sat with seamen around bamboo tables.

Amid the rumble of drunken men's voices, a high giggle drew Georgie's attention to where several sailors from the *Westerly* sat. One held a laughing native girl on his lap, a hand fondling her breast while his other slid past the grass strands of her skirt.

Georgie cringed and backed toward the exit. She'd seen saloon girls from time to time in Oregon and then in San Francisco, and their gowns had been cut low, but this was . . . She bumped against the doorjamb.

Turning to escape, she spotted Pierce leaning against the bar that ran along the side wall. And one of those near-naked heathens was untying his cravat!

"Pierce!" she cried and charged past a number of tables, jumping over several jutting legs, to reach him.

He wore a drunken leer as he turned to watch her advance, but that expression quickly disappeared. "Thought I tol' you t' get lost," he slurred.

Georgie ignored his rudeness. "I found a ship that's sailing on the morning tide."

"It's been a real experience knowin' ya, kid. But don' wait aroun' for me to see you off."

She wedged herself between him and the sloe-eyed whore. "You have to go pay the captain for our cabin *now*, before he goes to bed."

"Move along, kid. The lady and we were jus' gettin' acquainted." Pierce's mouth slackened into a lazy grin, and he reached for the native girl. "Isn' tha' right?"

Enraged by his betrayal, Georgie rammed her fist into his chest with all her might.

Stumbling back, he caught hold of the bar.

Before he could right himself, Georgie grabbed the front of his shirt. "*How could you?*"

"Hey, matie," caterwauled some sailor behind them. "Yer bonny li'l girly-boy gettin' jealous, there?"

Stiffening, Pierce scanned the room as he wrenched away Georgie's hands.

"Forget him." Georgie shook his shoulder. "What about Lark? I thought you cared about her."

Pierce leveled his attention on her again, with menace. "There is no Lark. Never was."

"Of course there is."

"Nope. I jus' dreamed her up one day. Tha's why no one ever knows anything about her. Hell, the only time you talk about her is when you want somethin'. Then you pull her outta your hat. Dangle her name in front of me. Well, it won't work anymore. Now take those damn eyes of yours and get the hell outta here." He grabbed his glass from the bar and downed its contents, then banged it hard on the counter. "Bartender! Another rum down here."

An unshaven saloonkeeper wiped his hands on his stained apron and plucked a jug from the shelf behind him, then moved along the bar toward them.

Georgie pulled on Pierce's shirtsleeve. "You don't need any more rum. Come on. The captain won't wait up much longer."

The barkeep shot Georgie a disapproving glance as he poured Pierce's drink. "This ain't no place for the youngster."

"Well," Pierce countered, "toss him out." He picked up his glass and emptied it in two big gulps.

"Sir." Georgie leaned forward across the bar. "Do you know someone who could help me get Mr. Kingston out of here? Our ship sails before dawn, and he hasn't even paid our passage yet.''

Pierce flung out a hand and yanked Georgie close. "Is that what it's gonna take to get ridda you?" He let go of her and groped around, trying to find the inside pocket of his coat. Eventually locating his money envelope, he fished it out.

Georgie shot forth a hand, snatched it from him, and hid it beneath her own coat. "You're even drunker than I thought. I'm surprised someone hasn't already taken it off you." She turned back to the bartender. "Can you help me?"

Pierce's eyes narrowed. "I never been thrown outta a saloon in m'life." Then, as if he'd lost something, he looked around the room. "Where'd my hula girl go?"

"Lad, you run along now," the barkeep said wearily. "I'll see he don't miss his ship. Which one is it?"

"The *Golden Duchess*. We'll be in the second cabin on deck." Georgie stared after Pierce as he staggered into the crowd, her heart turning into a heavy ball of pain. How could he even look at another woman after the night he'd spent with her? After the love they'd shared.

Unable to watch any longer, she turned and left.

Chapter
Fourteen

RAGE POUNDED BEHIND Georgie's eyes as she tore at her shirt. A button popped off, then another, and pinged against the mirror in front of her, and she couldn't have cared less as she stood in the center of this latest of a series of dreary, dark-paneled cabins.

Her breath came in sharp bursts. She'd never been so humiliated in her life. To watch her man—the one who'd asked her to marry him—chasing after some wagging tail like a dog on the scent. She shucked the shirt, then with trembling fingers, ripped at the knotted end of her chest bindings. She had to get free before she exploded.

Quickly but carefully, she unwrapped her breasts to minimize the first sparks of pain she always experienced upon releasing them. Rubbing away the hurt, she began to relax, and soon noticed her reflection in the good-sized mirror on the wall.

Letting her hands fall away, she studied her womanly endowments in the glow of the lone oil lamp bracketed beside the looking glass. Rarely before she met Pierce had she thought of her breasts as much more than a nuisance. But after seeing those native women earlier, brazenly flaunting their charms, she wondered if hers would seem as attractive to a man. To Pierce. Considering her rather tall, thin body, they certainly were a generous contradiction. Plumped full, yet they didn't sag like the breasts of a couple of the girls she'd seen dancing on the stage.

Imagine! Allowing their legs to peek through grass skirts that provided nothing more than a mocking pretense at modesty. And shoes? They didn't even wear them. No wonder the men were almost mad for the native women. Georgie had been schooled to show no more than a stockinged ankle, and then only when she felt flirtatious.

Spurred by wanton curiosity, she remove her boots and socks and kicked off her trousers to check her own limbs. Sticking one leg out to catch the light, she turned it slowly back and forth. Definitely longer and more slender than theirs, she thought with an objective tilt of her head. And weren't men supposed to be attracted to a slim ankle?

Not to mention long hair, she thought with a grimace. She moved closer to the mirror and gave a disgusted flip to the cropped cap that framed her face.

"It's all Pierce's fault. I did it because of him. The dirty rotten double-dealing Romeo. He's probably bedding one of those heathens right now."

As she wheeled away from the mirror, her eyes landed on the envelope of money she'd dropped onto his trunk. It was still stuffed with thousands of dollars, even after she'd paid for their return passage on the *Golden Duchess*. This trip would mean more weeks of being cooped up on a ship, but the alternative was to be stranded here in the middle of the Pacific. Then it occurred to her that it would serve Pierce right if he didn't get back to the ship before it sailed. Without his money he might have to stay there forever. She hoped he would. She hoped he would get some terrible disease like leprosy. "And I'll tell you one more thing, Pierce Kingston," she said aloud. "Even if you do come back tonight, I'm not going to torture my poor breasts day and night anymore. We'll just let the chips fall where they may."

A tapping came from the other side of the wall, and Georgie realized how loud she'd been talking.

She moved closer to the wall. "Sorry," she called, a bit mollified, but still impassioned. Stalking to her canvas bag, which she'd looped over the bunk post, she rammed in her bindings, then snatched up her shirt. She shoved her arms into the sleeves and fastened the buttons that remained. Who would care if it gaped here and there? she thought as she blew out the light. Even if Pierce came back, stinking of rum and some whore's perfume, he would be too drunk to notice.

She climbed up onto the top bunk, then grabbed her pillow as she lay down, huddling around it, willing herself not to think about the betraying bastard anymore. She hoped for sleep, dreamless, healing sleep.

Time dragged as she jumped at every sound, wondering if Pierce had come aboard. Finally drowsiness overtook her and she drifted off.

Sometime later, she awoke to more noise—loud whispers, shuffling sounds.

The door handle rattled.

"Locked," a man said in hushed tones. He rapped lightly.

She had no doubt Pierce stood outside with some of his drunken friends or, worse, one of those naked girls. She lay still and stared in the direction of the ruckus.

Knocking sounded again, this time loud enough to wake the whole blamed ship.

Her anger mounting, she climbed down from the bunk.

Upon opening the door, she found two men standing in the moonlight with Pierce hoisted between them.

Both stranger's eyes widened to a surprised gawk.

Realizing she had on nothing but a skimpy shirt, she quickly stepped back into the darkness of the doorway.

After a few seconds of silence one of the men asked, "Does he belong to you?"

"I'm afraid so."

Pierce's lolling head came up at the sound of her voice.

They shoved him closer.

"Lark?" His head bobbed, and he jerked it up again. "Though' I neve' fin' you again." It sagged again.

"You mean," said the other man, "we was puttin' up with his babblin' on about his long lost Lark all night, and you was here waitin' all the time? Guess the joke's on us."

"Leastwise," said the first, eyeing Georgie's shirt-front again, "now we know why Laughin' Mary couldn't drag him to her crib." Unwinding Pierce's arm from around his neck, he pushed the barely conscious man toward her. "G'night to you, ma'am."

Nearly buckling under the weight of Pierce's ungainly body, Georgie tried to move him far enough to one side to call after the men, to make sure she'd heard right— verify that Pierce hadn't lain with one of those whores after all. But by the time she managed to prop Pierce up against the doorjamb, the two had disappeared. "Fiddle," she muttered, but couldn't stop the smile that crept across her face as she looked up at the dear faithful man. Even bleary-eyed with rum, he couldn't have been more welcome. "Come on. Let's get you to bed."

She wrapped one of his arms around her shoulders,

then nudged him in the ribs. "Pierce," she said as loud as she dared. "Walk to the bed."

Like an obedient pup, he put one foot in front of the other.

"That's a good boy." Remembering the door, she swung back a leg and kicked it shut . . . just as Pierce stumbled over something.

He fell, taking her with him.

As she came down on top of his back, she broke her fall with a hand to the floor and discovered that he'd tripped over her carelessly discarded trousers. She had no one to blame but herself. But how was she going to get him up off the floor?

Beneath her, Pierce chuckled. "Whoops! Guess I fell." He sounded like a small boy who'd just been caught with pie all over his face. With a grunt, he started rolling over.

She dodged out of his way and rose to her knees.

"I had a wee bit too much to drink tonight."

"That's not all you had a bit too much of," she said, pulling him up to a sitting position. "What about those hula girls?"

"Now, Lark, you know I wouldn'—"

Without her realizing what he was up to, he reached for her—right past her gaping shirt to a breast.

She gasped.

He jerked away. "Lark?"

"I, uh . . ."

"Is it really you?" Groping in the dark, he found her shoulder.

She sprang to her feet, then felt around until she recovered one of his arms and tugged on it. "Pierce, you have to get up. Try to help me."

Surprising strength infused his legs. He almost leapt to

his feet and, catching the back of her neck, he ran his other hand across the front of her shirt and the thinly covered swells beneath.

Her own legs began to collapse at the shock, the thrill, of finally being touched by him again after such a torturously long time.

He drew her closer. "My God, it is you." He pressed his palm against one of her breasts, a shudder traveling through him.

Her own body did the same, and she swayed into him.

His grip tightened. He leaned down, brushing his lips softly across hers.

She couldn't help sighing as he drew away.

"Lark, Lark, thought I los' you. Tha' you were gone forever. But you came back." His mouth found hers again, this time with passionate possession, his hands now moving up and down her loosely shirted back.

For one brief instant Georgie knew she should stop him, tell him the truth. But she knew if she did, he'd cast her aside. The thought ripped through her chest like a knife.

She sent a fleeting silent prayer heavenward: Let me have just this one last night, and tomorrow I promise to tell him the truth. I promise.

Encircling his neck with her arms, she twined her fingers in his hair, pulled him closer, and deepened the kiss, meeting his seeking tongue.

His awakened manhood pressed against her belly.

She moved against it in an answer that sent a hungering ache to her core.

Too soon he pulled away. He took her face in his hands. "They lie' to me. They said you weren' here. But you knew I'd come, di'n' you? An' you waited for me to catch up. You love me as much as I love you, don' you?"

Despite the slurring, his tone bespoke the sincerest reverence.

He'd said he loved her. And, yes, she loved him, too, with all her heart. Her betrayal assailed her again with such force that she knew she couldn't trick him ever again. She reached up and touched his cheek. "Yes, but—"

He smothered her next words with his mouth, grinding it against hers in a pursuit so sensuous it erased all reasonable thought. He added a new dimension to his lovemaking by sliding his fingers in a languorous caress down her throat. They reached the first button on her shirt and undid it.

Georgie could feel the beat of her racing heart against his overheated palm.

His lips left hers, and he concentrated on the next button and unfastened it, then the next.

Her shirt fell open, and his hand moved inside to trace her curves, the fullness of her bosom, the tips that hardened to his touch.

She sucked in her breath and held it.

"I know I'm dreaming," he whispered hoarsely. "But for God's sake, don't wake me." He grazed her lips with the tip of his tongue, then moved down toward a breast.

As he descended, Georgie's legs began to melt. She grabbed for him.

He stumbled forward, almost going down with her, before catching his balance. He took her by her arms. "Maybe we better fin' the bed. Where is it?"

"Behind you."

As he stepped back with her, he slipped the shirt off her shoulders. His hands followed the garment downward until he reached her hips. He stopped. "You don' have anything else on, do you?"

"No. I, uh . . ."

"Don't be embarrassed. You couldn't have given me a more perfect gift than to be here in my bed waiting to make love to me." His hands moved across her skin to the center of her abdomen, and she quivered as he slid them downward.

Her eyes fell shut as her anticipation peaked.

Just short of reaching her most vulnerable spot, he trailed his hand upward again.

Her breath came out on a shudder.

Drawing her into his arms, he stepped back again, taking her with him until his leg bumped the lower bunk. "At last," he said on a chuckle.

Although she knew she should, she did not resist in the least as he pulled her down with him . . . cracking his head resoundingly on the frame of the above bunk.

He groaned low and let go of her. Grabbing his injury, he sank onto the mattress.

She knelt down. "Are you all right?" Straining to see him in the dark, she ran a hand upward until she found the sore spot on his head. "Please don't pass out on me now."

"Give me a minute," he said in a tight voice.

"Don't you worry about a thing," she said, stroking his temple. "You just lie there and rest a bit. I'll get your boots off."

Between her father and her three brothers, she'd had years of practice. She whipped the boots off in record time, then unbuckled his belt and started undoing his trousers.

A hand covered hers, and he leaned up on an elbow. "My head's much better now."

"You sure?"

"Yes." Coming to his feet, he brought her up with him, then wavered slightly.

She grabbed his arms, steadying him. "Pierce?"

"It's not my head. I've just had a little too much to drink. I was out drowning my sorrows and here you were, waiting for me all the time." He reached for his trouser buttons, as Georgie went for the ones on his shirt. "But don't worry, I'm all right. I'll be fine. I'll make up for leaving you here alone. Tonight, tomorrow, the day after that. I'll never leave you again."

His words cut Georgie to her soul. She knew this one last night was all they would ever have. Spreading his shirt, she laid her cheek against the expanse of his firm yet comforting chest and breathed deeply of the scent that was his alone. She felt the hard thumping of his heart and heard his lungs contract on a moan as she pressed herself against him.

"You're driving me mad." He held her away from him and pushed her down on the bed. Then, within seconds, he finished removing his clothes and crawled into her waiting arms.

Not an inch of her body was deprived as he spread himself over her, around her. His shaft, in the fullness of its power, held infinite promise.

His hands found her face, her eyes, her mouth, as the rest of him began to move slowly against her. "You feel so good," he whispered, his breath brushing her ear. "Why did you leave me? Promise you'll never do it again."

She answered him the only way she could. Capturing his head, she poured all of her love and longing into a desperate, demanding kiss. She crushed her lips against his, thrust her tongue into his mouth.

Returning her passion, he slanted his lips across hers,

driving her deeper into the pillow. A hand cupped her bottom and brought her hard against his waiting need.

Her body turned to flame. She wrapped her legs around him and wrenched her mouth away. "Make love to me," she panted, "like it was the very last time."

"And the first," came his rushed whisper as he rose up over her to make her his.

Long after Pierce's breathing settled into the steady cadence of slumber, Georgie continued to lie cradled in his arms, not wanting the sweet afterglow of their lovemaking to end. But she had no choice. She had to leave his bed before he awakened to the light of day and discovered the awful truth. She couldn't bear to have him find out in such a shocking manner. There had to be a gentler way.

In the distance she heard a door shut, then another. Muffled thuds and scrapes sounded from various areas of the deck, and she knew the crew was preparing to sail.

She could wait no longer. Slowly, carefully, she slipped out of Pierce's arms and eased over him and onto the floor. As she stood in the darkness, unable to make out his beloved features, a loneliness deeper than any she'd ever known seeped into her every fiber. Never again would he whisper her name or tell her how much he loved her, as he had done this night. Never again would she hear the desire in his urgent words, feel it in his touch. Once he learned the truth, he would throw her out, never to speak to her again. And when the ship docked in San Francisco, he'd be gone from her life forever. But who could blame him? She certainly couldn't.

Her toe scraped across some material. Reaching down, she discovered a shirt. His? Hers? What difference did it make? She picked it up and put it on. Then, grasping a ladder rung, she started up to the top bunk.

Suddenly a thought struck her, and she froze. This had been the only available cabin. When Pierce threw her out, where would she stay?

Recalling her vow, she looked skyward. ''I know what I said,'' she whispered. ''But you can see how impossible it would be to tell him now. And as drunk as he was, I'm sure I can convince him he was just dreaming. But I promise, just as soon as we reach California, I *will* confess. Honest.''

Vastly relieved at the postponement of her inevitable fate, she crawled to the foot of the bed and withdrew the long strip of binding from her bag. She'd have to wear it for a few more weeks. And since she and Pierce were again forced to share the same room, that meant nighttime as well. She cringed at the thought. Her breasts had begun to rebel at the constraints by becoming more tender with each passing day.

Brushing a hand across one, she remembered the searing thrill that had electrified it only moments ago when he'd taken it, then the other one, into his mouth, and to each in turn he'd done the most ardently carnal things.

For the last time.

Her breath caught on a sob.

Chapter
Fifteen

AFTER DRESSING WITH the dawn, Georgie sneaked out of their cabin with as little noise as possible. She couldn't bear the idea of being there when Pierce awakened and discovered that his Lark was missing. But she had no doubt how he would react. First, he'd stare at the bed, puzzled; then he would look around for some sign of her. After a moment, a heart-wrenching expression would replace his confused look as it struck him he'd just conjured her up in a drunken stupor. But even if he didn't figure it out on his own, even if he walked outside to search for her, a few words from Georgie would solve the problem, she was sure.

Fighting an urge to cry, she emerged onto the deck of the sleek three-masted ship, determined to put Pierce out of her mind, at least for a little while.

Under a spectacular display of sails filled with a warm but steady tropical breeze, she heard the hum of tightly secured lines and felt a strong vibration beneath her feet. She'd never been on a California clipper before, and with the wind at its stern, the ship was taking her fast, much faster than the British clipper had, faster than when she shot the rapids at The Dalles. Holding her cap in place, she hurried to the bow.

Reaching it, she let her gaze follow a bowsprit that

stretched out even farther. Then she looked up to the fluttering sails billowing above her on a line from the stem's tip to the foremast, from which strained an even more magnificent array of canvas. Looking down, she noticed that the prow also stretched forward, creating a considerable overhang. Standing at its point high above the water, she felt the same thrill as she had when she rode in the crow's nest of the coastal schooner.

"Well, young man," came a woman's voice from behind her. "I see you've found my favorite spot."

Georgie pivoted to find a rather tall, elegantly attired lady with a long straight nose and crisp blue eyes above precisely etched cheekbones. To her favor, a sprinkling of freckles and a fringe of unruly curls softened her gaunt features, as did her friendly smile.

"My name is Mrs. Gable." She extended one gloved hand in greeting as naturally as a man would.

Not knowing what else to do, Georgie shook it. And from the lack of surprise on the woman's face, Georgie knew she'd done the right thing. "How do you do? My name's Georgie Pacquing. My, uh, friend and I boarded last night."

"Yes, I know. The walls are quite thin."

In an instant Georgie's cheeks turned stove-hot.

"I do regret that I was compelled to knock on the wall. But now that you're aware of how readily loud talk carries, I'm sure we'll get along splendidly."

Exceedingly relieved that the lady referred to what had happened earlier in the evening, Georgie changed to a safer subject. "This is one fine ship."

"That it is." Mrs. Gable captured a flying strand of hair and tucked it into a tightly wound coil of faded red hair. "My husband and I chose to book passage on the *Golden Duchess* for precisely that reason. We prefer to travel on American ships. The officers and crew tend to be more to our liking.''

"Mine, too.'' Especially, she added to herself, since this woman was aboard. Mrs. Gable looked as if she had the same stiff backbone that had served Georgie's mother so well through the years. With her present, no sailor would dare give Georgie a hard time. ''When do they serve breakfast?'' Georgie asked, hoping to wangle an invitation to join the Gables. Even if the lady failed to live up to her appearance, perhaps Georgie could avoid the terrible moment a little longer.

Pierce, thank goodness, didn't arrive during the meal. Only the ship's officers, the Gables, and three male passengers ate at the two long tables in the dining hall.

With failing courage, Georgie stayed the rest of the morning with Mrs. Gable and her equally opinionated husband, a rather stout man in expertly tailored brown serge. At one of the tables, they taught her an ancient Hindu board game they'd picked up in India called pachisi.

All the while Georgie pretended interest, she watched the door for Pierce, her nerves as taut as banjo strings.

While rolling dice and moving the colorful wooden figures from space to space, the couple regaled her with stories of their extensive travels in the Orient. Then Mr. Gable, his waistcoat buttoned rather snugly across his ample torso, explained his plan for profiting quite handsomely from their grand tour. Georgie hoped she nodded at the appropriate times as he described the exotic riches and luxuries crated in the hold below—items for which the newly moneyed in San Francisco would be clamoring.

Noon arrived, bringing in the other three passengers

for dinner, and Pierce still hadn't made an appearance. Georgie did her best to enjoy a rather splendid meal, which included fresh pork and tropical fruits, since they'd so recently left port.

After finishing, the exceptionally fit elderly couple rose in unison.

"We generally take our constitutional now," Mrs. Gable said, articulating precisely. "Since your companion presumably hasn't found a reason to rise for the day, would you care to join us, young man?"

Georgie gave them her brightest smile, although she had no idea what a constitutional was. "Sure. Sounds like fun."

It turned out to be several brisk circuits of the deck. Dropping behind the couple where the pathway narrowed between a barrel and a coil of rope, Georgie almost bumped into them as they came to an abrupt halt.

"Is that the gentleman with whom you're traveling?" Mrs. Gable asked, her tone full of disapproval.

Georgie's mouth went cotton-dry. Afraid to look, yet more afraid not to, she peeked around the twosome.

Pierce stood at the entrance to the passageway. He glanced wildly about him. His shirt hung open over his trousers, his hair fell in disarray across his brow, and, worse, his feet were bare.

It took everything she had not to run to him, pull his troubled head to her bosom, tell him that his Lark was here for him now and forever more. But she knew that would only make matters worse. However, she still couldn't let him catch the brunt of the Gables' scorn. "Mr. Pierce has been ill. His fever must be on the rise again."

She broke past the couple and ran to the rescue.

Reaching Pierce, she caught his hand and pulled him into the shadows of the companionway.

"What? Wait!" He jerked away, then groaned and rubbed his forehead.

"I thought you might want to go back to the cabin and get your shoes," Georgie said in quiet, soothing tones.

"My shoes?" His words sounded hollow, and he looked down. "Yes, I see." He lifted his pain-filled gaze to hold hers for a couple of seconds; then his eyes faltered and drifted elsewhere. "Lark," he murmured.

Georgie held her breath, waiting for him to continue. He didn't.

She exhaled slowly. "Yes, what about her?"

Without looking her way, Pierce shook his head and sighed. "Nothing." Shoulders sagging, he walked back to their cabin and closed the door behind him.

Pierce's temples pounded with the ferocity of a giant bass drum as he eased out of his clothes. But he welcomed the pain. It distracted his thoughts. Letting his shirt and trousers drop where they may, he crawled back into bed. There was nothing left to do but to sleep it all away, especially the insane delusion. He rolled over, facing the wall, and closed his aching eyes.

A picture of Lark strolling toward him, stunningly beautiful in that sumptuous bouquet of pink roses and lace, stole into his thoughts. Her flirtatious eyes, the sound of her laughter—sometimes almost a tinkle, other times a deep throaty promise. So perfect . . . too perfect to be true. Especially for someone like him.

Pierce's eyes sprang open. Could it be possible? Could his father's wife have had him followed all the way to Oregon? Was all of this yet one more diabolical plot to destroy him? The vindictive witch had been the cause of

every travail in his life thus far. Why had he thought
Simone Lange would let a few thousand miles stop her?

After his father died and she found evidence of
Pierce's existence among her husband's papers, Simone
Lange, childless herself, had stopped at nothing to see
him branded as a high yellow bastard wherever he
went—at the school, for which she would no longer
provide tuition, and in New Orleans, to which he
returned to find his mother reduced to working in a
bordello for wealthy gentlemen.

Mrs. Wilton Chase Lange, or, as she was more widely
known, Simone Moreau Lange, daughter of the influen-
tial Charles Moreau, wielded the power of both houses
with the mercy of a cat-o'nine-tails slashing across a
naked back. Pierce's mother had felt the bite long before
he even knew of Simone Lange's existence.

As a six-year-old boy, he'd only known he was being
sent far away to a boys' school, never to be allowed to
come home again. He had no idea until he returned ten
years later that his weak-kneed father had been compelled to abandon Pierce's mother to the vengeance of
the shrew. At first his mother had turned to a friend of his
father, but after Simone Lange informed the man's wife,
there was nothing left for her but to become one of the
ladies of Madame LaRue's Sporting House—his exqui-
sitely beautiful mother, the elegant Sheenee of Kingston.

Pierce's head throbbed with renewed power at the
thought of the life forced upon his mother. And how it
had changed her. When he'd returned to New Orleans,
longing to see a gentle reassurance in her eyes, desperate
to be told it was all untrue, he saw only pity.

Although still stylish and beautiful, his mother was
resigned to her fate. Even after he'd accrued a small

fortune and begged her to come to California, she refused.

"No," she'd said with absolute finality. Sitting at her dressing table, she'd watched his reflection in the gilt-framed mirror, her gold-flecked hazel eyes unwavering as she rouged her cheeks in preparation for the evening's entertainment. "Eventually someone would show up who knew me from before. I couldn't bear to go through the shame again. I will not try to be someone I'm not, and neither should you. That woman will never let you be white. If she does, you'll be eligible to inherit."

Pierce's insides twisted, even now, at the remembrance of his worst fall at the Lange woman's hands. With the profits from a lucrative cotton deal in his pocket, he'd moved to St. Louis, hundreds of miles to the north of her far-reaching tentacles—he thought. It had been a beautiful summer morning, the sun turning the dew on the leaves to diamonds as he walked beneath the trees lining the lane to the Wingate Manse. He'd banged the brass knocker on the door with such high hopes—young Sally Wingate had accepted his marriage proposal the evening before. She didn't have the flirtatious charm of the southern belles who had strolled the decks of the river queens, but she was sweet and she adored her prospering young businessman. Pierce had come that day to speak to her father, knowing beforehand that approval would shine in the man's eyes.

But he never got past the front stoop. The butler, pompously stiff and proper, relayed his master's refusal and, with cruel bluntness, gave the reason: From an unimpeachable source, they had just learned that Mr. Kingston had represented himself falsely. Most falsely. And if he didn't vacate the premises immediately, officers of the law would be summoned.

Pierce should never have forgotten the lesson, because, as unbelievable as it seemed that Simone Lange's influence could reach this far, he was beginning to think she'd managed to set him up with Lark. Could it all have been an act? The expensive clothes, the southern belle accent? Could Lark then have become so infatuated with Pierce that she forgot Mrs. Lange's plan and gave him her most precious gift, her innocence?

Of course not. He was just letting his mind run scared. But if the witch had instigated a ruse, Lark and bumbling old Louie would surely have put a crimp in it. "Buck up, Pierce, my boy. If the Lange woman had been involved, you would be in much worse shape right now."

Pierce snorted and closed his eyes. How much worse could it get? If the incredibly real dream he had last night was any indication, he'd be tormented by Lark's memory until he found her. But only heaven—or maybe Georgie—knew where she'd gone.

As fleet as the *Golden Duchess* was with a steady wind at her back, the return to San Francisco had already taken more than three weeks. And Pierce felt that each of those twenty-two days took Lark farther away from him.

Pierce had spent hours each day out on the foredeck in self-imposed solitude, willing the ship to greater speed, but even more hours he spent brooding in his cabin. And more and more often he would find himself taking out his Fourth of July hat and smoothing his hand across it, checking the small dent Lark's parasol had made.

His socializing with the other passengers had been next to nonexistent. And from the looks they gave him, especially the Gables, he knew he was a prime topic of speculation. But then, he'd had years to get used to being the object of gossip.

Georgie gave him an especially wide berth after that first day. When Pierce had questioned him about where Lark might have gone, Georgie had screwed up his face, as usual, and wagged his head. The kid had then turned shifty-eyed when asked if Lark had friends in Oregon where she might be staying. He'd said no and muttered something about Lark probably being on her way back to her brothers on the Mississippi. Pierce refused to accept that possibility. He would never go back there, not even for Lark.

Nonetheless, he knew the kid was concealing something, because from that day on, he never spoke to Pierce unless it was absolutely necessary. He spent all his waking hours with the Gables and returned to the cabin only at bedtime. But before the ship docked, Pierce planned to have another dead serious talk with the lad.

A couple of days before reaching port, Pierce woke early to the jarring sway caused by a rough sea. He looked up and saw the slight indentation made in the upper bunk by Georgie's skinny body. He'd let the kid enjoy the trip thus far without any further questioning, but time was running out. "Georgie, you awake?"

The bed above moved and the boy groaned.

"Georgie, we need to talk."

"I, uh . . . Oh, no!" The kid's bed creaked wildly as he scrambled for the end of the bunk and practically slid down the ladder.

"What the—"

Before Pierce could finish, Georgie flung open the door and raced out in nothing but a flash of long red underwear.

Pierce threw on his shirt and trousers. He didn't know how the kid had guessed that an inquisition was about to take place, but running out wouldn't save him from it.

Wheeling out through the open door, Pierce charged down the passageway, uncaring that he hadn't taken time to put on his own shoes and stockings. He reached the deck and spotted Georgie instantly.

Showing mostly the seat of his red flannels, the boy hung over the closest stretch of railing, retching his guts out. The little water dog was seasick!

Smirking, Pierce walked up beside him. "I was just going in for some bacon and biscuits. Care to join me?"

Georgie swung his way. "Wha—uuhh!" He heaved all over Pierce's feet.

Pierce jumped back. "Damn." Wheeling around, he rushed over to a barrel of salt water that was used for swabbing the deck and scooped handful after handful onto his feet and the splatters on his pant legs. Then with one last glance at the boy still leaning over the rail, Pierce retreated to his cabin to change out of the soiled trousers. Questioning the boy would have to wait until later. Pierce had been seasick once himself, and he knew the poor kid would be in no condition to talk for a while.

Considering the wave-tossed floor, Pierce dressed as quickly as possible, then took the inside passage to the dining hall before Georgie returned in heaven only knew what sort of smelly disrepair.

Pierce walked into an empty dining hall, the obvious result of a choppy sea. He ate a light breakfast—his own concession to the erratically rocking ship—as he ran several ideas through his head for the best first steps to be taken in order to find Lark and Pegasus. Recovering the horse would probably take little effort. If he'd been raced even once, the fleet animal would already be famous in San Francisco. But unless he could get Georgie to talk . . .

Pierce downed the last of his coffee and stood up with

steely determination. The kid would talk if he didn't want to find himself chucked overboard!

As Pierce returned to his room, an uneasy thought slipped in. He couldn't remember seeing the horse's papers for some time. He went directly to the outrageously priced traveling trunk he'd purchased in San Francisco. Reaching down behind his straw hat perched atop his neatly folded clothing, he slid his hand across the bottom until he found an envelope. Relieved, he pulled it out, but discovered it was the one filled with money. It looked flatter and felt lighter than he'd remembered. He pulled out the bills and coins, shut the trunk lid, and crouched down to count them out on the slightly rounded surface. With the sea calming somewhat, he had to chase only a few sliding coins before reaching a total of a few dollars over fifteen thousand.

Rocking back on his heels, he relaxed. That was about right, considering he'd spent more than four hundred on fares, lodging, and clothing since he and Georgie had started out on this costly venture. He refilled the envelope and shoved it all the way to the bottom under his things, then continued his rummaging for the legal papers. He felt down the front and both sides without success. His concern mounting, he lifted out a pile of stacked shirts, and thank heaven, found the large brown packet lying on the bottom.

Pierce snatched it up and opened the end flap, then pulled out an assortment of contracts and receipts from his various investments. He sorted through them one at a time, but found neither the horse's pedigree nor the bill of sale. Uneasiness crawling up his spine, he spread the papers like a deck of cards, scanned them again, without success, then, becoming more disturbed, scattered them on the floor and rifled through them. No doubt remained. The horse's documents were missing.

Georgie. The little runt would even steal to cover his father's ass! Pierce should've known better than to start trusting him.

Springing to his feet, Pierce wheeled around, yanked up the kid's mattress, and looked beneath it. Nothing. Dropping it, he strode to the end of the bunks, unhooked Georgie's canvas bag from off the bedpost, and dumped the contents onto the top bed. Brushing the toilet articles aside, Pierce picked up each item of clothing and searched it for the hidden documents, then cast them away until nothing remained but a small cotton bag. Stuffed full and rather weighty, it was cinched and knotted at the top. He squeezed it, but didn't feel or hear the sound of crumpling paper—only something that felt like rope.

Strange. Why would the kid keep rope in a bag?

Then, his thoughts returning to the missing papers, he dropped the bag and strode to the door. The kid had a lot of questions to answer. And he'd better come up with the right answers this time.

Chapter
Sixteen

GEORGIE STOOD AT the bow, a brisk wind at his back. Fully dressed now in one of his navy blue suits, he'd apparently improved since his earlier bout with seasickness. Mrs. Gable was beside him, but in Pierce's state of mind, he couldn't have cared less.

He strode up between them. "Mrs. Gable, would you please excuse us? I need a word with the lad."

Her precise blue eyes widened a fraction. "Of course." Then, after checking the pin holding her bonnet, she turned into the wind and left them.

Georgie looked after her, then stared up at Pierce. "You should've said hello before rudely dismissing her."

Pierce snorted, grabbed the kid's skinny arm, and jerked him close. Compared to Georgie's misdeeds, rudeness could almost be considered a virtue. "I've had all the lies I'm going to take from you. But before we get to the rest, hand over my horse's papers."

Georgie tried to wiggle loose, but Pierce had no intention of letting go until he had some answers. The size of the boy's eyes doubled as if he'd been unjustly accused. "I don't know what you're talking about."

"I suppose you thought if you gave the documents to your father, I couldn't accuse him of theft. Well, it's like this, kid. You're not getting off this ship until I have 'em. In fact, I think a talk with Captain Bailey is in order. I'll have him lock up your little butt. See how you like that.''

Georgie clawed at Pierce's hand. "Let go! You're hurting me."

Pierce ripped the kid's fingers away. "I'll do more than that if you don't hand those papers over."

"I don't have them," Georgie rasped, his face red, his nose crinkling defiantly. "I don't! Why would I want 'em? Papa doesn't even have the horse anymore."

"Well, I still have his note, and that's proof enough to have the thief arrested. I wonder if horse-stealing is a hanging offense in California."

"You wouldn't do that!" Georgie cried, his face losing all color. "You . . . you . . ."

Georgie's eyes rolled back in his head, and he dropped like a rock. Pierce's hold on his arm was all that saved him from crashing onto the deck.

Caught completely by surprise, Pierce scooped up the dangling boy. So Georgie was really sick, after all.

Starting for their cabin, Pierce hadn't gone more than a few steps when Mrs. Gable intercepted him, her face drawn tight with anger.

She stopped directly in front of him. "It's bad enough," she accused, her neck stretching several inches as she jutted out her chin, "that you were brought aboard this vessel slobbering drunk, then spent the remaining weeks in a black mood, leaving the boy to his own devices, and forgoing any attempts at civil behavior toward your fellow travelers. *Now* you're resorting to violence. Just what, may I ask, did you do to that dear boy?"

"Madam," Pierce grated, his own anger surging, "I haven't laid a finger on the *dear boy*. He's—"

"Don't try to weasel your way out. I saw you jerking him around."

"Listen, lady. If anybody's doing the jerking around here, it's him. Now, if you'll let me pass, I need to get Georgie to his bed. He passed out. He must be a lot sicker than I thought."

"The boy swooned?" Concern ringing in her voice, she stepped aside. "I'll go with you. I've done volunteer work at the hospital in Boston."

With Mrs. Gable following close on his heels, Pierce carried Georgie inside and down the corridor to his cabin.

"Here, let me," the woman offered, stepping in front of him and opening the door. "Lay him on the lower bunk while I get my medicines. Then leave him to me. You've bullyragged the child enough for one day."

Manners forgotten, Pierce swung around to put her in her place, but the overstepping woman had already disappeared. Turning back with the kid, he had difficulty quelling the urge to just toss the squirt on the bed and leave. But, peering down at the feathered lashes, the slender smoothness of his exposed neck, so vulnerable, Pierce couldn't.

Shifting Georgie's weight to one arm, Pierce pulled back the covers and laid him down. As he began unlacing the scamp's shoes, his thoughts drifted to that one evening with Lark, when she, too, had fainted. Wilted like a lovely rose in his arms.

His reminiscence continued on to the scintillating lovemaking that had followed, and he'd managed to remove only one shoe when Mrs. Gable returned carrying a black leather case that would rival any doctor's.

"Thank you, Mr. Kingston. Now, if you'll excuse

us," she said, dismissing him in a tone crisper than
new-baked crackers.

"By all means," he returned, permitting every bit of
his own rekindled animosity to ride out on his words.
Letting the shoe he held fall haphazardly from his hand,
he stalked out the door.

Awakened by someone tucking the covers around her,
Georgie struggled to open heavy eyelids.

"And, pray tell, what do you have to say for yourself,
young lady?"

Georgie strained to remember what she'd done to
deserve a scolding from Mommy this time. Lifting
reluctant lashes, she could only make out a fuzzy form
sitting beside her.

"Well?"

The blur sharpened into a thin-lipped Mrs. Gable—
not her mother—and she remembered with a renewed
sense of loss that Mommy had been dead for almost
three years. Georgie glanced past Mrs. Gable to the
scattered contents of Pierce's usually neatly packed
trunk and wondered why the lady was sitting with her.
Then Pierce's fierce accusations flashed into her mind . . .
and the horrible threat. She wrenched herself off the pillow.

Mrs. Gable pushed her back down. "I'm waiting for
an explanation, *Miss* Pacquing, if that's even your
name."

Miss Pacquing? Swiftly Georgie slapped her hands
against her chest and found it bare. Sliding them down,
she noted she had no other clothes on, either. My God,
she'd fainted, and this woman must have undressed her.

"Yes, young lady, I've learned your little secret, and
I want you to know I'm simply appalled. Undoubtedly

there's a Mrs. Kingston out there somewhere who would be even more so.''

''A Mrs. Kingston?'' Georgie's buzzing head couldn't keep up with the woman.

''We'll worry about that matter later. At this particular moment we're discussing you. Healthy young ladies do not faint without reason. Exactly when was your last menses? I assume you've at least had enough sense to keep track of them.''

''Menses?'' What was the woman talking about now?

Mrs. Gable's eyes narrowed to thin slits. ''Your monthly flow.''

That Georgie understood. She paled, felt herself slipping into another fog.

At the strong sting of ammonia in her nostrils, she sprang back to full consciousness.

''I assume, by your reaction, you've missed one or two,'' the woman said as she shoved a cork into a small vial and dropped it into a leather valise beside her.

Georgie couldn't believe she hadn't given the possibility of pregnancy a single thought. And now that she thought about it, she hadn't been plagued with the complication of her monthly since she'd been traveling with Pierce. But how long had that been? ''What's the date?''

Mrs. Gable arched a thin brow. ''The twentieth. September twentieth.''

The information dropped Georgie deeper into a well of self-pity. Tears blurred her vision. There would be no gifts, no hugs and kisses this year. And she was pregnant! ''Tomorrow's my birthday.''

''Your birthday? I see. And after your mother risked her life to bring you into this world, just what do you think she'd say about this mess you let *that man* get you into? It's just as well she didn't live to see this day . . . *if* you were telling the truth about her demise. Everything else about you seems to be a lie.''

Georgie closed her eyes, and a flood of tears rolled off her cheeks. ''You're right,'' she choked out. ''Mommy would've—'' Sobs broke forth with unstoppable force, cutting off any more words.

Surprisingly, Mrs. Gable gathered Georgie into her arms and began to rock her and stroke her hair. ''There, there, child,'' she crooned over and over until several minutes later, Georgie, limp and exhausted from weeping, slumped against her. The older woman gently lifted Georgie's chin up to her and smiled. ''It's going to be all right. You just get your rest. You have the baby's well-being as well as your own to consider now. *I'll* take care of the rest.''

Georgie jerked upright. ''What do you mean?''

The staunch lady patted her cheek. ''Now, you mustn't get any more upset. It's not good for the baby.''

''But you mustn't—''

She covered Georgie's lips with her fingers. ''Now, now. I'm quite capable of handling this situation. You just leave everything to me.''

Her breathing becoming labored again, Georgie brushed Mrs. Gable's hand aside. ''No! You can't! You mustn't tell him. Not anyone.''

''My dear, you're getting entirely too distraught. Lie down and inhale slowly while I find something to calm you.'' After shoving Georgie back onto the pillow, she rummaged through her valise, then withdrew a tall, slim bottle.

Georgie sprang up again. ''You have to promise you won't say anything.''

''Yes, this should do quite nicely,'' she said, unscrewing the cap. She held the bottle against Georgie's lips. "Take a small sip."

Opening her mouth to protest, Georgie bumped her lips against the rim and ended up with a mouthful of bitter-tasting medicine. She quickly swallowed in order to speak. "*Promise.*"

Mrs. Gable looked at the bottle and wagged her head. "Oh, dear, that was quite a bit more than you were supposed to take." Replacing the cap, she shrugged. "It's probably for the best. You'll be asleep in no time."

The warmest, laziest sensation flowed into Georgie's limbs, and her tongue began to thicken. "Please, promise," she mumbled through numb lips.

"Of course, my dear." The motherly woman pushed her down and drew the covers up to her chin. "You just get some rest. There's nothing to worry about."

Pierce stood at the rail, a healthy wind at his back, looking to the east. Clutching the smooth wood, he urged the tiniest speck of land to come into view. Anything— the peak of a mountain, a jutting peninsula. Although the California-designed clipper swept along in the high wind faster than any of the clumsier seagoing steamers, he'd never felt so frustrated in his life. Pierce was sure the captain'd had no idea how irritating his casual announcement had been when he passed by moments before and reminded Pierce that today was the first day of fall.

Fall. He'd lost the entire spring and summer aboard ship. First, on the tedious journey to the West, then on this wild-goose chase.

But Captain Bailey had given him a small piece of good news. If the wind remained steady, if it didn't die down or increase to a gale, forcing them to strike the sails, they would blow into San Francisco in two days instead of three. Pierce appreciated the news, but if anything, it only made him more frustrated.

He pulled out his timepiece and discovered it had been more than half an hour since he'd left Georgie in Mrs. Gable's care. There should be some word by now. He sighed, hoping nothing was seriously wrong. He couldn't help caring for the kid, even if he did want to tan Georgie's britches at the moment. Replacing the watch in his vest pocket, he swung around to go check on Georgie . . . and bumped into Mrs. Gable coming up behind him.

Pierce stepped back. "Forgive my clumsiness."

Her expression alarmed him.

"I was just coming to look for you. How's Georgie?"

"Your little game is up, Mr. Kingston. And don't bother to waste your breath. I'm marching up to the bridge to inform Captain Bailey at once. But first, I have only one question for you, and I want a direct, honest yes or no. Are you married?"

The woman was angrier than a wounded bear. What in the world had Georgie told her? "Mrs. Gable, I don't know what—"

"A simple yes or no, if you please."

"No," he blurted, his own anger evident. "But what has that got to do with anything? What's the matter with the boy?"

The woman's eyes flared and she inhaled harshly, expanding her sparse bosom. "You'll do right by her, or I'll shoot you myself. I've given her a dose of laudanum to calm her. But when she wakes up, this *will* be attended to." Chin thrust skyward, Mrs. Gable whirled around.

Pierce caught her arm. "For God's sake, woman, what are you talking about?"

"Don't you use profanity with me, young man. And I'll thank you to unhand me this instant."

Pierce took a step back. "I still want an answer."

"Come, now, Mr. Kingston. Don't act so surprised that Georgie is with child."

"With what?"

"Are you deaf? I said Georgie is pregnant." Her pointing finger almost jabbed Pierce's nose. "And you will do right by her."

Dumbfounded, Pierce stared after the woman as she strode haughtily away. Unable to move, he watched until she disappeared into a doorway.

Georgie was a girl?

Could it be?

In a rage, Pierce started for his cabin.

But by the time he walked in, his steps had slowed. It seemed too inconceivable—even for Georgie.

The floor was strewn with his belongings. Then he recalled the papers he'd been searching for. And why.

He swung his attention to Georgie. Although limited sunlight streamed past the partially curtained window, Pierce could easily see a healthy flush on the delicately curved cheeks of the apparently sleeping lad. His gaze lingered a moment on the spray of long auburn lashes, then moved to the full lips, pouty in repose. The delicate curve of the jaw.

Pierce shook his head. "No. Impossible."

Beneath the blankets, Georgie's chest rose and fell with the slow, even cadence of breathing. The kid was either sound asleep or doing one heck of a job faking it.

Knowing Georgie, Pierce opted for the latter. He reached down and nudged his shoulder. "Stop pretending. You have a lot of questions to answer. What the hell did you tell that woman?''

Georgie didn't flicker so much as an eyelash.

''Fine. If that's the way you want to play the game.'' He grabbed hold of the covers and flung them back.

Chapter
Seventeen

AT THE SIGHT of a nude female body, Pierce threw the covers into place again and sprang back.

He stared in stunned silence at the sleeping form for a minute or more before moving close again. He bent over the face. It was still Georgie's.

Slowly, uncertainly, Pierce reached for the blanket once more. Starting to lift it, he darted a glance to her eyes.

She lay flat on her back, as unmoving as before.

Feeling like a Peeping Tom, Pierce raised the cover only a few inches. The full swell of a breast greeted him.

My God, the brat was a girl!

Spurred to action, Pierce smoothed back Georgie's hair and imagined a cascading cluster of auburn locks.

"Lark?"

Joy swept through him like a grass fire.

Just as swiftly, it turned to a rage so intense his temples throbbed from it. His vision blurred, and he had an almost uncontrollable urge to strangle that creamy and oh-so-vulnerable throat.

But first he wanted some answers.

Grabbing her shoulders, he lifted her off the pillow and gave her several shakes. "Georgie? Lark? Whoever the hell you are, wake up!"

Her head bobbed around as if she had a broken neck. A breathy low moan, the only sign of life, escaped. It was useless to try to rouse her. Whatever Mrs. Gable had given her must have been very powerful. ''Damn!''

Pierce lurched off the bed, still so filled with anger there was scant room to inhale. He glared down at that face, so peaceful-looking in slumber, so innocent. Yet he couldn't begin to count the number of times and ways she'd made a fool of him. Tricked him. Lied to him. And even now that he'd discovered her secret, he didn't know if she was Lark pretending to be Georgie or vice versa.

But then, did it really matter? The result was the same. She'd made a complete jackass of him. His skin crawled at the thought of all the times he'd mooned over Lark in front of her, and how many times she'd taken advantage of his weakness.

One thing he did know: No one, not even his father's wife, had ever vanquished him so thoroughly.

The idea of staying another minute in the same room with the lying piece of river trash galled him, but he wasn't up to going another round with Mrs. Gable just yet.

Feeling suddenly drained of all strength, Pierce trudged to the end of the bunks and climbed up to the top one. He swiped at Lark's spilled belongings, sweeping them out of his way. As he did so, the small cinched bag again caught his attention. No one would take such good care of a piece of rope.

With jerky fingers, he unknotted the strings and, reaching inside, withdrew the contents.

Braids! Two long coppery braids.

The little liar had even gone so far as to cut off all that gorgeous hair. Anything to fool him into taking her to her worthless father.

Pierce flung them off the bed and flopped down, only to be taunted by all the days he'd spent worrying about the fate of his "fragile lady," all the dreams, the unceasing yearning.

Cringing, he closed his eyes and rubbed the sides of his throbbing head, willing his mind to go blank. But in popped a picture of Mrs. Gable's accusing glare. Her pointing finger, her snide tone when she said, "Georgie is pregnant."

Pregnant? Pierce shot straight up and cracked his head against the ceiling . . . and sank into a black swirl.

Pierce's pocket watch ticked out a seemingly unending march as he, nursing a lump on his head with a succession of damp cloths, waited for Georgie to awaken. Over the hours, his impatience had settled into a deadly resolve while he lay on the bed above. By the time he heard her stirring, he knew that nothing the lying wench could say—no excuse, no pitiful wide-eyed pleading—would alter his decision. This time she would dance to his tune.

She moaned, and the covers rustled.

He rolled onto his side and propped his head on a hand, ready for the first battle in a long time he knew without a doubt he would win.

Georgie staggered out of bed as naked as a jaybird and almost collapsed before catching hold of the bedstead. "Heavens to Betsy, what did that woman give me?" she muttered as she raised her drooping head, totally unaware that Pierce was watching her. She shook it back and forth, then abruptly stiffened. *"Oh, my God!"* Still hanging on to the post for support, she swung down and scooped up a very long strip of cotton. Then, letting go of the bed, she flung herself to the door and rammed the bolt home.

While she leaned the palms of her hands against the door and took a series of deep breaths, Pierce felt not the slightest twinge of guilt as he memorized every inch of her figure. Taking his sweet time, he started at the nape of her slender neck and meandered to the fragile shoulder blades, then down the creamy smoothness of her back to a waist that gently dipped in before curving out into the cutest, roundest derriere. He wandered on down the long, tapered legs that seemed to go on forever. How such grace and femininity had been disguised as a boy, he'd never know.

Weakening at the tempting sight, Pierce gave himself a mental shake. But she'd done it. Had been doing it for years. Everyone who knew her thought she was a boy. Pierce was just the last in a long line of fools.

Georgie pushed away from the door and turned around. Pierce expected her to notice him, but instead of looking up, she began fiddling with the cloth in her hands.

While she ran the narrow strip across one palm, Pierce took the opportunity to view the front of her body. As much as he'd appreciated the other side, he had to admit he'd never seen more tempting breasts, from the full swells that more than filled a man's hands to the pouty crests that tilted audaciously upward—nothing shy about them. No wonder he hadn't been able to forget her. It was a pure shame that Providence had seen fit to endow one so deceitful with such perfection. His eyes moved downward.

Having reached one end of the yardage, Georgie began to wrap it around herself just beneath her arms, then secured it with a knot before winding a second strip, overlapping the first.

The chit was binding her bosom. She obviously thought her secret was still safe. Pierce snorted. "I wouldn't bother if I were you."

Georgie's big bronze-colored eyes flew up to him and widened. A shriek turned into a croaking gasp as she tried to cover her nakedness with the cotton, which unraveled in her frantic fingers. She shot a glance down, then back up to Pierce. Then, in a blurring dash, she dove for the bottom bunk.

Pierce didn't even try to stop his ungentlemanly chuckle as he heard the flutter and flap of sheets and blankets. Grinning, he leaned over the edge and looked down at her but could see only a large woolen lump. She didn't really think covering her head would save her, did she?

Pierce vaulted off the top bunk and dropped down on the bed beside her.

The huddled heap scooted closer to the wall.

Enjoying the moment, Pierce plucked his frock coat from off the footboard. After retrieving a cheroot and a match from an inside pocket, he tossed the garment aside, then casually struck the sulfur tip on the bedpost and lit up. Making himself more comfortable, he leaned against the headboard, propped one leg across the other, and took several drags off his smoke, all the while relishing the rapid rise and fall of her scratchy gray covering.

She was scared as a cornered rabbit, and with good reason.

Thoughts of murdering her had surfaced more than once while he'd waited for her to wake up. He'd remembered the times she called him a gulling gambler . . .

when all the while, this "fair daughter of the South" had been nothing but a matchless fraud. An arrogant, mouthy, lying she-wolf.

Only one thing had kept his fingers from choking the life out of her—the baby. And, he thought, allowing himself a moment of weakness, the haunting memory of a wonderfully witty young lady who had given herself to him once, lovingly, completely. For one magical evening, she'd forgotten herself, believed in him and the game she played.

Unwilling to ever succumb again, Pierce quickly restored his ire. "I'll be speaking with Captain Bailey this evening," he began.

She jumped at the sound of his first words, but made no other move.

"I'm sure he'll be more than delighted to make an honest woman of you. I'll arrange for a marriage service tomorrow afternoon."

She hurled herself his way, banging into him. Then, just as quickly, she scooted away, and her face popped out from under the cover wearing an incredulous expression. "You plan to marry me? What about all I—uh . . ." Her gaze wavered, and she threw the blanket over her head again.

"Believe me," he said, not letting any of his own turmoil creep into his steady tone, "I'm not doing it for you but for the baby. No child of mine will ever be branded a bastard. Therefore I'll see to your needs until it's born and I find a nursemaid. Then I'm shipping you back to your scourge of a father. You two deserve each other."

That head of tousled hair emerged again. *"You want to keep the baby?"*

Pierce rose to his feet and stared down at the desperate

expression in those deceptive eyes. "You don't really think I'd leave my child with you to corrupt, do you?" Not waiting for a response, he wheeled around, strode to the door, threw the bolt, and slammed out.

Everything that was necessary had been said.

The following afternoon Pierce had yet to return. And much to Georgie's relief, Mrs. Gable had furnished her meals, since the idea of facing the passengers and crew sent her stomach rolling worse than the choppy sea.

Georgie assumed, however, that Pierce had not broadcast the truth of her duplicitous behavior, since Mrs. Gable's attitude toward her, though stern, held a measure of sympathy. And, blessing of blessings, the indomitable matron had yet to question her.

Now, one mere hour before the fateful moment, Georgie stood on a small stool in the Gables' more spacious cabin, doing her utmost to hide her misery. She hung on to the bedpost to balance herself while the older lady wrapped and draped her in an exquisite red silk sarong trimmed in gold. "I don't know how to thank you for letting me wear this Malayan wedding costume. It's far more than I deserve after deceiving you the way I did."

Mrs. Gable paused from adjusting the folds of the shimmery fabric clinging to Georgie's hips. "I don't know what caused your lapse of morality with Mr. Kingston, and frankly I'd prefer not to know. But despite your deception, you've been a polite and pleasant traveling companion. Consider this loan my birthday gift to you. How many is it?"

"Eighteen."

"So young," Mrs. Gable murmured as she fetched a jeweled brooch from an intricately carved chest resting on the narrow table attached to the side wall. Catching up the gathers at Georgie's shoulder, she ran the pin through and closed it, then moved back and studied the Oriental gown. "Yes, gorgeous. You may step down now."

Georgie inspected the fit, then looked back at the elderly matron. "It *is* beautiful. But considering my circumstances, don't you think wearing red is inappropriate?"

"In our culture, perhaps. But everyone on this ship knows that in the Far East it's considered *the* color for celebrating. And what's more festive than a wedding? I paid a fortune for the costume and all its accessories. But, as I reminded my dear stubborn husband, some young Chinaman who's just struck it rich in the gold fields will be only too glad to relieve us of it for his newly purchased bride . . . and give us a tidy profit to boot. Besides, who knows, maybe the good Lord knew you'd be needing something to lift your spirits today."

Just the thought that the Lord knew all she'd said and done renewed her guilt with almost paralyzing force. How would she find the strength to walk out on deck in one short hour? How could she face Pierce and everyone else on board?

Mrs. Gable stared at her as if waiting for a response.

"I—uh . . . You plan to sell this beautiful costume then. Did you say for a *purchased* bride?"

"Yes, some Orientals place little value on their girl children. If a father is in need of money, he will sell a daughter."

"How dreadful." She couldn't imagine her own father ever selling her, his only daughter. But she herself had done worse. She'd valued her sex so little, she'd tossed it aside for the free life of a boy. Could this be retribution for rejecting what God created her to be? A forced marriage to a man she loved with all her heart, but who had every right to hate her with just as much passion.

"Speaking of eager grooms," Mrs. Gable said in a lighthearted tone that added an extra pang to the ache in Georgie's chest. "Your Mr. Kingston insisted on an immediate wedding—a sure sign that he's an honorable man and regards you with affection. So pick up your chin before it hits the floor and come sit at the dressing table. The past is past. Think of today as a new beginning."

Even the cool caress and soft swish of the sheer fabric could not allay Georgie's malaise as she stepped off the stool and moved to the waiting chair. She knew Pierce's true motive—to gain legal control over her until the child was born. But Mrs. Gable was treating her with the utmost kindness in these trying circumstances and shouldn't have to endure her morose mood. Exerting considerable effort, Georgie forced her lips to curl into a smile.

Mrs. Gable pulled several gold bands ajangle with tinkling bells from the small chest and slipped them onto Georgie's arms. "Before I'm through with you, Mr. Kingston will think he's marrying a Siamese princess."

Dangerously close to tears, Georgie wanted to cry out that even the lowliest coolie would be preferable to her. Instead, she fingered her saved tresses, which Mrs. Gable had fashioned into a hairpiece, and tried her darnedest to concentrate on the long auburn locks. In the softest of waves, they emerged from a thick braided coil along with strings of golden bells.

"Here, darling, let me put this around your neck." Mrs. Gable held forth a lacy gold necklace at least two inches wide with a clear amber stone suspended from its V-shaped center. "Yes, my dear, when you walk out to marry your Mr. Kingston, he'll be so overwhelmed by your beauty that any doubts he might've had will be whisked away on the clouds.''

The wind died down to a faint breeze, and the sounds of lapping water and flapping sails diminished to a soft whisper as Pierce waited on the foredeck for Georgie and Mrs. Gable to appear. Beside him stood the captain, and, to a man, the twenty or so crew and passengers faced them in a half circle, dressed in their finest to mark the occasion.

The wedding had been set for two o'clock, yet Pierce had no doubt it was a good ten minutes past. Irritated, he fought the urge to check his timepiece. He wouldn't give the already amused onlookers any more ammunition. He'd spoken to no one about the situation except Captain Bailey. Even then he'd given no excuse and only the barest explanation. But word of Pierce sharing his cabin with a masquerading young lady had spread faster than hot butter.

Catching Pierce by surprise, the ship sailed at that moment from the bright warm sunshine into a bank of thick, damp fog.

The tall, rather stiff captain tucked his Bible under an arm and withdrew a pair of white gloves from his navy jacket pocket. He chuckled. ''From summer to winter in a matter of seconds. But it's a welcome sign. Means the California coast is just beyond.''

''How much farther, would you say?'' Mr. Gable asked, standing off to one side.

''Thirty, forty miles.'' The captain looked up at the now sagging sails. Then, with a frown creasing the bridge of his long nose, he pulled out his own pocket watch. ''Where is that bride?''

Just then a group of sailors across the circle from

Pierce turned their heads and began murmuring. Two stepped aside and swept off their banded dark blue caps while clearing a path.

"It's about time," Pierce muttered under his breath while straining to see through a foggy swirl.

The mist gave way to a shimmer of brilliant red and gold that was mystically transformed into a vision of gossamer grace in motion. Eyes demurely lowered, she moved into the circle as whispered exclamations fell to a hush. The only sound came from the delicate music of myriad tiny gleaming bells. They streamed among cascading locks, dripped from rows of bracelets and ankle bands, and even dangled from the crescent-shaped toes of her golden slippers.

Stunned by her beauty as she slowly walked toward him, Pierce reeled as his thoughts returned to the first moment he'd discovered Lark. She'd been equally as overwhelming that day as she parted a sea of homesteaders to come to him in a bounty of hoops and frills, sporting that audacious smile.

She moved nearer, and Pierce saw none of Lark's spirit in her downcast expression, nor did he detect a wisp of Georgie's fight and energy. They'd both disappeared, and a creature of exquisite sadness had replaced them. Profound loneliness weighted Pierce's chest, and he realized he would sorely miss them both . . . even Georgie. Somehow, when he wasn't looking, the smart-mouthed kid had also stolen his heart.

The lovely stranger reached him.

Taking her hand, he felt the faint tremor of her melancholy. The deepest compassion filled him, and he gave her fingers a reassuring squeeze as he turned with her to face Captain Bailey.

"May I have your full names, please?" The captain's

gray eyes mirrored Pierce's empathy as the firm-jawed officer looked from her to Pierce.

"Pierce Lange Kingston." Stating his middle name reminded Pierce of his illegitimacy. At least it was within his power to prevent his child from suffering this one curse. And the other, God willing, would never be discovered.

Glancing away, he let his gaze settle on the lustrous hairpiece artfully concealing his bride's shorn locks, and he suddenly realized how it must have hurt her to cut off all that radiant beauty to protect her secret. He began to understand some of what she'd sacrificed . . . and all to save her father. As misguided as her deceptions had been, her motives were no less than noble.

Lost in his thoughts, Pierce gradually became aware of a considerable pause. Then she startled him with her quiet words.

"My name is Lark Ellen Georgette Pacquing." She lifted her lashes, and her great bronzed-colored eyes sparkled as if tears waited in the wings.

Further touched, Pierce placed his other hand over hers.

Her chin trembling, she moved her plaintive gaze up to him.

Hoping to ease her distress, he smiled.

Her quivering lips tried to form themselves into a smile of their own while a tear slipped over the fragile curve of her cheek.

Despite all his resolve, Pierce felt the deepest desire to take her into his arms there and then, hold her close until he'd absorbed all her pain.

But Captain Bailey began. "Dearly beloved, we are gathered here today . . ." His resonant monotone con-

veyed the seriousness of the occasion as he instructed the
two on the duties of marriage.

When the captain charged them to be faithful in
sickness and in health, Pierce recalled the night he had to
be half carried aboard the ship. Too drunk to navigate on
his own, he'd been dumped in Georgie's arms. Suddenly
he realized he probably hadn't been hallucinating that
night. Lark might very well have been with him, let him
make love to her.

"Do you, Pierce Lange Kingston, take this woman to
be your lawfully wedded wife?"

Pierce looked down at Lark—Georgie—whoever. He
no longer knew what to call her.

She lifted woe-filled eyes.

Tightening his grip on her hand, he turned to the
captain. "Yes, I do."

"Do you, Lark Ellen Georgette Pacquing, take this
man to be your lawfully wedded husband?"

Wind gusted, sending a salty spray across the deck and
setting her bells to tinkling. The sails above billowed and
snapped, drowning out her reply.

The captain tucked his Bible inside his coat and yelled
above the sudden squall. "What did you say?"

Pierce glanced her way and saw her head bob up and
down.

"Splendid!" Captain Bailey shouted and took an
awkward step to balance himself as the ship rode a
mighty wave.

Pierce instinctively threw an arm around Lark to
steady her.

"I now pronounce you man and wife," the captain
finished in a loud voice. He grabbed Pierce's free hand
and gave it a hearty shake, then bent down and pecked
Lark's cheek. "Guess we were just having a little calm

before the storm.'' Straightening, he stepped past them. ''Rickman,'' he yelled. ''Get to the helm. Lefty, Mike, Saunders. Strike the top sails. The rest of you, heave to. ''Looks like we're in for quite a blow.''

Lark broke out of Pierce's hold. She bumped past the Gables in an unsteady run across the perilously pitching deck to the rail. Hanging on, she leaned over the side.

Seawater blasted across her.

One of her hands lost its grip. Then the other as the wave washed her across the deck.

Pierce started for her.

Mrs. Gable, staggering in the same direction, caught his arm. ''The crew needs your help,'' she cried above the gale. ''I'll take care of your bride.''

Pierce saw a sailor at the foremast struggling with a line, then turned back to see the older woman helping Lark to her feet. A fine start for a honeymoon, he thought, making his way to the seaman. But could it have been any other way?

Chapter
Eighteen

THE AFTERNOON DRAGGED into a cold, miserable night of the wind howling under the door, creaking timbers, bumps, and bangs as the ship was tossed about like a rider on a bucking bronco.

Georgie's seasickness raged with the same unrelenting vengeance. Often in the worst throes of nausea she wondered if death wouldn't be preferable.

Mrs. Gable checked on her a few times during the long hours, and Pierce, dripping wet in yellow oilskin, came more often, but only for a minute or two. Each time he appeared, he looked more haggard and his voice sounded wearier when he knelt down to ask about her condition. Georgie knew how much strength was required to man the sails in fair weather and how much more challenging, more dangerous, it was in a storm. Yet each time he arrived, his concern seemed genuine.

In the predawn light Georgie watched Pierce leave after yet another quick visit. He tiptoed out of the cabin and quietly closed the door behind him.

With her own energy drained, Georgie curled into a ball, fighting to contain tears that formed because of this last caring gesture, undeserved though it was, then cursed herself for turning into such a weepy mess.

Before she and Pierce had made love that first night,

she'd rarely cried. She couldn't fathom what had befallen her. And as for the seasickness, she'd never before been even remotely queasy on a vessel, river or seagoing, in any kind of weather. If Papa and the boys could see her now, they wouldn't believe their eyes.

At the thought of her absent family, a fresh batch of tears spilled down her cheeks, further soaking her pillow as she waited for the next dreaded wave of nausea.

Then the howling gale ceased as abruptly as it had begun. Although the ocean calmed more gradually, within minutes her bed settled to a near-stillness.

Again a surge of gratitude spilled her into another blasted attack of emotion.

"Enough's enough!" she railed into the growing morning light. Swiping at her moist eyes, Georgie rose on feeble red-flannel-clad legs and stumbled to the small porthole. She unlatched it and swung it open.

Crisp briny air met her, and she took several deep breaths. Its freshness had a soothing effect on her raw insides. Maybe she would live after all.

After a revitalizing moment, she craned her neck out the opening. She looked to the east and found the sky still ominously dark. But in the opposite direction the storm had passed, and sunlight laced the upper edges of the diminishing clouds.

"Hoist the sails," came the captain's voice from somewhere toward the stern.

Although Georgie could see no one from her cabin amidships, she heard shouts of "Aye, aye, sir," from fore to aft.

Soon she identified the screech of damp hemp against iron rings as men heaved to, then the dull slap of wet sails catching the salty breeze.

Leaving the porthole ajar, Georgie made her way back

to bed, still exhausted but exceedingly relieved. She lay down with the fervent wish that when she next awakened, land would be in sight, all her queasiness would be gone, and by some miracle Pierce would truly care for her, not just for the health of his baby's mother.

"My dear," Mrs. Gable called against the blustery breeze as she stepped from the top rung of a pier ladder onto the hustle and bustle of the crowded embarcadero.

Her own energy drained from the ascent, Georgie turned and waited for the imperious lady to join her. The few hours of undisturbed rest before entering the bay had only partially revived her.

Plumed bonnet firmly pinned to her chignon, the stately matron strode with purpose. She gave no evidence of labored breathing after the long climb, though, unlike Georgie who still wore boys' garb for lack of anything else, Mrs. Gable had to contend with heavy skirts. "My dear, this may be my last chance to speak to you alone. Come with me before the men catch up with us."

She took Georgie's hand into her own tan-gloved one and led her to the far side of a freight wagon into which two dockworkers were tossing sugar-filled cotton sacks. She shot a reproachful glance at the gawking laborers, then moved closer to Georgie and spoke to her in hushed tones. "Mr. Kingston obviously cares for you very much. He married you quite readily once he learned of your condition. However, I really don't understand what possessed you to run away with him without a proper wedding. You could've been ruined for life. The only thing I can think . . . Was there some problem with your family? Did they disapprove of the match?"

Georgie had hoped to bid the motherly lady good-bye without having to divulge the truth about her recent behavior. She picked an imaginary speck of lint from her navy coat. "It's really a long story."

Mrs. Gable's attention shifted, and she peeked around the end of the wagon.

Following her lead, Georgie saw Pierce and Mr. Gable circling a cluster of arguing travelers to reach them. Although both were nattily attired in starched collars and recently pressed suits, the stout older man looked dowdy beside Pierce. As he strode toward her, his lean, virile build filled her with pride. She desperately wanted to believe he would forgive her, that she hadn't mistaken the kindness in his eyes when he'd awakened her to prepare for their departure.

And now those same intensely blue eyes set against his smooth tan beheld Georgie again.

The sight sent a giddy twitter through her belly.

"My husband spoke to your Mr. Kingston this morning," Mrs. Gable continued in a hurried whisper. "I just want you to know that your husband gave his word that you will be well cared for. He said that you and your child will want for nothing."

"Darling," her husband said as the two men reached them, "since our crates won't be unloaded for a couple of days, Mr. Kingston has suggested we stay at the St. Francis Hotel, where he did when he was last in town. That is, if it hasn't burned down."

Mrs. Gable turned to Pierce. "I did notice a considerable number of buildings under construction as we sailed into the bay. Did you hear something about a recent fire?"

"No," Pierce said, "but this city is famous for them. Too much celebrating, I'll warrant. In fact, I suggest you prepare yourself for some shocking sights."

The lady gave his hand a patronizing pat. "My

husband and I have visited any number of unruly ports. We are really quite well traveled."

Pierce acquiesced with a nod and a smile, then shifted his attention to Georgie . . . and all the animation left his expression. "I have several matters to attend to. Mr. Gable has offered to take you with them to the hotel. I'll be there in time for supper."

What a fool she'd been! Instant rage swept through her. Addled by her illness, she'd forgotten his threats against Papa, but they were as imminent as ever. "What *matters*?"

At her demand, a jaw muscle twitched in his otherwise expressionless face. "My racehorse, of course."

"You're not going without me."

Butting in, Mrs. Gable cajoled, "I'm sure your husband is only thinking of your welfare."

Georgie stopped glaring at Pierce long enough to turn to the busybody. "There are things you don't know, Mrs. Gable."

Pierce snorted. "That's a sure bet."

Georgie swung back to the arrogant rat. "I'm going with you!"

"Suit yourself. But you'd better keep up."

She turned back to the obviously offended older woman who'd swelled up until she looked as if she might start sputtering any second. "Thank you for your concern, Mrs. Gable. We'll join you at suppertime."

"I'll reserve a room for you," Mr. Gable said, firmly gripping his wife's elbow and leading her away.

Swinging back to Pierce, Georgie found that he was already striding into the milling throng.

Her anger stoked again, she shoved her way through a group rowdier than a bunch of Mardi Gras drunks. But the few yards' sprint to reach him rendered her out of breath. She caught his arm to prevent him from escaping again.

Halting, he glowered down at her. "Button your coat. All I need is for you to catch a chill."

Stifling a useless retort, she did as she was told while looking toward the nearest ship's bow. The *Pride of Kate*, not Papa's ship, the *Flying Cloud*. "You should've awakened me before we dropped anchor. Did you see Papa's ship when we sailed in?"

"Captain Bailey said it's berthed at the end of the Market Street wharf." He again broke into a healthy stride.

Georgie struggled on wilting legs to keep up. She wouldn't give him the satisfaction of hearing her complain. Instead, she put as much force as she could muster into her voice. "You were going to go after Papa and confront him without me, weren't you?"

He stopped short and wheeled on her. "Look here, Georgie—Lark. . . . What the hell am I supposed to call you?"

Not about to be intimidated, she arched a brow. "Whatever suits your fancy."

A sudden gust lifted his hat, which he caught and held in his hand. The wind riffled through his jet-black hair, making him look even more dashing.

She refused to let his looks affect her. She barreled past him in the direction he'd been walking.

In a couple of long strides, he caught up, then matched her pace.

They wove their way through a crowd of excited prospectors disembarking from a large steam-powered ship and merging with a horde of pitchmen, who vied for their money.

Breaking out on the other side of the crowd, Georgie

sighted the *Flying Cloud* docked alongside a jutting pier. In a flash of panic, she grabbed Pierce's gray sleeve again. "What are you going to do to Papa?"

He glanced down at his arm. "You're wrinkling my coat. Again."

Letting go, she stepped closer. "Answer me."

He leaned down, meeting her eye to eye. "Nothing. *If* you hand over my papers."

Georgie swallowed a foul word behind tightly pressed lips and took a quick breath. "I already told you. I don't have your blasted papers. And if you had a brain in your head, you would've figured out by now that Blackwell took 'em. Why do you think he stopped dogging our every move?"

From the menace in his expression, Georgie thought he might hit her. He grabbed her arm instead and started toward the gangplank.

At its foot, an emaciated cargo officer stood, manifest in hand, marking off a crate being carted away.

"If I might, I'd appreciate a moment of your time," Pierce said.

An apparently recent victim of malaria, the officer lifted weary yellow-tinged eyes. "As you can see, I'm occupied."

Pierce pulled a ten-dollar gold piece from his pocket and placed it on the cargo list.

The man snatched up the coin and stuffed it in his pocket, then favored Pierce with a forced smile. "What can I do for you?"

"I'm looking for one of your crewmen, Louie Pacquing."

"Oh, him. He transferred onto a Pacific mail steamer headed for the Panama Isthmus. Did it while we were still anchored in the bay waiting for a berth."

Gone again? All the fight drained from Georgie. Papa had already left for Louisiana, thinking he'd find her there with Cadie. When he discovered she'd been left behind in Oregon, he'd go back there for her . . . back to the trouble waiting for him. Somehow she had to catch up with him before he did. She stepped forward. "Sir, do you know of another steamer in the bay that will be leaving for Panama in the next day or two?" She couldn't take a chance on a sailing ship and the whimsy of the wind.

"Only that one over there." The officer pointed to the ship they'd passed moments before. "She'll make a fast turnaround. They're doing a brisk business, transporting passengers from Panama."

"Thank you very much." She turned and started back.

Before she'd gotten more than three or four steps, Pierce latched on to her shoulder. "Just where do you think you're going?"

She shrugged out of his grasp. "Where do you think? To see about passage to the isthmus."

"You don't listen at all, do you? I'm keeping you with me until after the baby's born. And I'm through with chasing your no-account father."

"But if I don't catch up to Papa before he gets back home, he'll be beside himself with worry about me."

"You think I give a damn?"

"He'll go back to Oregon for me. Probably get arrested."

"Not likely. Blackwell and I are no longer there to press charges. Unless he managed to rob a few other suckers I don't know about."

"You don't understand about Papa."

"Good. I plan to keep it that way."

Georgie gave him her meanest narrow-eyed glare. "Fine! You just do that. But I'm going. With or without you. I'll work my way to New Orleans, just as Papa's doing." She spun away and took off at a run down the wide-planked pier. In less than a second her feet were churning on nothing but air—Pierce had hooked his arm around her waist.

He hauled her up beneath his arm.

"Put me down!"

"Shut up."

From off the *Flying Cloud* came a high-pitched singsong from a definitely male voice. "What's the matter?"

Wielded like some old sack of potatoes, Georgie couldn't lift her head high enough to see who had called out, especially since Pierce had marched away, ignoring the heckler.

"Hey, pretty boy," the voice called again, but in normal tones. "You don' have ta take that off a him. If you wanna be treated right, meet me down at the Eagle Saloon tonight. I'll show you the time a yer life."

"Yeah, right," Pierce muttered as he tightened his hold around Georgie's ribs and lengthened his stride.

Incredibly embarrassed, Georgie kept her head down, not looking up to see the faces that belonged to the snickers and guffaws as people stopped and turned their way.

Pierce didn't slow down when he reached the end of the wharf. After stepping off it and onto the muddy road, he kept up his pace for what seemed like forever before he finally stopped. He plunked Georgie down on her feet in front of a beached ship that had been turned into several business establishments. Partially buried, it was wedged between a liquor store . . . and the two-story Eagle Saloon!

"You're not going to—"

Before Georgie could finish, Pierce took her hand and pulled her through the wide doors of a general store whose false front hid part of the ship's hull. He didn't slow down until he had passed barrels and crates to reach a counter and the aproned proprietor, a stout man with a stringy mop of light hair.

The man looked up from an open ledger. "Vat I can do for you?" he asked in an accent Georgie couldn't place.

Pierce said, "Do you know of a store that sells ready-made ladies' dresses?"

Georgie's mouth dropped open. She clamped it shut again. There'd already been too many scenes in front of strangers for one day.

Closing his book, the storekeeper broke into a big grin that reminded Georgie of her papa. At the sight tears stung the backs of her eyes, and she looked away.

"You come to right place," the man said with enthusiasm as he came from behind the counter. He pointed to the rear of the shelf-lined room. "Yust valk trough dat back door an' go out da udder side. My vife haf ladies' shop over dere."

"Thanks." Pierce took Georgie's hand again and dragged her into a dank back room. Only one suspended lantern lit the narrow path between rows of boxed goods stacked head-high.

Georgie halted and tried to jerk free.

Tightening his grip, Pierce also stopped. "What now?" he growled.

"I am not going to wear a dress in this hellhole. I wouldn't be able to go out on the street alone."

"And I'm not going to be made sport of anymore." He started walking again.

She dug in her heels and pulled back—to no avail. She stumbled after him until he reached the next door.

He put a hand out to open it, then paused and turned, his face taking on an evil appearance in the shadowy slant of light. "You will *not* embarrass me when we go in there. You *will* let the proprietress fit you for at least three dresses—and shoes and bonnets and everything else that goes with them. Even if you aren't a lady, as long as you're with me you're going to look like one. Do I make myself clear?"

Georgie's fingers itched to scratch out his eyes, furious with the way he was lording over her. "You think if you get me out of my britches and into girls' clothes, I won't be able to sign on with a ship, don't you?"

"I think if you don't settle down and start obeying your husband, I'll take you to a blacksmith and have him chain us together."

"Just because you're a man and stronger, you think—"

"That's right. And it would pay you to remember that, *Mrs. Kingston.*" He yanked open the door and hustled her into the shop.

Georgie burst through the door and, to her amazement, stepped in a richly carpeted room virtually draped on two sides with scores of hanging dresses. She'd never seen so many ready-made clothes for sale in her life.

Two women stood in the middle before a tall swivel mirror. They whirled around.

"Goot day," said a thin woman with severe black eyes, a black dress, and a tightly knotted bun to match. She fingered a measuring tape draped around her neck. "I help you, ya?" Her accent was similar to her husband's.

Pierce politely tipped his hat and stepped forward. "Yes. That would be most kind of you."

The other woman, in a garishly overplumed bright green bonnet and a velvet day gown that displayed far more of her charms than could be remotely considered decent, smiled at Pierce in an overly familiar manner.

And the scoundrel returned it.

Shooting him a glare that Georgie hoped would shrivel his lust-filled musings, she stepped up to the proprietress. "Madam, I am truly fortunate to find you and this wealth of clothing. My entire wardrobe was lost in a fire, and as you can see, I was reduced to borrowing a young lad's attire."

The woman's hands went to her sallow cheeks. "Oh, ya! I tink you is a . . ." Her eyes skittered up and down Georgie. "Such a terrible ting."

"Got your hair, too, I see," quipped the wanton one as she slinked closer. She was not so easily fooled.

"No," Georgie countered. "Actually, I suffered an illness, and my physician ordered it cut because its luxuriant overabundance was sapping my strength. In fact," she said, turning back to the shop owner, "my dear generous husband wants to make up for my recent tragedies. He told me to buy anything I fancy." Making sure a winsome smile was firmly in place, she gazed up at Pierce with what she hoped would be construed as adoring eyes.

Pierce's face became a shade more colorful as he fumbled with his watch fob. He pulled out his timepiece. "This won't take too long, will it? We have a considerable amount of other business to take care of."

"Sir," the shopkeeper said, spreading an arm. "You see? I haf much clothes. All fine. Ve find one dress, I know, maybe more ve no haf to alter. Udders you come get in two, tree days. Very quick. I am modern business-voman vit many workers and two machines dat sew. But if you vant, you can go. Come back in one hour. I haf your vife ready and vaiting for you den.''

Pierce's jaw relaxed, and he looked profoundly relieved. He glanced down at Georgie and his expression turned wooden. ''No, I think I'll stay here with my bride. I haven't been able to bring myself to leave her side since our wedding.'' He wrapped an arm around Georgie's shoulders and gave her a quick squeeze.

''But, darling,'' she said, deftly stepping out of his mocking embrace, ''I don't want to keep you from locating your horse. I'm sure if you ask in a few of the gambling halls, or perhaps the Eagle Saloon next door, someone will know of his whereabouts. After all, Pegasus is such a stylish stallion.''

''Pegasus?'' The flamboyantly dressed woman laid one of her scheming hands on Pierce's arm. ''The racehorse?''

Pierce didn't seem to notice. ''Yes. You've heard of him? A dapple gray.''

''Oh, la, yes. He's the talk of the town. I saw him run twice myself. Once at the Pioneer Racetrack and once at the Union.'' Her brows, not much more than pencil lines, dipped with a frown. ''You say he's yours? I thought a man named Jasper Blackwell owned him. He created quite a stir when he produced some legal papers and had the horse confiscated from Norton Oakes.''

''*Papers he stole from Pierce!*'' Georgie spat without thinking.

He shot her a silencing glower, then turned back to the woman. ''Do you happen to know where Blackwell is staying?''

''Oh, I'm afraid he took the horse and left town.

Thought he'd get better odds where Pegasus isn't so well known yet.''

"And where's that?" Pierce asked, his voice rough with what Georgie knew was barely suppressed rage.

"Up to Hangtown in the gold country. He took a riverboat to Sacramento just the other day.''

Pierce turned so red, Georgie envisioned a volcano erupting out the top of his head any second. "A boat?" He shoved clenched hands into his pockets. "*Another* boat?"

Chapter
Nineteen

SHORTLY BEFORE DARK Pierce ushered a bedraggled Lark through the entrance of the St. Francis Hotel. With his arm around her waist to help her along, he could feel her tremble even through their various layers of clothing. Obviously she shouldn't have been walking up and down the hills of San Francisco so soon after her illness, especially in her delicate state. But considering her obstinacy, there'd been no other recourse. A wardrobe for her had had to be purchased, then a trunk to hold her new things. He'd made arrangements to have everything delivered and loaded onto the steamship, *Senator*, which would return from Sacramento later that night. Then there'd been a lawyer to see and letters to write and post.

As they approached the register counter on the far side of a marble tile floor, they moved beneath a lit chandelier, and Pierce noticed a tinge of blue around Lark's pale lips. He steered her instead to a group of upholstered chairs. "Sit here while I see about our room."

Despite her exhaustion, Lark shot him a defiant glance as she collapsed onto a brocade cushion. "So I'm to be trusted now, am I?"

Pierce didn't dignify her remark with an answer. He strode swiftly to the desk. Yet he couldn't help watching for a flash of escaping dusty yellow, the color of her velvet traveling costume, while he talked with the clerk.

When Pierce returned to her with their room key in his pocket, he noted how slowly she rose to her feet. Guilt mingled with his concern. But just for a second. She had only herself to blame. "The man at the desk said the Gables went in to supper only moments ago and are expecting us to join them."

"I'm too tired to eat."

"You can't go to bed without eating something." He took her arm. "And try to act like a lady while we're with them, if not for my sake, then for the Gables'."

Lark pulled out of his hold on the pretext of straightening the ties of her ruffled bonnet. "That would be a lot easier if you were more of a gentleman."

"And let you run off to New Orleans with my baby? You'd probably have it out on the street picking pockets by the time it was three."

"That couldn't be any worse than you teaching it how to deal from the bottom of the deck."

Pierce clamped his jaw shut before he created a scene in the middle of the lobby. Nonetheless, if it hadn't been for her condition, he would gladly have suffered the embarrassment for the supreme pleasure of turning her over his knee. While savoring the picture, he took a slow, calming breath.

"What's so funny?" Her uncertain tone told him that the grin that had crept across his face must've unnerved her.

"Nothing for you to worry about. At least for now," he added with a quirk of his brow. "Right now you need to eat in a relaxing atmosphere. You don't look all that well. Please, a truce. At least until after supper."

Lark snugged her hand into the crook of his arm.

"Very well. Through supper. For the sake of the Gables."

Pierce kept a firm grip on Lark's velvet-clad waist lest she try to jump overboard as the *Senator* eased away from the dock.

She hung over the side of the deep-drafted side-wheeler, waving farewell to the Gables in the misty dawn. Tears—no doubt for their benefit—trickled down her cheeks.

Mr. Gable's glum appearance was certainly more credible. While hundreds of excited argonauts had climbed aboard along with Pierce, who was going after the money-making stallion, he was forced to stay behind to attend to his cargo.

Mrs. Gable returned Lark's smile with her own until her attention shifted to Pierce. Her expression immediately soured as it had done every time she'd looked at him since he'd refused to let Lark remain with them until his return. Of course they weren't privy to the fact that she would've taken off for Louisiana one second after he left. Yesterday he'd allowed her to post letters to her father and brothers—some to New Orleans and others to Natchez—but that hadn't diminished her determination one iota.

The side-wheels picked up speed, and soon the Gables were no more than two specks among the dozen or so other well-wishers.

Lark retrieved a lace hanky from a small beaded reticule suspended from her wrist and dabbed at those gorgeous eyes with ladylike grace.

Pierce still couldn't get over how, with a few hoops and crinolines, she could transform herself to such a point that even her facial expressions calmed into the perfection of genteel charm. "Well, my dear, I want to thank you. You've left those good people thinking I'm a heartless ogre."

She tilted her face up to him and stuck out her bottom lip in a mocking pout. "I suppose we all have our crosses to bear. And you can let go of me now. You really don't think I could swim in this getup, do you?" She spun out of his hand, setting her hoops into motion. They continued to bounce as she wedged her way past scores of male passengers and headed for the crowded staircase.

As she made her way through, the adventurers' exuberant gold talk died into soft murmurs. Several young bucks turned to follow her.

Pierce more than understood how they felt. No matter what a fraud she was, he couldn't deny that she looked stunning in the snug satin-trimmed jacket that provocatively flared out from her waist to accent the yards and yards of velvet in her muted yellow skirt.

She parted the men like a prow, and in waves they stopped talking and gawked.

Despite himself, Pierce became uneasy for her. But the little fool should've known better than to take off without him. He briefly scanned the passengers on the main deck and the one above. Including two Chinese girls and one who looked Mexican, he counted only five females aboard the packed ship, and each one had the good sense to be safely attached to some man's arm.

Pierce was tempted to take his time before rescuing Lark from the swarm of woman-hungry men, but the sight of a crewman unfurling a sable herald flag changed his mind. He hadn't been able to secure their passage the day before, and if he didn't get them to the captain's office ahead of this mob, his chances of booking a private cabin looked mighty slim.

Practically running, he recklessly shoved his way through the crowd.

The men seemed oblivious to his rudeness, however, for one thing alone held their attention—the elegant young woman in yellow, the belle from Oregon who'd duped him just as completely.

As she started up the stairs ahead of the parade, Pierce overtook her. He swiftly seized her gloved hand and placed it on his arm.

A ground swell of groans came from behind.

The men's disappointment sounded so pitiful that Pierce felt almost sorry for the fools. Almost.

She glanced at him only briefly before continuing her ascent.

Pierce leaned close to her and whispered, "Walk faster. The sable herald is being raised. Any second now the bell's going to start ringing."

"Then what are we waiting for?" Lifting her skirts above her silk-stockinged ankles, she fairly flew up the steps.

Surprised but undaunted, Pierce held on to his hat and chased close behind.

At the top, she didn't slow a step as she dodged past more men to duck inside an enclosed central promenade flanked by small shops. And that same abandoned laughter that had bewitched Pierce on the Fourth of July spilled out of her.

Joy swelled within him. The Lark he remembered had returned to him.

Just then the ship's bell began ringing, and Pierce felt it confirmed his realization. Even his feet felt lighter as he trailed her up the next flight to become the first passengers to reach the captain's office.

But as Pierce knocked, Lark slumped against the wall

next to a Dutch door, her eyes closed, her heavy breathing straining the buttons of her fitted jacket.

"Are you all right?"

She raised her auburn lashes, and her lips trembled into a smile. "Give me a minute. I guess I still haven't completely recovered from the seasickness."

The upper half of the door swung open, and a pudgy older officer, presumably the purser, laid a register book and a pencil on the shelved bottom half. He looked over the top of his wire-rimmed spectacles. "May I help you, sir?"

The thunder of footsteps nearly drowned out his words as an unruly herd of passengers hurried to get in line.

"Yes," Pierce said, drawing Lark to him and out of harm's way. "Your ship hadn't returned when I came by yestereve. I do hope there's still a private cabin to be had."

The officer's watery eyes left Pierce. They lingered on Lark, and his fat lips puckered into a disgusting smile. "Actually we have several still available."

"I'm pleased but surprised," Pierce said, louder than was necessary, even considering the rumble of converging men.

Reluctantly, the purser returned his attention to Pierce. "Most passengers prefer to stay out on the deck, since it's just for the one night."

"Well, we'd like the roomiest cabin available."

"That will be thirty-five apiece. Seventy dollars."

"*What?*" Lark moved into the opening. "That's highway robbery."

The officer edged back. "I know, ma'am. But that's the going rate."

She leaned farther in, her eyes narrowing. "Then we'll

sleep on the deck with everyone else." His lovely lady had disappeared into the mouthy brat again.

Pierce wouldn't allow her to spend the night on deck with two or three hundred men on a spree, but before he could voice his objection, the purser said, "That'll be thirty dollars. Fifteen apiece."

She crashed her fist down on the shelf, sending the ledger and pencil bouncing. "I'll swim first!" She whirled around. "Where's the captain of this thieving hulk?"

Pierce hooked an arm around her and snagged her back, then picked up the pencil. "Where do I sign for a cabin?"

The purser's sausagelike finger pointed to a line, and Pierce started to write.

Lark dropped her hand over his. "You're not going to let him cheat you like this, are you?"

Inhaling deeply, Pierce glared hard at her.

Her own intent gaze began to waver, and finally she looked away. "It *is* your money. I suppose you can throw it away on anything you please."

"Thank you. And now would you please let me finish here? I'm sure those behind us would appreciate a turn."

"No, not really," said a towhead behind them with a plundering grin turned on Lark. "Watchin' your missus in an uproar is a sight more fun than handin' my hard-earned cash over to them ring-tailed pirates."

That's all Pierce needed—someone to encourage her to continue ranting. He quickly signed the ledger and counted out the outrageous price.

"Cabin three," said the purser as he handed Pierce a key that surely had to be worth its weight in gold. "And if you've a mind to eat, it'll be two dollars a plate."

With her rebellious arm firmly trapped within his,

Pierce bought several of the grossly overpriced meal tickets, then left the window and started back past a line that snaked out into the stairwell and down the steps. As they walked, he could hardly hear himself think for the swish of rapidly removed hats and the eager greetings of "Mornin', ma'am."

Lark aroused the horny bunch even more with one of her bedazzling southern-belle smiles.

She might be enjoying her little game, but the hair on the back of Pierce's neck began to prickle. Considering the bounty of handguns and knives tucked and strapped on in every conceivable manner, those argonauts looked more prepared to wage war than to go prospecting. And he had the strongest feeling that at least half of them were at that very moment envisioning his swift demise.

Reaching the lower deck, Pierce felt immensely relieved to find the promenade almost deserted. They easily walked through and out onto the aft deck. "Come along," he said as Lark veered toward the stairwell that led down to the sleeping quarters. "I need to arrange for our trunks to be brought up."

She stopped and slipped out of his grasp. "Fine. Give me the key. I'll wait for you in the cabin."

"I don't think so."

She planted her hands defiantly on her hips. "Do you really think I'd try to jump ship this far from shore?" One hand swung wide. "Look back there, for heaven's sake. We must be a mile from the dock."

Pierce chuckled wryly. How dumb did she think he was? "But not from that island over there." He nodded toward the closest of the hilly forested knolls rising up in the great bay—the one they would pass in the next minute or two.

"So it's going to be like yesterday, is it? You not letting me out of your sight for one minute."

"You do catch on quick."

"And I suppose you'll spend the night sleeping in a chair propped against the door again."

Refusing to be baited any further, Pierce took her arm and started toward the ground staircase.

She came along without protest . . . this time.

But would she never cease bucking him at every turn? And how many more hours of sleep would she cost him? Especially when he couldn't keep his mind off her restless, lying little body. Her every roll, her every soft sigh . . .

A dull thud and slight jarring awakened Georgie. They'd docked. What was she doing in bed when there was work to be done? She tossed off the sheet and swung her feet to the floor . . . and caught a flash of lace ruffles over her knees. She had on girls' drawers and a chemise.

Immediate awareness of her circumstance hit her, and she sank back onto the pillow.

In the vague light of dusk, she listened to the slap of the giant wheels until they slowed to a stop. The *Senator* had moored for the night. She must've slept through the dinner bell.

She rose and walked to the window she'd left open to catch any possible breeze stirring in the hot, sluggish air that had caused her to retreat to her cabin earlier in the afternoon. She'd been dressed too warmly when the boat left behind the ocean-cooled air of the San Francisco and Suisun bays and began making its way slowly up the Sacramento River, the temperature steadily rising with each serpentine mile.

She looked past the bank, expecting to see a village, but saw nothing except the last rays of daylight, which turned the stripped stalks of a cornfield to orange and gold. A little to her right, a white frame house, a barn, and a couple of sheds stood in a space that had been cleared of all save a couple of craggy old oaks. The *Senator* must have docked at an isolated wood stop for the night.

Light flared and settled into a steady glow inside a window of the home, attesting to life within.

After the ripsnorting craziness of San Francisco and a ship filled with shouting, stomping gold seekers, the sleepy little farm seemed out of place in California. Yet no more so than she.

Although she had spent years working and laughing alongside her father and brothers, free from the constraints of hoops and whalebone, she hadn't been able to keep her way of life from slipping away any more than she could stop the sun from setting. Her gaze gravitated to the fading glow in the west. Tomorrow the sun would rise again, but she would still be thousands of miles from her family, trapped in a marriage to a man who apparently resented her even more for not being the lady of his dreams than for tricking him. And he wouldn't even consider her need to go after her father. He cared only about himself, his child, his horse.

Her spirits dipping ever lower, she decided that a constitutional around the deck might help. If nothing else, the worn yet still plush rivercraft might bring back a few happy memories.

She turned away from the window to get dressed and spotted her corset on top of her trunk.

"Bilge water!" The very thought of lacing herself into it made her ribs ache.

The corset, she knew, was mandatory, but she'd be darned if she'd wear all the petticoats heaped on the floor. "It's too danged hot."

She shoved aside all but the hooped crinoline, which was made of an airy open-weave fabric. After stepping into it, she pulled it up. While tying it at her waist, she noticed Pierce's pin-striped coat and vest neatly placed on his trunk—always the tidy one. Then she realized he'd come in to leave them while she'd slept.

She snorted. More likely, he'd come in to see if she was still there. "And," she said aloud, raising her voice and hoping it would carry, "he's probably outside sitting against the door right now." She charged to the door and flung it open.

He wasn't there. And, thank goodness, no one else was in the corridor either, since she stood there in nothing but her undergarments.

Muttering to herself, she slammed the door shut and went to her trunk to retrieve one of the lightweight frocks she'd purchased the day before. "Well, it's not like he trusts me. I practically had to sign a blood oath just to be allowed to come in here and take a nap." Rummaging about, she found a dimity dress striped with a soft green and pulled it out. "And if we hadn't been traveling through some stinking tule swamp at the time, he never would've conceded to that."

Venting her anger, she savagely shook out the dress. "He never believes anything I say."

At the ludicrous accusation, Georgie burst into giggles. Of course, he didn't. He'd be the biggest kind of fool if he thought she wasn't going to escape to find Papa the first chance she got. Her laughter faded at the thought of her father. The poor dear must need her by now something awful. But not Pierce. That self-righteous wall of stone needed no one. Particularly not a smart talking tomboy. "No, I would never do. Not in his perfectly planned future."

Why she'd ever let herself fall in love with him she'd never know. All he wanted was some prissy bit of fluff to show off—just like all the rest of them. Well, she'd learned her lesson. She would never even look at another man, much less let one within ten feet of her.

At the thought of never being near Pierce again, her resolve melted into the deepest sadness. How could she walk away from the tenderness and passion they shared. "And there's the baby," she breathed, placing her hands on her belly. Soon she would have to give some real thought to the tiny life growing inside her.

By the time Georgie finished dressing and walked out onto the river side of the unoccupied lower deck, the air had cooled to a satiny softness and a million stars twinkled overhead. In the gentle glow of an occasional lamp, the night was perfect, except for the loud talk and clanging piano music coming from the salon above.

She started away from the noise as several boisterous off-key voices broke into song: "Buffalo gals, won't you come out tonight, come out tonight, come out tonight; Buffalo gals, won't you come out tonight and dance by the light of the moon."

Georgie increased her pace until the racket diminished to a low roar. Then she slowed to a stop. She rested her arm on the railing and looked out at the wavering reflections of the ship's lights on the slowly streaming water. Very restful.

"Four!" came a shout from the bow deck. "Gimme another four!"

Looking in that direction, she saw a cluster of men shooting craps. She'd never understand why men were so hell-bent on gambling away what they'd worked so hard to earn. She wagged her head in disgust. "You'd think after a while they'd learn. But they don't. Papa sure never did."

Swinging around, she retreated to the stern, then meandered over to the other side.

A young lady in a bell-shaped skirt as wide as hers strolled on the arm of a properly attired gentleman who even wore a stovepipe hat. Georgie heard their light chatter as they moved to the railing and paused, their eyes on one another, seemingly oblivious of all else. The man's arm came to rest about the woman's shoulders, and he bent close to her ear. He must've whispered something funny, because she laughed.

As Georgie passed them, she had no doubt that they, too, were newlyweds. Through the years she'd seen any number of young couples honeymooning on her family's old river queen. Loneliness, envy, and self-pity assaulted her by turn.

She continued on for several yards, feeling sorrier for herself with each step, until she drifted to a stop. Against her will, she looked back at the couple, saw the young man kiss his bride on the lips, watched her wrap her arms around his neck, pull him closer, watched one of his hands move to the back of her head. . . .

The couple became a blur as her chest began to ache and tears filled her eyes. One spilled down her cheek.

Pierce should be here with her, strolling with her, telling her amusing stories, scattering kisses across her face.

Pierce quietly pushed open the door of the cabin while balancing a tray of food on one hand. Once inside, he stepped gingerly in the direction of the scarcely visible washstand. Fingers stretched before him, he touched the smooth surface and moved the bowl and pitcher back far enough to gently set down the tray. He then searched his shirt pocket for a match to light the wall lamp. He didn't want to frighten Lark by awakening her in the dark. She'd looked entirely too flushed when she retired that afternoon. Between the surprising heat of the interior country and her heavy attire, she'd sagged as rapidly as a plucked flower.

No, he sighed, this wildflower didn't fare well when caged in a corset any more than a poppy did in a vase. The lovely belle he'd dreamed about so often had been just that—a dream, a puff of smoke.

Pulling out a match, he snapped the sulfur head with his nail. It burst into flame, and he lit the lamp before turning toward the bed.

It was empty. Lark was gone! The lying little hellcat had tricked him again. She'd sneaked off as soon as it got dark.

Pierce wheeled and started out the door at a dead run, then halted just as suddenly. The minx was smarter than that. She wouldn't simply wander off into the night with no way of getting back to San Francisco. She just wanted him to think that. Fool him again.

Well, not this time. Not anymore. Lark knew every nook and cranny on these steam monsters. She'd tuck herself away in some hole until the *Senator* returned to the bay.

Pierce started off again in long, determined strides. He'd begin at one end and not quit searching until he found her. Reaching the deck, he turned onto it.

And saw her.

He stopped short.

She stood gazing off into the distance, looking like a

goddess. No, an angel. The glow from a deck light cast a shimmer of gold on her complexion and set her artfully arranged auburn hair to a coppery blaze.

His chest swelled. All that beauty belonged to him. Only him.

But to claim her was unthinkable.

Engrossed in watching a couple several yards away, she didn't seem to notice Pierce's approach.

Curious as to why they enthralled her, Pierce paused.

The couple stood so close together in the dim light, they blended into one. They appeared to be talking, but the unceasing hubbub from the salon above prevented him from hearing their voices. But what they said wasn't important. What mattered was that they were together. And any idiot could see they were in love.

Pierce swung his gaze back to his own bride, who had yet to spot him.

Something on her cheek sparkled like a diamond, then diminished to a glistening streak as it moved downward. A tear.

At the sight, his heart lurched. God, how he wished they could return to that first day! If only she were really that delightful enchantress.

As he moved closer, she turned and looked up at him with eyes of liquid bronze. Abruptly her fingers flew to them and wiped away the evidence of her sorrow.

That small act stole all reason. He had to take her into his arms, hold her until there were no more tears. He stepped against her hoops, shoving them back, until he came within inches of her face.

Although her gaze eventually fell to one side, she didn't retreat as Pierce took her chin in his hand and gently brought her face back to him. "Are you feeling better?"

"Yes. It's much cooler now." A streak of wetness marred the side of her cheek.

Pierce's fingers moved to brush it away with a naturalness he didn't dare ponder. "That marsh was pretty muggy, all right, and the mosquitoes were ferocious."

His touch didn't appear to offend her. If anything, Pierce was almost certain she'd pressed into it.

"I was told," he continued, his voice dwindling to a husky whisper, "that from now on it won't be so humid, but it'll still be hot. So maybe you shouldn't wear so many petticoats."

Her lips skittered into a smile. Then slowly, sensuously, they returned to a soft, barely parted fullness, so ripe, so ready to be taken. Begging to be.

He rubbed his thumb across their satiny tenderness. Unable to resist, he bent to taste their sweetness.

"Kingston?"

Startled, Pierce swung in the direction of the intrusive voice. The man's timing couldn't have been worse.

One of the young fellows with whom he'd been playing poker stood at the edge of the stairwell leading up to the salon. "We been waitin' fer ya. Thought y'all was comin' right back."

Pierce waved him off. "Maybe later."

The hayseed, who looked as if someone had put a bowl on his head to cut his hair, took a couple of steps closer and dropped his hand onto the butt of a revolver stuffed into his wrinkled trousers. "Mister, I lost a heap of money ta y'all. You said you'd gimme a chance ta win it back."

"By all means, Mr. Kingston." Lark swept past him, her hoopskirts grazing Pierce's legs. "Do get on with your sheepshearing."

Pierce watched in defeat as she breezed past the brainless clod-buster and disappeared inside. If she couldn't even abide the fact that he played cards for a living, how could she ever accept his heritage? With more certainty now than ever, he knew he could never let her lure him back to Louisiana, no matter what she said or did. If there was any hope that they could make a life together after the baby came, they would have to stay in the West.

A life together? Had he lost his mind? He was sending the fraud back to her father, and that would be the end of it. And in the meantime he was getting tired of her making him out to be the villain, especially in front of other people. He'd been looked down on enough to last him ten lifetimes, and he wouldn't put up with it anymore, particularly from her.

"Well, are ya comin'?" the stubborn hayseed asked.

"I said later. I have a few things to straighten out first, once and for all."

Chapter
Twenty

GEORGIE'S WIDE SKIRT caught at the narrow entrance to her cabin. Too angry to care, she shoved her way through. She expected to hear a rip, but didn't. Too bad, she thought. It would serve him right to have one of his expensive new dresses ruined.

She slammed the door shut and reached for the buttons at the back of the deeply scooped neckline. How dare he treat her as if he felt she wasn't fit to be his wife, let alone the mother of his child, when he made his living off of others' weaknesses.

Struggling to reach a fastening at the center of her spine, Georgie caught a whiff of food, and her stomach knotted. She looked up and saw a tray on the wash-stand containing a bowl of beef stew, a large hunk of bread, and a glass of milk. She hadn't realized how hungry she was.

But Pierce had.

It was so hard to stay mad at him when he always saw to her needs even before she asked.

All her needs that is, except the most important one—the need to be forgiven, not pitied. And loved. But he didn't even care enough to take her to find her papa. Sighing, she walked to the table and picked up the bread.

The door burst open.

Dropping the chunk of bread, Georgie swung around.

Pierce filled the entry, his eyes dark and glowering. "I've had all the lies and innuendos I'm going to take from you." He slammed the door shut behind him and crossed the floor in three fast strides.

Spurred by fear, she backed up till she hit the wall.

Pierce loomed over her. "You've never even seen me play cards, yet you accuse me of cheating at every turn."

That was true, but she sure wasn't going to admit it. She met his challenge. "Well, if you don't cheat, you must be the luckiest man alive. Not once have I ever heard of you losing."

"Lucky?" A chuckle that sounded more like a growl followed. "You've seen my luck the past couple of months. It wouldn't pay for a lollipop."

"There! You said it yourself." She shrugged, and her partly unbuttoned bodice started sliding down. She snatched it up again.

Pierce undoubtedly noticed. Several seconds passed before his attention left her low frilly neckline and returned to her face. "I'm sure you've gone through my things more than once. Have you ever seen a deck of cards, marked or otherwise? I don't palm them or hide them up my sleeves, either."

"You're doing something underhanded."

"I don't have to cheat to win. Gambling is my profession. I figure the odds and play with care, and I never drink on the job."

"I see. You just take advantage of those who do. You wait till they get drunk and take their money. Well, one thing is certain: I'm never going to let you make me feel guilty again." She pushed past him and scooped the bread up off the floor.

Pierce followed her every move with astonished eyes. "You feel guilty? That's a revelation. A daughter of Louie Pacquing with a conscience!"

"Don't you talk about him that way," she said, shaking the crust at him. "He was a good father to me. Better than some riverboat gambler could ever be. And as for my baby, I'm taking—"

"No, you're not. You're not running back to that damned place with my child."

Damned place? "It's not just the horse, is it? There's something back in Louisiana that you don't want to face. Maybe your own conscience. . . . I'm right. I can see by your expression."

"You see nothing but what you want to see. Oh, what's the use? Schemes and lies. That's all you know about." Wheeling around, Pierce strode to the double bed—the only bed—and sat down. He propped one leg on the other and tugged at his boot.

"You're going to get undressed now? In front of me?"

"It's not as if I haven't done it before, is it, *Georgie my boy*?"

"That's not true. I always gave you your privacy. It would've been wrong not to."

Pierce's mouth went slack. Then he grinned and shook his head. "Of course. How dumb can I be?" With one last pull, the boot came off in his hand. He dropped it, then reached for the other.

Hastily rebuttoning her dress, Georgie edged toward the door. "I'll go fetch some extra blankets and make a pallet on the floor."

"Forget it. You're not to leave this room again without me."

"I thought we'd already had this discussion. I promised you this afternoon that I wouldn't try to escape from here if you stop watching my every step."

"And if you promised, it must be so." With scoffing laughter he started working off his other boot. "Besides, with this many men on the loose, you'd get yourself in trouble for sure. Eat your supper and come to bed. It's been a long day."

Aghast, Georgie looked from his arrogant face to the bed. "I thought you were going to play cards again."

"I don't feel like working anymore tonight."

"You don't really expect me—Louie Pacquing's lying whelp—to share the same bed with you."

The boot came off in Pierce's hand. Staring at her with eyes of ice, he held it aloft.

For a second Georgie thought he would throw it at her.

But he let it fall. It hit the floor with an unnerving thud. "If you don't try to leave this room, you've got nothing to worry about. Absolutely nothing."

Georgie's hoopskirt seemed to grow in size as she tried to put space between herself and the man on the bed. If he wanted the bunk, fine. She'd simply find another place to sleep. The purser had implied that there would be plenty of extra cabins. She'd just dawdle a bit, take her time eating, until he fell asleep. Then she could sneak out. It shouldn't take too long, considering he'd spent the night before in a hard-backed chair with only a pillow for comfort. A smile tickled the corners of her mouth as she remembered hearing him squirming around during the night. And to think that she'd almost felt sorry for him!

"Shoot the bolt on the door."

She jumped at the unexpected command, then felt like telling him to do it himself. But the rustling sounds behind her told her he was removing his trousers. And all she needed to weaken her willpower was to see him go traipsing across the room half naked. Besides, the last thing she wanted was to have to slide some noisy bolt aside when she made her escape. "I'll do it in a minute. I'm eating." Replacing her bread on the tray, she took the spoon and bent forward to scoop up some stew.

"I said, lock the door," he ordered, his tone even more steely this time. "Unless you'd rather I tie us together."

Hating him was becoming no trouble at all. She slammed the spoon into the bowl, uncaring of the splatters, then whirled around . . . and found him sitting there in nothing but some cotton drawers. But she refused to let his bare throat, his shoulders, his muscle-padded chest, affect her in the least. Averting her gaze, she stormed to the door and rammed the bolt home. Naturally the blasted rusty thing made a loud screech. "Satisfied?" She flounced back to her meal.

He didn't reply, and an uneasy silence followed.

After she took several more bites, he still hadn't said a word, and the hairs on the back of her neck began to prickle. She just knew he was sneaking up behind her. She picked up the glass of milk—not much of a weapon, but it would have to suffice. Trying to appear nonchalant, she turned slowly around . . . to thin air.

The rat lay in bed, his face to the wall, a sheet covering most of his back. *He was ignoring her.*

Fine. Good. All the better. She certainly didn't want him watching her and thinking about things that simply were not going to happen . . . unless . . . No, never.

Georgie's food disappeared much sooner than she'd expected. Without even a chair to sit in or rug to lie upon, she'd either have to leave the room or get on the bed. Dabbing her mouth with a napkin, she turned to survey the situation. She studied Pierce's back. His steady breathing told her he'd already fallen asleep despite the continuous drone coming from the salon. He no doubt was as used to noisy riverboats as she.

Then maybe he wouldn't wake up easily. She checked the shutters at the window, but soon saw they didn't swing open. And of course the rusty old bolt could be heard by the deaf.

But, maybe . . . As she scanned the cabin, her gaze fell upon the big earthenware pitcher on the washstand. A healthy crack on the head with that and he wouldn't awaken for quite a while. She lifted it out of its matching bowl.

Full of water, it weighed a considerable amount. Too much. It might kill him. She tipped it to pour out the liquid.

Then stopped.

What was she thinking of? If she was going to do something this rash, she needed to do it when there was a boat traveling downstream that she could board. The traffic was much heavier on this river than on either the Columbia or the Willamette, and the right moment would surely come. She couldn't afford to cause trouble now just because she didn't want to lie down beside the hateful man.

With a sigh, Georgie poured a small amount of water into the bowl and retrieved a cloth from the shelf above. She washed her face and neck, then unbuttoned her bodice and dropped the strap of her chemise to reach more areas.

As she ran the cloth downward, she heard movement from behind her. She swung around.

Pierce had rolled onto his back, but he appeared not to have awakened.

Several seconds ticked by as she stood frozen, holding up her dress. Finally she let out a breath she hadn't known she held, then quickly scooted over to the wall lamp and blew it out, sending the room into darkness.

It seemed like forever before she'd finished her toilette, removed her hairpiece, and changed into a new nightgown, all the while listening for any telltale sounds from Pierce. Yet, too soon, she couldn't think of one more thing to do. After checking the ribbons tied at her throat, she tiptoed on cold feet to the bed dimly striped by the faint light coming from the small slatted window. Folding back the sheet, she gingerly ran her hand along the surface to see if Pierce had stayed on his own side. She reminded herself for the thousandth time that he wouldn't bother her. After all, he *had* said that as long as she didn't try to escape, she had *absolutely nothing to fear.* And so far, he'd never lied to her. At least she didn't think so.

Her side of the bed appeared safe, yet the batiste of her summer gown felt incredibly thin—why she'd let that shop lady talk her into buying it, she'd never know. Carefully, very carefully, she lay down on her side at the edge and inched the sheet over her. Rigid with apprehension, she waited . . . and waited. And waited.

The dirty rat. He really wasn't going to try anything! If she ever needed proof, she had it now. He didn't care one whit about her. Well, fine. But if he thought he could hold her prisoner until he got his hands on her baby, he didn't know Georgie Pacquing.

A long narrow pier jutted into the gray distance of a stormy sea. Just beyond, Georgie spotted a passing clipper ship braving the buffeting winds.

She kicked aside a tangle of skirts and sprinted forward. An infinitely long pier lay before her, but she had to reach the end of it. Had to signal the ship.

With her every leaping step, the distance ahead of her stretched. Georgie strained forward, trying harder.

Flags flying, a bounty of sails billowing from the masts, the ship rapidly slipped farther away.

Racing faster, Georgie waved her arms wildly. "Wait! Don't leave me!"

At last she came to the end of the jetty. "Wait!" she yelled again, but her cry was lost in the blustery wind.

The ship grew smaller.

Pain, agony, ripped across her chest. They hadn't seen her. She would be stranded here forever. Never again to see her family. And Papa. Papa would die.

No! The ship was coming back! Joy soaring, she watched the vessel turn slowly around. With its flying jib pointing her way, the ship's bow cut a swath through the giant swells. She was saved.

The tide receded, exposing a great jagged rock in the vessel's path.

"Look out!" *Georgie frantically pointed at the lethal projection, but saw no one on deck.*

In that instant the ship careened against the crag with an explosion of cracking boards and screeching joints. The mortal sounds continued as wave after wave tossed the clipper onto the giant boulder, breaking it apart.

Georgie heard faint shouts above the tumult, then sighted several men clambering up the masts of the sinking wreck. She couldn't believe her eyes. Pierce! He'd come to rescue her, and now he would die if she didn't do something fast.

She ran to one side of the pier and looked down its length for a moored boat, a dinghy, anything. None bobbed down below. She whirled around and dashed to the other side. But the dark water was just as empty.

At the sound of a wretched cry, Georgie looked back at the ship and watched in horror as a sailor dropped into the swirling turbulence.

A yardarm broke away, taking another down in a tangle of canvas and rigging.

Georgie sucked in a scream as Pierce's eyes reached across to hers.

She had to do something.

On the beach she spotted a palm-thatched shanty. As fast as her legs would take her, she ran.

She burst through the swinging doors.

Men, hundreds of them, milled about, all drinking, all talking at once.

She grabbed the arm of the nearest sailor. "Help me! My husband's ship is sinking!"

The concern on the burly man's face slowly changed to a slack grin. "Georgie! Look maties!" he shouted above the hubbub. "Georgie's here with another one of her tall tales." He hoisted her to his shoulder as if she were nothing more than an empty sack, then tossed her onto a high stage.

She looked down into a field of laughing faces.

"We love a good story," the gap-toothed limey called.

"Please!" she cried. "You have to believe me. My husband's ship is sinking. Help me!"

"No!" yelled the burly one. "That's boring. Tell us about the lovely Lark."

"Lady Lark," they chanted. "Lady Lark."

Several pounded their fists on tables.

Someone split the air with a sharp whistle.

"Please believe me! Please!"

"Lark! Lark! Lark!"

"No! Listen!"

"Lark!"

"Help me!"

"Lark? Wake up!"

"Wh-what?"

"You were having a nightmare." The voice came from behind her. A hand lay on her shoulder.

Rolling over, she grabbed for him. "But I have to— He's . . . You're—"

"Shh, quiet down." He gathered her close. "My God, you're heart's beating faster than a hummingbird's. It was just a bad dream, sweetheart. Calm down." His hand made soothing circles on her back.

Nestled in the hollow of his neck, she inhaled deeply of Pierce's manly scent. It reassured her somewhat. She reached up, found his face. "You're really safe?"

His own breath caught, and his yes was barely audible as his mouth moved across her seeking fingers.

Relief flooded through her, choking her with emotion. She melted against him and lowered her hand to the warm safety of his throat. "I was . . . so scared."

"I know." His lips touched her forehead, her cheek. "But you're with me. I'd die before I let any harm come to you."

She moved away, trying to see his expression in the darkness. "Really?"

He closed the space she'd vacated, his mouth a breath from hers. "I promise."

He'd die for me. His loving vow replaced her fear, filled her every lonely place to overflowing. He did love her. Spilling into tears, she wrapped her arms around him, hugged him tight, and sought the comfort of his lips.

Pierce felt the tenderness of her mouth, so giving beneath his. Felt her breasts, so soft, so full, as they molded to him.

Her pulse again beat a hasty staccato against his chest.

Tasting her, he throbbed with his own need. *What was he thinking?* She was all wrong for him!

She moaned, a soft mewling sound, and arched against him.

Pierce's heart stopped, then tripped over itself, and, his desire mounting, all reason took wing.

He ravished her lips, then entered them. Testing. Teasing. Her tongue joined his, and the kiss deepened into a fiery duel. With each parry, he felt himself harden more until he feared he'd burst. He had to slow down. Breathing fast, he tore away from her. "Let go."

She stiffened. *"What?"*

"I'm going to light the lamp. This time I want to see you, see the beauty I touch. Your eyes."

She relaxed, and her hands dropped from his shoulders.

He bounded off the bed. Then, quickly, finding a match, he lit the lamp and adjusted the flame to the softest glow. He turned back to find her gaze, dark and languid, on him. He reached out and pulled her to her feet.

Her sensual stare turned shy, then fell away.

His attention left the childlike innocence of her face to wander down the slender column of her throat to her bold breasts concealed by the thinnest layer of white. The taut peaks beckoned to him.

He reached for the pale blue ribbons at the ruffled neck of her nightgown.

She jumped slightly and caught his wrists as her gaze darted to his.

Her uncertainty caused him to hesitate. Slowly he took her hands and raised them to his lips. He kissed each palm, his tongue making leisurely circles at their centers.

She inhaled raggedly.

Pierce looked up and saw warmth return to her eyes. "You're so beautiful," he said in hushed tones as he released her and raised his hands to her hair, playing his fingers through her short auburn locks. "I loved your hair when it was long, but there's something incredibly enchanting about it now, the way it feathers about your face. Like a wood nymph's."

"And your eyes," she said, her words sliding like silk as she reached up and took his head, "could bewitch even the cleverest sprite."

Knowing her shyness had disappeared, Pierce pulled loose the first ribbon, then the next two. Then, lowering her hands to her sides, he slipped the batiste fabric from her delicately rounded shoulders. It fell without a whisper, unveiling creamy breasts whose rosy upslanted tips seemed to defy gravity. The quickness of her breath thrust them toward him in repeated entreaties . . . lush, pouting, inviting.

He tore his attention away. He wanted to see all of her, her tiny waist and the soft, almost imperceptible roundness of her belly, the tender place where she now cradled his child.

A rush of wonder overwhelmed him. He felt his eyes sting with tears as he placed his hand over the spot.

Georgie's breath caught as she felt the quicksilver of Pierce's touch. Her legs trembled with intense emotion at this tenderest of gestures. My God, how she loved him. She held on to his shoulders to keep from falling.

His blue satin gaze slid adoringly upward again. "Such a gift," he said, his words barely audible above the gentle hum of the flickering oil lamp. He took her face in his hands and gently pressed his mouth to hers.

His light touch sent her senses reeling. She flamed to her core and turned to liquid. When she swayed against his chest, her skin came to life against his. She needed more. She grasped his hair and plundered his mouth.

Groaning, he pulled her tight against his chest, his arms encasing her in a powerful grip as he met her tongue in his own impassioned conquest.

Georgie felt the hardness of his need pressing hungrily against her abdomen, begging to be freed. She beckoned with her own undulations until she thought she'd go crazy. Wrenching away, she ripped at the strings of his underdrawers.

The intensity of her desire sparked in him a wildfire

beyond anything Pierce had ever known. He grabbed her hands. "Let me. I can do it faster."

She looked up at him, her eyes dusky. "Hurry."

Lark turned away from Pierce, giving him a most enticing view of her behind as she walked to the bed. He watched her lie down with the grace of a swan before she turned to face him.

"Hurry," she repeated.

The crescent shape of her upturned hip framed a velvety patch of bronze—the tiny grove that hid her most alluring secret.

"You're still standing there."

Realizing he had not moved, Pierce quickly shucked his underclothing.

She smothered a gasp that quickly turned into a giggle.

"What's the matter?"

She made a miserable attempt at straightening her face. "I'm sorry. I just never knew you were . . . that there was . . . so much of you."

She never ceased to amaze him with her outbursts. Nonetheless, he couldn't help feeling a measure of pride as he dropped onto the bed beside her. Holding her in his gaze, he watched her eyes lose focus as he ran a hand down her silken throat and captured a supple breast. He rubbed his thumb across her nipple, reveling in how readily it responded, then, unable to resist any longer, took it into his mouth.

When Pierce drew on Georgie's breast, ecstasy bolted from it down to her lower depths. "Oh, yes," she sighed.

After sending her to the edge of sanity, he released her and smiled smugly as he lifted knowing eyes to her.

She should've been embarrassed to let him see her naked passion, but she was enjoying him too much. She reached for his neck and pulled him with her as she settled onto her back.

Without offering the slightest resistance, Pierce spread himself over her, flowing across her like a sea of molten lava. Searing. Inflaming.

His hand slid down to the entrance of her greatest hunger and moved inside.

She met his questing finger again and again, asking for more, much more. She reached for that part of him that she most desired. When she wrapped her hand around his length, Pierce stopped moving, stopped breathing. Then slowly he began to thrust through her hand with a lover's rhythm.

Feeling his manhood pulsate with life and grow even harder, she let it slide through her enclosing palm as her body began its own dance again, matching the tempo of his entreating hand, his eager shaft.

When neither could bear the ever-hastening taunts another second, he withdrew his finger and she guided him inside.

Pierce buried his hands in her hair and vanquished her with a wrenching kiss. His tongue drove into her mouth. At the same instant he drove into her, careening down, filling her to the depth of her need.

Moaning, she threw her arms around him and arched her hips to meet his.

Pierce withdrew himself, slowly, feeling every moist, quivering inch of her. He wanted to savor it, experience every nuance. But the fevered pitch of her grasping hands and his own hunger wouldn't let him. He took her again, hard. Then again and again. Faster. Deeper.

She opened herself to him, luring him to her farthest reaches until he thought he might never return. Every part of her strained for him as she panted with a need equal to his.

In that moment his desire for her swelled to such fullness that it spilled forth and, with it, his seed.

She felt him burst within her. The impact sent her head into its own explosion, spiraling her into a shower of stars. Crying out, she wrapped her legs around him and held fast, lest she soar away, without him.

"My sweet, sweet Lark bird," Pierce murmured in her ear.

After a long moment, he gently pulled away and, breathing more slowly now, collapsed beside her.

Georgie opened her eyes and saw in his all the love she could ever want, ever need. Unable to express the depth of her feelings, she rolled toward him and ran her fingers over his pleasuring lips.

Her touch sent a tremor through his heart, and he knew his need for her would never be fully sated. He molded her to him and ran his hands across the hot, moist skin of her back while sprinkling kisses over her damp face.

She returned them, kiss for kiss, sliding her own hand down his ribs and over his thigh, then back again, reveling in the smooth hardness of his body until the last of her energy drained away. She dropped her head on the pillow and yawned, smiling her sincerest thank-you. "Good night, my love."

In rapid succession, Pierce's expression changed from surprise to delight and then, strangely, to regret as he rolled onto his back.

Puzzled, Georgie thought she'd done something wrong and couldn't fathom what it was.

Then she decided she must have been mistaken, because he pulled her within the comfort of his arms. "Yes, sleep well. Until tomorrow."

Snuggling into the hollow of his shoulder, she inhaled the warm musky scent of this lover of hers, this husband. Content in the afterglow, she drifted off on the heavenly promise of his words, words that she was almost certain meant ''I love you.''

Chapter
Twenty-one

PIERCE LAY SPRAWLED on the bed with his bride, thoroughly exhausted, but relishing the reason. He and Lark had spent most of the day making love, napping only during the hottest part of the afternoon. The only time they'd parted was when he left her to fetch their meals, and he did so only out of necessity, since they'd generated such ravenous appetites.

A surprisingly cool breeze wafted through the partly open shutters and washed over his damp body.

Rolling onto his side, he saw that the light peeking through the slats had faded considerably. He turned back to his beauty and rested his tanned hand on her pale, silken belly. He loved the contrast. "It must be well past six. We should reach Sacramento soon."

Lark's wide, expressive mouth meandered into a smile as she stretched those slender yet shapely arms. The smile broadened, then her eyes took on an impish glint, and she started to giggle.

Her laughter unnerved him a little. She could be wholly unpredictable. "What's so funny?"

She pressed a hand to her mouth and shook her head. "Nothing."

"Tell me."

Her laughter died to a fidgety grin. "I was just thinking how dumb I can be about some things."

"Like what?"

Lark's brows rose, and she rolled her eyes. "Well, you know how animals mate? I thought that's how it was with people, too."

The remark conjured some provocative images, but he decided to play it safe. "I don't know what you mean."

"You know," she singsonged. "A dog mates with a bitch. Then, his goal achieved, he trots on down the road."

"So?"

She lowered her gaze to his shoulder and scooted closer in what seemed to be a shy effort to hide her nakedness. She curled her finger around some hairs on his chest. "You know."

Pierce lifted her chin. "No, I don't."

"Well, you made love with me over and over. I just never knew it would be so . . . so . . ." Her voice dropped to a whisper. "Now I know why young married couples smile all the time."

Chuckling, Pierce wrapped his arms around her. "I aim to please."

"Then why did we make love only once last night?"

Taken aback, Pierce stared at her, then pressed his lips to her forehead. "You bade me good night. If you were tired, I didn't want to force myself on you. I only wanted to do whatever would make you happy."

The ship's bell began a loud clanging, and the constant hubbub of voices on the deck grew more excited.

Pierce groaned and sat up. "We'd better get dressed. We'll be landing in a few minutes."

Lark sat up behind him, her breath tickling his neck,

the tips of her breasts teasing his back. "Do we have to?"

The woman was insatiable. And he loved it. But they'd run out of time. "'Fraid so, sweetheart."

She slid her hands over his shoulders. "I'm sure the purser wouldn't mind of we just stayed on in the same cabin."

"That's not possible." He turned to face her. "As greedy as our captain is, they'll be unloading, reloading, and cleaning all tonight. This ship leaves again for San Francisco at first light."

"The sooner the better. We've already lost precious time." She spoke as if they were returning with the *Senator.*

"Lark, I thought you'd accepted the fact that we're going on to Hangtown to retrieve my horse and see that thief Blackwell punished."

Her eyes sharpened along with her tone. "But you said— I thought— You said you wanted to please me. And I have to go after Papa. After all the other messes he's gotten himself into, I don't know what he'll do if he thinks he deserted me, too."

"When are you going to stop feeling responsible for him?" Pierce took hold of her arms. "He's the parent, not you. And, besides, we sent him several letters. One of them's bound to reach him. And, as you recall, I saw to it that you told him in the letter that you were married to me and being well cared for."

Lark shrugged away from him, then leapt off the bed. "You don't *know* if he'll get my letter before he finds out I'm missing. We have to go back." She snatched her ruffle-trimmed drawers from off her trunk and thrust in a leg.

He sprang to his feet. "Forget it!"

Pulling up her underdrawers, she met his challenge. "Just because you cared nothing for your father doesn't mean I should forget mine. I'm going, with or without you."

Pierce was beginning to feel entirely too naked himself. He lifted his own underwear from a wall hook. "I'm not spending another penny to chase after him. Your father's not fit to—"

"*My father's not fit?*" Lark scooped up her chemise and wiggled into it. "I'll have you know he's a far better father than some low-life gambler could ever be. And as for my baby—"

"At least I don't lie and steal," he grated, rage exploding inside his head. The hellcat had hookwinked him again, this time by using her body. He stalked toward her. "And I don't prostitute myself to get what I want, either."

Lark slapped him hard.

Instinctively he swung back a fist, then stopped himself before delivering the blow. He couldn't hit that face. And no matter what else she was, she carried his child.

Unflinching, she stood her ground. "How dare you say that to me after we . . . we . . ." Her gaze wavered.

Shaky himself, he turned away and plucked the trousers off his trunk. He rammed in a foot. "Hurry up and finish dressing. I need to beat all these yahoos to the stage office or all the seats on the next coach to Hangtown will be gone."

"Don't waste your money buying me a ticket."

"Oh, you're going all right."

"We'll see about that."

Pierce chose to ignore her last remark. He had no

doubt who would be the victor. And if she had any sense, neither did she. He lifted his shirt off the bedpost and put it on.

Lark stepped into her loosely laced corset and pulled it up, grumbling something he couldn't make out.

A grin stole across his face, and he turned away to hide it. If nothing else could keep her in line, that whalebone contraption surely would.

His shirt and boots on, Pierce raised his trunk lid. Shoving aside his fool straw hat, he lifted out the pistol and holster he'd won in a card game the afternoon before. He swung the weighty gun belt around his hips and buckled it, then adjusted the slant so that his palm met the gun butt with ease. Testing his speed, he dropped his hand, then went for the revolver. He drew it less swiftly than he would've preferred. He needed to practice.

"Where did you get that awful thing?"

Holstering the weapon, Pierce turned to meet her scowling face. "Where I get everything else. I won it off some young idiot. I doubt he'll miss it, though, since he still had a matching belt strapped on as well as another six-shooter stuffed in his waistband to keep his knife company. You would've thought he was going off to war—him and everyone else in this country."

"So you have to do it, too," she sniped while still struggling with the upper laces of her corset. "In Oregon a man could—"

"This isn't Oregon. Here, let me help you. At the rate you're going, we'll be here all night."

"Well," she retorted, turning her back to him, "if I didn't have to wear this damned thing—"

"*Damn*, you say?" He hooked his fingers into the loose lacings. "And from *such a lady*."

She jerked forward, unintentionally aiding Pierce's efforts. She gasped. "*Not so tight.* And as for my coarse language, I think it suits my new profession."

Pierce couldn't help smiling. Or admiring the delicate lines of her bare neck and shoulders. "You're probably right." He finished pulling the corset together and tied it, then couldn't resist patting her cute behind.

"Stop that!" She spun around, glaring.

He pretended not to notice. One thing was for sure, life with her was always exciting. "Hurry up. Sacramento's waiting for us."

Georgie had lain beside the bully for hours in their stark room at Carpenter's Hotel, waiting for him to fall into a deep slumber. She'd almost drifted off a time or two herself. But at last he inhaled deep, even, *safe* breaths. Slowly and with stealth, she eased herself off the bed and tiptoed across the bare floor to the opposite wall where she'd hung her clothing. Gingerly, she lifted her dress off a hook and dropped it over her head.

The bedsprings squeaked.

She froze. Listened. Then heard Pierce's steady breathing again. Satisfied he still slept, she slipped her arms into the sleeves, then smoothed the ribbon-trimmed print muslin over her chemise. She smiled, recalling how her *clever* husband had outsmarted himself when he left their trunks at the stage station to be loaded for their early morning departure for Hangtown. She'd been *forced* to sleep in her underclothes. And as for the blasted corset and petticoats, he could keep them or eat them for breakfast for all she cared.

Reaching behind her, she fastened enough buttons to hold her dress together, then felt around the darkness-shrouded floor with her foot until she located her shoes and stockings. As she picked them up, her face brushed against Pierce's coat hanging above her, and she remembered the money.

Georgie felt a twinge of guilt.

Then, reminding herself how he'd dragged her off the boat and all over town the evening before, she squelched her conscience. She reached into his inner pocket and filched several bills, then shoved them into one of her shoes.

She cast a derisive glance at the barricaded entrance—as if some heavy chest of drawers shoved in front of the door would stop her—then headed back past the foot of the bed, her eyes never leaving Pierce's unmoving figure until she reached the window. It stood wide open to catch the breeze . . . and looked out over the veranda roof. She lifted a leg over the sill, and it landed with ease on the corrugated tin roof.

Taking a last look at Pierce, she felt an achy heaviness in her chest. She had no doubt that in the years to come she would never regret another loss as much. If only . . . Sighing, she bent low and climbed out onto the steeply slanted roof and into a balmy moonlit night.

Hanging on to the wall, she took a tentative step forward.

The tin popped beneath her foot.

Georgie ducked down on her hands and knees, then stretched out on her belly, as much to spread her weight as to hide. She waited, but heard nothing except her own pulse pounding in her ears. Holding her shoes aloft, she began to slither down the slope, sure that at any second she'd hear the clatter of Pierce's pursuing footsteps.

She didn't, thank goodness.

Reaching the lower edge of the veranda roof, she peeked over.

Heavens! The ground was a good fifteen feet below—
or at least that's how far down it appeared to be in the
dark. If she dropped off from there, she might break a leg
or hurt the baby—she couldn't chance that. She'd have to
find another way down. And fast. Not just Pierce, but any
one of the argonauts in the crowded hotel might wander
to a window and see her.

Georgie started wriggling, feetfirst, up the slant. The
task proved much more difficult than the descent had
been. With every small measure of success, her skirt rose
higher up her legs.

A knee scraped across the edge of a tin strip, and she
very nearly yelped.

She would have to turn around. Slowly she left the
relative safety of the grooves, and worked her way across
the tops of the smooth humps where the chance of sliding
off was far greater, especially since her hands were
occupied with her shoes. Finally, when she faced the
building, she shot a quick glance up at Pierce's window.
No one there. Her luck still held . . . for the moment.
But she simply had to think of another way off.

Then it occurred to her: She could climb in through
someone else's window and sneak out their door. She
could've kicked herself. If she had thought of it sooner,
she could've been out on the street already.

She scooted sideways across the rows of ridges for
several yards, then made the laborious crawl up to the
second-story wall. The window just above her was open
wide, due, undoubtedly, to the balmy night. She rose up
and peeked over the sill.

A raucous chorus of snores from at least three men
greeted her. How any of them could sleep, she'd never
know, but she thanked her lucky stars they did.

After carefully transferring both shoes to one hand,

she used the free one to feel around the interior of the room—it wouldn't do to climb inside and land on someone's stomach. Almost satisfied, she stuck her right foot inside and carefully swung it across the floor. The space appeared to be clear of obstacles. Steeling herself with a big gulp of air, she ducked her head inside and started to pull in her left leg.

Something outside the window gripped her left ankle and jerked hard. She swallowed a scream and slapped at her captor.

Another hand caught her arm and pulled her back out onto the roof.

She banged her head on the window frame and almost dropped her shoes.

But that didn't slow the bully as he yanked her close to him. "Out for a stroll?" Pierce's sarcasm rode out on a harsh whisper.

Taking a tighter hold on her shoes, Georgie had the strongest urge to hit him. But she was standing on a slanted tin roof! Oh, what the heck! She rammed the toes of her leather shoes into his belly.

He grunted and stumbled back.

Her shoes went flying.

Pierce lost his footing and crashed onto his rear, but the rat still hung on to her.

Splatting down on top of him, she heard a number of additional bumps and bangs before her shoes disappeared over the edge of the veranda roof.

And beneath her, Pierce was sliding.

She clung desperately to him.

Holding her snugly, he wedged his feet into crevices, stopping their descent, and they came to a halt, thanks to his quick thinking. But not before they'd slipped halfway down.

"Who's out there?" came a gravelly voice from one of the windows.

"I got 'em in me sights," yelled another.

Pierce was breathing in jerky bursts, and one of his hands had inched dangerously close to her throat, so Georgie thought it best to try to smooth things over. "Sorry," she called. "I was sleepwalking, and my dear husband came out here to save me."

"You expect us to believe that?" returned another of the many shadows leaning out the row of windows.

"You'd be a fool if you did," Pierce bellowed in return. "My wife couldn't tell the truth if her life depended on it. She stole my money and was trying to sneak out on me."

"Your wife, you say?" someone hollered, his voice close to laughter.

"'Fraid so." Pierce sounded almost nonchalant, almost calm.

Their audience guffawed like the coarse fellows they undoubtedly were.

But at least Pierce's hand had stopped short of her neck, and although her heart still beat like a war drum—which he surely felt, with her pressed against his chest—Georgie experienced a small spark of hope.

"As much as I'd like to toss her off the roof," Pierce continued amid the laughter, "she's carrying my child. So if one of you would throw us a rope, I'd appreciate it."

"Sure, be right with ya," called a man with an unmistakable Kentucky twang.

A match flared inside the room as someone lit a lamp. Seconds later a shirtless, bearded man returned to the window with the light. Another joined him and tossed a length of line to them.

Quick as a flash, Pierce snatched it out of the air, again demonstrating a strength and agility that Georgie had, till now, taken for granted.

"Got it?" asked the man.

"Yeah. Keep it taut." Winding it around his wrist, Pierce rose to his feet, hauling Georgie up with him. "Grab the rope and work your way up it," he ordered.

Georgie, who prided herself on her own agility, had no problem complying. Soon she and Pierce both reached the window and the several leering men whose disrespectful eyes roved over her. "Thank you," she mumbled as she released the rope and hurriedly edged along the outside wall toward her own room next door.

"Looks like you got a handful there," called one of the gapers, hanging out the open window just beyond hers.

"That I do," Pierce answered from close behind.

"'Twill teach ye to marry up wi' a redhead." The Scottish burr came from somewhere behind them and sent the jackasses into another round of hee-hawing and hooting.

Fervently wishing she had a hefty handful of stones to sling, Georgie reached her room and crawled inside and out of their sight. Then, remembering her shoes, she whirled back to Pierce, who was having trouble wedging his much larger frame through. "My shoes. The money's in them."

Both feet now on the floor, he straightened. With the faint moonlight behind him, Georgie saw his silhouetted hands as he repeatedly clenched and unclenched them. After several long seconds he spoke in a weary voice. "By all means, the shoes." He stalked to the door and, putting his shoulder to the big chest of drawers, shoved it aside, caring not a whit how much it squawked as it scraped across the floor. Flinging open the door, he spread an arm in a grand gesture. "After you, m'lady."

Giving him as wide a berth as possible, Georgie hurried into the dimly glowing hall.

She hadn't taken more than two steps before he caught her arm and, holding it uncomfortably tight, steered her toward the stairs.

Georgie glanced up at his face and read the barely contained violence in the thin line of his mouth, the knotted muscles in his jaw. She just might have pushed him too far this time. Maybe an apology would help . . . a little anyway. They reached the head of the staircase, and she opened her mouth to speak, then snapped it shut. The rat had his clothes on!

Georgie latched on to the banister and halted. "You're dressed! You knew I was out there all the time. You left me to crawl around on that slick tin, scraping up my knees, almost getting myself killed, while you were inside leisurely buckling your belt."

"Yeah," Pierce drawled, his mouth sliding into a one-sided grin. "And you were more fun to watch than a colt drunk on sour mash."

Chapter
Twenty-two

FOR OUT-AND-OUT physical misery, only Georgie's seasickness could possibly have surpassed what the stage driver had blithely called "hell-bent for Hangtown." The first leg of the journey through the countryside at breakneck speed was bad, but it couldn't begin to compare with what she endured after they left the valley floor and started the winding climb into the foothills. Since then, she'd been bounced, bumped, squashed, elbowed, and kneed while being forced to sit as straight as a rod because of her dratted corset. And if that wasn't bad enough, she'd developed a case of heartburn that threatened to turn into nausea. Wedged between Pierce and some bony fellow, she suffered in the oppressive heat. A few times they stopped to change horses, and she could get out to stretch her cramped body, but while the coach was in motion her only relief was the dusty breeze coming through the windows.

The three men seated across from her weren't so lucky. Facing the rear, they caught precious little of the wind. Sweat rolled off their temples and inside the collars of their sturdy cotton shirts. Like almost everyone else she'd encountered since leaving San Francisco, they wore practical clothes, were heavily armed, and seemed oblivious of the discomfort. They talked loud enough to be heard over the creaks and the cracking whip, rumbling wheels, and thundering hooves. On and on they prattled about all the gold they would find and the things they'd spend it on once they'd struck it rich.

She ignored most of the enthusiastic talk by pretending to sleep or by staring out at mile after mile of dry grass shaded only by an occasional oak. Except for a farm or two, the steady stream of freight wagons they passed in the uninhabited land provided the only sign of life. Gradually, as they climbed higher into the rolling hills, towering pines joined the sparse greenery, but the evergreens served only to remind her of Oregon, and her spirits plummeted even further.

Pierce, however, seemed quite contented, even if he did contribute very little to the ongoing conversation. But of course he'd gotten his way. Again. Acting like a perfect gentleman throughout the journey, as if he truly thought she deserved his courtesy, he helped her out whenever they stopped to rest or change horses. He also inquired at regular intervals about her comfort. Any onlooker would have thought he truly cared.

But last night he'd shown his true colors. Her own husband calling her a liar in front of all of those buffoons. He had enjoyed every minute of their laughter, of her shame. Well, that made him no more of a gentlemen than she was a lady. He should've called them out, shot everyone of them with that stupid gun he was so proud of.

A whalebone stay jabbed her under the bosom as a coach wheel jounced across another rut.

The desire to reach into her bodice and readjust it was almost irresistible, but after last night, there was no way she'd allow herself to be a laughingstock again.

Never again, she vowed while stretching to ease the

poking, would she put herself in the position of getting caught in a stupid lie. From now on nothing but the truth would come out of her *ladylike* mouth. And Pierce was right—about one thing, anyway: Papa was a grown man, and it was time he started taking responsibility for his own actions. She had enough troubles of her own. And besides, the little life growing within her had to be her first concern. By sliding around on that roof she had endangered the baby. She couldn't, *wouldn't*, do anything so foolish again. Not even for Papa.

"Look!" shouted Deke Mallery, the lanky prospector crowded next to Georgie. "There's a tent. An' another. We must be gettin' close."

The other men craned their necks out the windows as the coach neared the top of a rise dotted with hundreds of tents.

Cresting the hill, the stage raced at full speed down a steep incline, and Georgie couldn't believe the sprawling town that lay before her. Two huge brickyards bordered the road, and although only a sprinkling of tents dotted the outskirts, thousands of cabins and houses filled a broad ravine. Toward the center of the metropolis stood a number of larger buildings with false fronts. The largest building had a name—Empire—printed boldly on its side and stood out from the rest because it was painted stark white.

"One thing's fer sure," bawled the short red-faced man across from Georgie as he settled back into his seat. "I'm gonna be lookin' after myself real good. Any place what calls itself Hangtown sounds downright unhealthy."

"Stick with me, Thayer." The swarthy one next to him patted the pistol in his holster. "I'll watch your back if you watch mine."

"Yeah," Mallery agreed. "An' we gotta do more'n that. From what I was told, the monte dealers are all dishonest, and those Frenchy girls are worse."

The temptation to expose Pierce's profession was almost irresistible as Georgie gave him a sidelong glance that he pretended not to notice. Since he didn't wear the gambler's traditional black coat and brocade vest, the men hadn't guessed that he was a gambler, and he hadn't seen fit to so inform them. As usual.

"I heard," piped up the youngest traveler, who looked barely old enough to shave, "that it ain't even safe to go to the outhouse by yerself." Suddenly aware that a woman was present, the youth, seated across from Pierce, quickly tipped his hat. "Beggin' yer pardon, ma'am. We shouldn't be talkin' 'bout such things in front a y'all."

Mallery broke in. "There's nothing for you to worry about, Mrs. Kingston. The worst cutthroat would never lay a finger on a lady such as you."

Pierce teased Georgie with the same knowing look she'd given him mere seconds before.

She'd show him. From now on she'd be more of a lady than he could keep up with, despite his posturing. She turned away without responding to him or to the unfitting talk of the men.

But they didn't notice. The stage had reached the center of town, and everyone's attention had returned to the windows.

As the road curved downward, they passed between rows of slapped-together cabins that soon gave way to all manner of stores, shops, banks, and saloons, an express company, even a printer's shop—all equally as astounding in this wilderness as the mushrooming of San Francisco.

The stage was forced to slow down considerably to weave its way past lumbering wagons, riders on horseback, and crisscrossing pedestrians—few of whom were female. Georgie had not expected to see many women, but she was astounded by the large number of men lounging on the boardwalk with bottles dangling from their hands. Beside two of these disreputable drifters, an outrageous sign was posted on Mr. Bell's Boomerang, one of the larger gambling houses:

BED FOR THE NIGHT

Crockery Crate with Straw: $7.50
Crockery Crate without Straw: $5.75
Billiard Table: $5.00
Under the Table: $3.00

Georgie wondered if any amount of money would purchase them a room for the night, let alone what she longed for more than anything—one with a soft feather bed.

''Whoa!'' the stage driver yelled from above. Then she heard him slam his boot onto the brake.

The stage rolled to a halt in front of the City Hotel.

While the two passengers who'd ridden on top with the luggage vaulted off the rear, Pierce opened the door and jumped down. ''My dear,'' he said smoothly, and held out his hand.

Rising, Georgie accepted it with a full measure of affected grace and stepped out into the midafternoon sun.

Pierce's hands went to her waist. He swung her away from the coach and set her gently into the shade of a covered boardwalk.

Gripping his shoulders for balance, she couldn't help admiring the muscles that saw little need to flex with the effort. Her wayward mind flashed to what he looked like unclothed . . . until she gradually became aware that she'd forgotten to let go.

But then, he hadn't released her, either. His gaze exuded warmth as he leaned toward her mouth.

She couldn't believe he planned to kiss her. She certainly shouldn't let the bully do that!

Georgie needn't have worried. He veered to an ear and whispered, "Your hat's lopsided."

A flush burned her cheeks. She quickly adjusted the straw bonnet adorned with peach and russet silk flowers. She'd purchased it to complement the dainty flowered print of her muslin dress, not to mention her hair and eyes. Why she'd bothered, she didn't know.

While she smoothed her skirt over her petticoats, Pierce—*his* hat, of course, positioned at just the perfect angle—strode to the stage driver and handed him a coin. "Would you please see that our luggage is placed in the lobby until I've secured accommodations here or elsewhere?"

The big, paunchy man grinned, showing haphazardly arrayed teeth. "Sure thing." He patted his protruding belly. "Then I gotta see about gettin' some vittles in me afore I head out again."

"Thank you. I appreciate it. Is the food in the hotel edible?"

"Wouldn't know. Too expensive for my pocket. But I ain't never heard no complaints."

Turning back, Pierce stopped and stared at a sign beside the front doors.

Curious, Georgie turned to look.

HORSE RACE IN HANGTOWN

SATURDAY, OCTOBER 2

AT 2:00 P.M.

FLIEDNER'S VELVET THUNDER

AGAINST

BLACKWELL'S PEGASUS

Two young men swaggered up to them and stopped between Georgie and the poster. Their guns slung low, they grinned and tipped their rakishly slanted hats.

"Afternoon, ma'am," the shorter, dimple-cheeked one said, emitting the foul odor of whiskey. "A purty thing like you shouldn't be standin' here all alone."

She took a step back.

Undaunted, they closed the space.

"Yeah," a skinny fellow with a pimpled face said as another man approached her from the side. "We're the town welcomin' party, an' we'd be plumb tickled if you'd let us see you safely to your destination."

"That's mighty kind of you," Pierce's proprietorial tone cut in from behind. "But my wife is sufficiently attended."

As one, they swung their attention to him.

Pierce's show-nothing gambler's expression intimidated them. They backed away from Georgie, tipping their hats again, and retreated. But she couldn't help noticing the swift glances they shot at her ringless left hand before drifting into the stream of pedestrians.

Obviously Pierce didn't, either. "As soon as we're settled, we're going to a jewelry store. I'll get a wedding band on that finger." Taking her arm, he started for the hotel entrance.

"Before we do anything, could we please have something cool to drink? A glass of lemonade would be heaven-sent."

Pierce stopped and tilted up her chin. "You're looking even worse than you did an hour ago. Now you've got circles under your eyes, too."

Georgie jerked away, but then, remembering her vow, she spoke in carefully modulated tones. "What a lovely compliment."

"It was a rough trip. Next time I'll hire a buggy, and we'll take it slow."

"I'm not some old woman in her dotage."

"Believe me, no one could ever accuse you of that. But you are with child, and certain adjustments will be necessary." He started forward again, escorting her into a surprisingly opulent lobby.

Red paisley paper covered the walls, and mahogany chairs were upholstered in matching velvet. The usual symbol of elegance, a crystal chandelier, hung from the high paneled ceiling.

"Let's go into the dining room," he continued, guiding her toward the wide archway off the lobby, "and get that drink you wanted. Then we'll order a meal, and while we're waiting for it, I'll register at the desk—that is, if you promise not to try anything foolish while I'm gone."

"If you can get a room with a big comfortable bed, you can count on me not to escape. At least not today."

"Sounds promising."

Georgie looked up and saw an incredibly smug grin. "Well, I wouldn't get my hopes up if I were you. I doubt if there's a room to be had. And even if there is, nothing's going to happen between us, since you're so reluctant to meet my price."

Sure enough, the smile vanished. Without another word, Pierce led her into a large empty dining room decorated much like the lobby. He seated her at a table by a large window overlooking the busy street and then took his own chair.

Almost immediately a short, plump Mexican woman, white apron covering most of her peasant blouse and calico skirt, arrived at their table. Her friendly smile made Georgie feel at home even in these circumstances. "Señor, Señora."

Pierce, too, must've felt her warmth. He relaxed against the spool-backed chair. "My wife and I would like some cool lemonade if you have it."

"*Si, no problema*. Thees ees California. *Un momento*." She turned away and hurried toward a rear door, her skirts all a-bounce from the roll of her round hips.

In less than a minute she returned, breaking into their awkward silence by placing two tall glasses before them. "Anything more you like?"

"Yes," Pierce said. "I know it's well past noon, but could we get something to eat?"

"I have cook fry you steak and some potatoes. No?"

"That would be fine."

While Pierce finished ordering, Georgie took several swallows of the soothing beverage. It settled her stomach and refreshed her, body and spirit. By the time he'd turned toward her and picked up his own glass, she felt equal to anything he might dish out. In fact . . . "Pierce darling, you never did tell me why you're so afraid to take me back to New Orleans."

His eyes turned to ice, and the muscles jumped in his jaws. No doubt she'd pricked a very tender spot. Standing up, he picked up his lemonade and downed it in several fast gulps. "I'll go see about our room. Then I think I'll take a quick walk down to the printshop. Most likely that's where the race announcement was made. Maybe the proprietor knows Blackwell's whereabouts.''

''Even if you find him, do you really think he's simply going to hand Pegasus over to you? Blackwell is dangerous. He's capable of anything.''

''You've always given him more credit than he deserves.''

She gave him a patronizing smile. ''Whatever you say. But don't forget—he *is* the one with the horse's papers.''

''I'm counting on that. And if I bring the authorities with me, he'll have to produce them. I'm sure I'll easily be able to prove he forged my signature. I have a number of other documents with my name on them.''

She waved him off. ''Fine. Looks like you have things—''

At the sound of boisterous laughter, Georgie looked past Pierce to the entrance and saw coming in the same ne'er-do-wells who'd accosted her just moments before.

''I think I'd better stay,'' Pierce said, taking hold of his chair again.

''Don't be silly. They're not going to bother me in here. Go on. The sooner we get this business over, the better.''

Jabbering on about a recent game of blackjack, the three young men didn't so much as glance their way as they took seats at a table across the room.

Pierce remained motionless for several seconds, then stepped next to her. ''This is not their kind of place. They must've seen you through the window. You're the only reason they'd come in here.'' With his back to the men, he pushed aside his gray coat and drew his revolver.

''My God, what are you going to do?'' Georgie whispered frantically.

"Take your napkin off the table and place it on your lap. I'll slip you the gun."

"I don't want it. I don't even know how to shoot."

Ignoring her, he dropped her napkin onto her skirt and slid the weapon beneath it. "If one of them starts to come your way, just casually lay the revolver on the table with the barrel facing them. That'll be enough to keep 'em at bay until I return. I won't be gone more than ten minutes." Without waiting for her objection, he spun on his heel and strode across the polished floor and out of the dining room.

The noisy talk on the other side of the room softened to whispers and giggles punctuated by the squeaking and scraping of their chairs as they moved about.

The heavy gun lying in Georgie's lap only added to her distress. After all, they, too, had weapons. And no doubt they knew how to use them.

The servingwoman returned. Her mouth curled downward when she spotted the newcomers. She approached them with purposeful steps, glancing several times toward the lobby, hoping, Georgie assumed, someone would come and throw them out. She stopped well short of arm's reach. "*Hombres*, what you want?"

"A smile, to begin with," Georgie heard one of them say.

The woman's diminutive form stiffened. Her hands went to her round hips, and Georgie knew she could keep the rowdies in line.

Paying no more heed to them, Georgie picked up her glass and turned to look out the window.

Every few seconds someone either walked, rode, or drove by, looking busy. And the number and variety of establishments staggered the imagination. All these people had come to Hangtown for one reason alone—to get rich off those who lusted after gold. One sign on a saloon even advertised "swimming baths"—whatever that meant.

Pierce came into view, and Georgie's heart fluttered as she watched him cross the packed-dirt street in long strides that bordered on a strut. Wearing his perfectly tailored gray suit and with his jet-black hair catching the sun beneath his rakish hat, he was far and away the handsomest man who had passed her window today . . . or any other day, for that matter. Too bad he was so blasted arrogant. Too bad all he wanted was some phony southern belle instead of a real live woman. And why couldn't he see that she was more, so much more? Why?

Discouragement weighted her heart as she watched him reach the other side of the street, where he stepped onto the boardwalk and stomped the dust from his boots, then headed west with obviously only one thing on his mind—finding that blasted racehorse.

Remembering the nuisances across the room, Georgie took a sip from her glass while sliding a covert glance their way and saw that one of them had produced a deck of cards and was dealing a hand.

Relieved, Georgie returned her attention to the window to watch her dashing husband while he was still hers to watch. He had stopped by a group of men hoisting sacks from a feed store to their wagon.

Another man stepped up uncomfortably close behind Pierce and reached into his pocket. Something flashed in his hand as he brought it forward.

Pierce stiffened, started to turn, then stopped.

Blackwell! Georgie realized it was Blackwell! And he was holding a gun at Pierce's back.

Georgie sprang to her feet.

Her revolver hit the floor with a loud clatter.

Shoving back her chair, she scooped up the gun and ran for the door. Pierce had left her the gun, and now he desperately needed it.

She raced out of the dining room and through the lobby only vaguely hearing the waitress cry, "Señora, your food!" above the banging of her own shoes against the hardwood floor. Just as she reached the door, it swung open, and she crashed into someone entering. The gun fell from her hand and bounced off to the side.

"Pardon me," an older man said, grabbing her while she regained her footing.

"Sorry," she blurted before snatching up the weapon and banging out the door. Picking up her skirts, she sprinted across the street, dodged past a slow wagon, and headed for the feed store.

Men turned to watch her making a spectacle of herself, but she didn't have time to care.

A tall lumbering beer wagon blocked her view.

She wheeled around it to reach the boardwalk.

Pierce and Blackwell were gone!

She ran inside the building, which smelled of barley and oats, past the stacked sacks and barrels, all the way to the back, but she saw nothing.

"May I help you?" the proprietor asked as she shot past him again on her way out.

She halted. "Have you seen a tall good-looking man in a gray suit with an ugly man in black?"

"I don't believe so."

At the entrance, she looked both ways and across the street without success. She peeked into the assay office next door, then raced to the printshop, where Pierce had been headed, and barged inside.

No one was in the front room.

She slammed through a rear door into a room containing cumbersome printing equipment.

Also empty.

Resisting an overwhelming urge to cry, she slumped against a desk, breathing hard. The gun in her hand also bumped into it, reminding her of the urgency. She inhaled deeply, then ran out the way she'd come.

Down the boardwalk she rushed, scanning every curious face, ignoring questions she had no time for, peering inside every establishment until she came to a side street. Devoid of traffic, it curved out of sight behind some houses on the side of the ravine.

Hesitating, she spun around, searching behind her, across the main street, and ahead. Her instinct told her Blackwell had forced Pierce to walk up the lane. "Lord God, let me be right," she called heavenward. Then, taking a tighter grip on the gun and her skirts, she leapt off the boardwalk and flew up the lane.

Rounding the curve, she slowed, praying she would see Pierce, but the deserted road ended a few hundred feet ahead, where the hill grew steeper. Oh, no! She'd been wrong.

A movement from above caught her eye.

At the top of the ridge, Blackwell was pushing Pierce ahead of him and they were disappearing down the other side.

A door slammed to her left, and a young man with a sunburned face came out of a shack toward her. "You look lost. Can I help?"

She felt herself cave in at his offer. "Yes—yes," she sputtered, out of breath. "A man—took my husband at gunpoint—over the hill. He's going to shoot him. I just know it."

"I'll get my gun." He turned toward his cabin again.

"*Thank you*!"

"Don't do it!" yelled someone across the way.

Georgie swung her head to see a figure standing in the shadow of another shanty.

"What?" the first one asked.

"Don't you know an ambush when you see one?"

"No!" she cried. "I'm not lying. You've got to help me!"

"She acts like she's telling the truth," the skinny one said.

"Believe me," Georgie said, looking from one to the other, "I wouldn't lie about something this urgent."

The second man, with small bitter eyes beneath an overhanging brow, stepped into the sunlight wearing only red underclothes. "Think, Clem. If a young lady as beautiful as she is really needed help, every man jack in town would've come up here with her."

"Sure," the other said, "but what if she didn't know—"

"I don't have time for this." Georgie hiked up her skirts and took off again.

"See? I told you," the suspicious one's voice followed after. "And look! She's got a revolver hidden in the folds of her skirt."

She clambered up the dry grass of the hill, which steepened to a slide of loose gravel and shale. After losing her footing, she fell to her knees, scraping the palm of her free hand and the knuckles of the one holding the weapon.

As she neared the top, her dress caught on a bush. She tugged at the prickly brush in frantic frustration and then finally beat down the branches with the barrel of the gun . . . and her recent nightmare flashed before her.

The long pier, Pierce hanging helpless from the battered ship, and the disbelievers who refused to help.

And now she was actually living the nightmare. After years of successfully deceiving folks along the Columbia, then months of lying to Pierce, she had finally told the truth, needing desperately to be believed, but no one would listen.

Was this her punishment? Would Pierce be sacrificed for her sins, here and now, before she had a chance to tell him how much she really did love him?

Chapter
Twenty-three

"THIS IS AS far as I go." Halting on the sandy bottom of a narrow gully, Pierce felt the poke of Blackwell's gun barrel against his spine.

The bastard shoved hard. "I say when we stop."

Pierce held his ground and swiveled until he could see the sallow-skinned man's bulging dark eyes. "I'm not letting you take me out of the town's hearing range. I've only gone along with you this far because you were acting so crazy back there, I thought you might shoot me and get yourself hanged before you regained your senses."

"Turn around!" Blackwell still sounded hysterical. "Start walking." He rammed the weapon into Pierce's back again.

"I'm not alone. Someone knows why I'm here. You can't get away with this."

"I know. I saw you get off the stage. I'll figure out what to do about the woman later."

Pierce's apprehension heightened tenfold. If Blackwell murdered him, he'd have to kill Lark, too. "There's no need for violence. I'm sure we can come to an agreement that will satisfy us both."

"I still can't figure out how the hell you got back here from Hong Kong so soon. *Move*." He jabbed again.

"Look, Blackwell, no damned horse is worth dying over. If you want Pegasus, he's yours. Just give me what I paid for him, and we'll call it even. I'll be perfectly happy just to bet on him."

"Yeah, you're one smooth talker, all right," Blackwell sneered. "Even if I did believe you, I don't have the money. I ain't no rich smartass like you. Don't have no bulgin' pocketbook to bet, just the piddlin' amount I make off'n my harness sales. And what with the high price of everything in this godforsaken country, I barely been able to keep me and that glutton of a horse fed. No, I'm keepin' Pegasus and takin' that wad of money you got to boot. Guess I really oughta thank you for showin' up like you done. *Get going.*"

Pierce knew he was as good as dead. The weasel had been digging a hole in his back with that revolver since he'd first come up behind Pierce. No fancy move on Pierce's part could hope to compete with the man's trigger finger. . . . But to save Lark, he had to try. He started to walk again in feigned obedience, with Blackwell keeping pace. Pierce decided to take a couple more steps, then drop to the ground and roll into him. One. Two. *Now.*

But before he had a chance to act, an explosion from another direction nearly deafened him. A shriek rang in his ears, but he felt nothing except his own wildly pounding heart.

"*What the hell*?" Blackwell's gun barrel scraped across Pierce's back as he swung it away.

Pierce spun around to see Blackwell aiming at a whirl of skirts tumbling down the hill. *Lark!* He slammed his fist down on the man's wrist.

The gun went off as it flew out of Blackwell's hand.

Hearing the bullet ricochet off a rock, Pierce knew it had missed Lark.

Blackwell lunged for the gun.

Pierce leapt on top of him and scrambled for it.

The weasel beat him to it.

Pierce ripped at the clutching fingers.

Blackwell's teeth sank into his wrist.

Bringing up his knee, Pierce slammed it against Blackwell's ear, breaking free of the bite, but losing his grip on the weapon.

Blackwell came up, swinging the gun in his direction.

Pierce blocked it with one arm and smashed a fist into the vile face.

The gun exploded again.

Pierce caught Blackwell's hands and yanked them and the weapon above their heads. More powerful than his opponent, Pierce forced the struggling man's arms off to one side.

Blackwell slammed a knee into Pierce's belly.

He doubled over, losing his grip for just a second—but long enough for Blackwell to turn the barrel in his direction.

The revolver went off.

Pierce felt the bullet breeze past his ear. Spurred to greater strength, he wrestled the gun down toward the ground again.

"Move, Pierce!" Lark cried from directly behind him. "I'll get him!"

"Get back!" he yelled as Blackwell suddenly gave way. Pierce tumbled into the man, and something bashed his head. His vision blurred.

"Oh, my God," came Lark's voice from somewhere in the fog. "I missed."

He shook his head to clear it and found himself on his back with Blackwell standing over him, gun aimed.

Lark leapt onto Blackwell's back, one arm around his neck, the other over his eyes. "Get up, Pierce! Run! I've got him!"

Pierce threw himself to the side, dodging the next bullet, and jumped to his feet as Blackwell clawed at the hand clamped over his face.

"Bitch!" the bastard rasped and batted at her with the revolver.

Pierce grabbed for him.

Blackwell spun away, engulfing Pierce in a swirl of Lark's petticoats.

He caught only the bonnet on Lark's bobbing head. It came off in his hand. He tossed it aside. "Let go of him. You're going to get hurt."

"No!" she cried. "I've got him. You get him from the front."

Blackwell's gun barrel connected with her head. She yelped and lost her hold on his face, but still held on to his neck as he swung toward Pierce, the revolver now gripped in both hands.

Pierce hurled himself at Blackwell's feet.

The bastard stumbled over Pierce, bringing Lark down with him. Her skirts tented over them, blinding Pierce.

"Get off!" he yelled as he scrambled desperately among the flailing arms and legs for the gun. He felt hard steel and grabbed for it, but Blackwell snatched it first.

It went off.

Lark gasped and tumbled away from the struggling pair.

Fear and rage like nothing he'd ever known infused

Pierce. He lunged for Blackwell, caring not where the barrel pointed. Trapping Blackwell's head in both hands, he slammed his knee upward, ramming the bastard's nose into his skull.

A bullet stung Pierce's side as Blackwell sagged in death, but it didn't matter. Nothing mattered but Lark. He wheeled around to her.

She sat in the dirt, alive, thank God, clutching her arm and staring up at him with a smudged face and the widest eyes. "You're—shot!"

"So are you!" He dropped down to his knees and ripped the bloody sleeve away from her wound to find she'd only been grazed. Relief turned him into jelly. With a shaky hand, he pulled out a hanky and pressed it to the gash, then looked fiercely into her face. "Don't you ever do anything like that again. Do you know how close you came to getting killed?" He felt like strangling her, but instead he caught the back of her neck and pulled her to him, breathing in her scent. He kissed the top of her head hard and long. Tears stung his eyes, and he squeezed her tighter. "Don't you ever scare me like that again."

She reared back. "Scare you? It wasn't me Blackwell was taking off into some gully to shoot. If I hadn't seen you through the window, you'd be dead now."

"Not necessarily. I had a plan."

"Criminy sakes! I must be rubbing off on you. That sounds about as dumb as something I'd say."

Her brash Georgie-words caught him off guard, but no more than those lush Lark-lips as they widened into a big grin. Still holding the kerchief to her scratch, he couldn't resist bending to kiss them.

Her smile died, and she swerved away. "What about you? Let me see your wound."

Pierce looked down. "Couldn't be much. It doesn't hurt."

With her free hand she hooked his coat behind his empty holster and untucked his red-splotched shirt. She leaned close. "You're right. Nothing but a little nick. It's already stopped bleeding." Her smile returned. "Blackwell wasn't much of a shot, was he?"

"What in tarnation's going on down there?" The shout came from the ridge.

Looking up, Pierce spotted a man with a grizzled beard, his legs spraddled and a short-barreled rifle resting in the crook of his arm. Two younger men popped up beside him. One looked quite ludicrous with a gun belt strapped on over his red underdrawers. Farther away, another rose into view, then three more.

"What's all the shooting about?" shouted one.

"'Pears like someone got hisself kilt," hollered the older man as he carefully sidestepped down the sheer incline. Partway down, he stopped and picked up a revolver that looked like the one Pierce had given Lark.

Pierce placed her hand over the kerchief he'd pressed to her wound, then rose and helped her up. Keeping one eye on the armed men who were swiftly descending the hill, he picked up her bonnet. Casually he dusted it off, then slipped it onto her head. He tied the beige ribbons while speaking softly. "Let me do the talking. This is too serious a matter for one of your tall tales."

Lark opened her mouth, obviously to object.

With pleading eyes, Pierce placed a finger over her lips, and she relaxed.

As the men converged, each took a close look at the body crumpled on the ground, blood oozing from its face. All turned to Pierce with grim expressions. One toyed menacingly with the hammer of his revolver.

The bearded fellow picked up Blackwell's gun and, shifting a wad of tobacco in his mouth, stared at Pierce. "'Pears to me like ya shot him clean 'tween the eyes. He looks familiar, but I can't quite place him."

"Yeah, he does," agreed the one in the underdrawers. "Me an' Clem shoulda followed the woman on up here. Looks like she and her partner found someone else to bushwhack right quick." His deep-set eyes gravitated from Lark to Pierce.

The other men, guns aimed, stepped closer, shrinking the circle.

"Gentlemen," Pierce said. "You're jumping to the wrong conclusion. This man brought *me* out here and tried to shoot me. *I* was the one who was unarmed."

"You say?" spouted a short New Englander, defiantly expanding his chest. "Then how come 'tis he who has a bullet in his brain?"

"I got a new rope back at the house," the one in baggy red offered.

"He has *not* been shot. Get a doctor. He'll verify what I say. I butted his nose into his skull after he shot my wife."

All eyes turned to Lark.

She pulled the bloodstained cloth from her scratch, and a couple of the men sucked in their breath.

The bearded one spat tobacco juice off to the side, then turned back. "How do we know that's from a bullet? Stick coulda done that. This could all be a setup."

Pierce lifted his shirt, exposing his nick. "He shot at me, too. And you yourself retrieved my gun up on the hill where my wife dropped it. She foolishly came after me, trying to save me from Blackwell."

"Great God!" the short man spewed. "'Tis Mr. Blackwell. They killed the man who brought the horse for Saturday's race."

"Hank, maybe you best climb on outta here and get that rope, after all," the older man said, stroking his beard.

The biggest, brawniest man in the mob slammed his fist into his other hand. "Yeah, you do that. I got my mule-skinnin' wages fer a whole month ridin' on Velvet Thunder."

Lark moved closer to Pierce.

He placed an arm around her. "You men are frightening my wife, and she's already had too much excitement for one day. If you'll check in Blackwell's coat, I'm sure you'll find all the evidence you need to understand why he wanted me dead."

Everyone's attention returned to the body.

"We'll just see about that." Along with another man, the muleteer stooped down beside Blackwell. "What are we searching for?"

"Papers. He stole my racehorse and the bill of sale I received at an auction in Oregon. I've been trying to catch up to him, have him brought to justice. When I arrived today, he saw me first. And I was unarmed."

"This it?" The large, strapping man brought forth a long envelope.

The gray-bearded one took it and pulled out a sheaf of folded papers. He sorted through a number of shipping orders from an eastern harness manufacturer. "Ain't here. . . . Wait . . . here it is!"

Immeasurably relieved, Pierce felt Lark sag against him. Holding her more firmly, he looked beneath the rim of her straw bonnet and saw perspiration beading her forehead. He needed to get this ugly business taken care of posthaste. "If you'll look on the second page, you'll find my name, Pierce Kingston, along with the auctioneer's. And I'm assuming Blackwell wrote his own name below, then forged my signature."

"Yep," the older man said, spitting.

Pierce reached inside his coat and pulled out a purchasing contract. "My signature here should verify what I've said."

"I see. Blackwell didn't do a very good job of it, neither. He forgot the *s* in your name. Where are you stayin'?"

"The City Hotel."

"Good." He turned to a young man with a sunburned face and peeling nose. "Clem, run back to town an' get the law an' the undertaker. Me an' the boys here'll stay an' set things straight. Kingston, why don't you get your missus on outta here? She's lookin' mighty peaked. This ain't no fittin' sight for her."

"I appreciate that." Suddenly realizing that Lark had not spoken since the men arrived, Pierce wondered if she'd finally decided to obey him—for once—or had become too ill to say anything. Not taking a chance, he scooped her up into his arms. "After our roll in the dirt, my wife and I could use a long soak in a tub."

"Yeah," the bearded man said. "''Pears like you got yourself a purty good dustin' there. I'll see to it you get all your papers soon as ever'thing's cleared up. And by the way, in case you don't know, that horse of yours is stabled at the livery on the downwind side of town. You do still plan to race him, don't you?''

"Absolutely. Wouldn't want to disappoint folks."

"And if you want the best bath west of the Mississippi," interjected the muleteer, "go on over to Mr. Bell's Boomerang. His swim baths are a sight better than some piddly little tub the hotel can provide. Ain't that right, boys?''

Nods and grins replaced the hostile expressions of a mob that moments earlier had had lynching in mind. A couple of men raised their brows suggestively.

"Here's your hat," offered the stubby fellow.

"Thanks." Shifting Lark's weight to one arm, Pierce took it. Dirty and smashed in, it looked as bad as his head felt after Lark hit him with the rock. He eased it over the bump on his crown.

Lark tightened her grip on Pierce's neck and scanned the men. She then favored them with a heart-stopping smile that completely overshadowed her smudged and rumpled appearance. "A swim bath sounds truly delightful. I'm sure my husband and I will find it most pleasurable.'' She tilted her head up to him, her long auburn lashes fanning heavenward, teasing him with a sultry gaze. "Isn't that right, darling?''

Even knowing—hell, especially knowing she was toying with him, Pierce felt a tightening in his trousers as he passed between the men.

The others weren't faring much better. Stepping aside, they doffed hats, shuffled their feet, and sighed.

"Afternoon, ma'am."

"See you at the race, ma'am."

"Hope you're feelin' better soon."

Starting up the incline carrying his beauty, Pierce turned back and nodded farewell. As he did, he noticed the fellow with the sunburned face nudge the one in red. "See? I told you she was a real lady. Not no ambushin' liar, like you said."

Pierce choked down a chuckle. If they only knew.

Mr. Bell's swim baths turned out to be half-barrels measuring a good four feet high and at least eight feet across. Three of them, each filled almost to the brim and surrounded by curtains, stood on the enclosed back porch of a sizable gambling hall. Great cast-iron kettles rested on the cold hearth of a huge fireplace set in the long outer wall. Standard-size water barrels lined either side.

In contrast to the heat of the September afternoon, the porch, lighted only by a high window, offered a cavelike coolness. She smiled with gratitude at the attendant as the balding and pockmarked man took their money and handed her and Pierce each a bar of soap, a washcloth, and a towel.

"Ye got the place to yerselves. But take the last tub down," he said, with traces of a British accent. "It'll gi' ye more privacy. And since its early fer me usual customers, I'll keep out any that might happen by, fer the lady's sake." He grinned at Georgie, and his spritely green eyes more than made up for his other flaws.

Georgie returned his smile as Pierce handed the man an extra coin and said, "Thank you. We won't forget your kindness."

"And I thank ye, too, sir," he called after them, as Pierce escorted Georgie to the other end of the porch.

They reached the assigned area and laid their towels on the long bench next to the side wall. Then Pierce drew the canvas curtains around them while Georgie moved next to the huge half-barrel. She dipped in her fingers.

The water running through had just enough warmth not to chill. It couldn't have been more inviting.

After removing her bonnet, she hung it on a hook, then hiked a foot up onto the bench and loosened her shoe lacings. She couldn't wait to get out of her suffocating clothes. She looked up at Pierce as he pulled the last section of tarpaulin closed. "Hurry up. The water's perfect."

Pierce turned around and broke into a smile. He tossed his own hat with practiced expertise onto the hook next to Georgie's and began working loose his black cravat. "I see you're back to your old self again."

Sitting down to kick off her shoes, she eyed him quizzically. "What do you mean?"

"You've been as docile as a lamb since the incident in the gulch." Necktie off, he set to work on his shirt buttons. "It was getting a little scary."

Georgie stood. The coolness of the plank floor soothed her hot feet as she sidled up to him. "Li'l ol' me?" she said in her best southern belle drawl. "How could I possibly scare a great big handsome knight like you?"

He stiffened slightly, his expression becoming suspicious as she twined her arms around his neck and lolled back her head to view him. Then his face slowly relaxed again into the beginnings of a smile.

"You deserve any reward this poor helpless damsel has to offer, after y'all came so valiantly to mah rescue." Drawing back slightly, she eyed him with mocking innocence. "Or," she quipped, "was it the other way around?"

Pierce's expression lost all its humor. He hauled her to him. "I meant what I said before. Don't you ever deliberately put yourself in danger like that again. I couldn't bear it if anything happened to you."

She pushed away. "You mean if anything happened to the baby. Well, you needn't worry. From now on—"

"No," he chided, pulling her to him again. "I mean you. You've not only stolen your crooked little way into my life, you've stolen my heart. And the mystery is, I can't figure out why. You're a lady only when it pleases you to act like one, and you lie at the drop of a hat. But when Blackwell shot you . . . Lark—Georgie . . . You never did say which name you prefer."

"It doesn't matter, as long as you know that I'm both."

"Oh, believe me, nothing about you has escaped my attention. Especially that tender neck of yours." He bent toward it.

She leaned back, dodging his advance, and looked him squarely in the eye. "Then you don't mind being married to me?"

"*Mind*? Not since I finally came to realize it's the Georgie in you that gives Lark her sparkle. And believe me, I know it was the tomboy, not some helpless belle, who came to save me."

Could it be that he actually cared for her? The real her? "Well, maybe I will stay with you for a while. I'm beginning to think you need looking after more than Papa ever did. At least he knows when to run. But you, you really thought you could reason with Blackwell." She shook her head. "You're too danged forthright for your own good. How you ever made a living as a gambler, I'll never know. But enough of this talk, when all that luscious water is waiting for us." She spun around. "Unbutton me. I'm going to die if I don't get out of these clothes soon."

He reached for the fastener at the nape of her neck. "I may be overly forthright, but you always do a fine job of making up for my *failing*. No one would ever accuse you of being too honest."

"Actually, lying could start becoming a problem."

"Start?"

"No, silly. A few hours ago I promised myself I'd never tell another lie. It's too much work trying to keep it all straight. And besides, I hate being laughed at. . . . But now I hope I don't become too dull and boring for you."

Chuckling, he slipped the dress off her shoulders. Then, with shocking tenderness, his lips brushed her back.

A moan escaped her.

He worked his way up. "Impossible," he breathed. His tongue traced her ear as he untied her petticoat strings and shoved her skirts to the floor.

"Wh-what?" she asked, not quite comprehending his words in the midst of his tantalizing overtures. She fumbled for her corset strings.

He replaced her hands with his. "Boring. You could never be boring." The stiff undergarment loosened, and he pushed it down over her hips.

She sighed, stepped out of the heap of clothing, and turned to face him, then saw that he'd gotten only as far as unbuttoning his own shirt. "Hurry up. You've still got most of your clothes on."

He reached for his belt buckle. "Such a bold request! Doth this mean the fair maiden hath a small measure of affection for the gentleman? That you might even find it in your heart to love this low-life gambler just a little?"

Oh, my, he wanted to hear the words. But could she truly trust him enough? He'd never actually said those words himself. "It all depends. How do you feel about me?"

"This from the young lady who just professed she would never lie again?"

"Yes, but this is different."

"I don't see how."

"I could get— You might— Oh, all right. I love you. Satisfied?"

He moved closer and took her face in his hands, the blue in his eyes turning dark as midnight. "Tell me again," he murmured, only inches from her mouth.

The pulse at her temples banged against his fingers. She knew he could feel it, could tell how enormously he affected her. Her mouth went dry.

He continued to wait.

"I love you." The words came out on a tremulous whisper.

He exhaled, and she realized he'd been holding his breath. "I love you, too." His gaze roved over her face. "I love your eyes, the color of your hair. More than anything, I love the fact that you're carrying my baby."

Georgie stiffened and stepped out of his hold. "How could I have been such a fool? The baby is what you really care about. If you'd ever cared about me one bit, you would've taken me back home. You knew how urgently I needed to go."

His stare turned cold. "I told you, I *will not* go back there. And with a baby on the way, I'm even more determined to stay away from Louisiana."

Georgie snatched up her dress to put it on again. She'd be damned if she would stay and endure his selfish arrogance one minute longer. He loved her? And she thought *she* was a good liar.

Pierce grabbed her arm and whirled her to him. "All right. You win. I had hoped I'd never have to tell you this, but here it is: I'm a bastard."

''You think that's news to me?'' She tried to jerk away, but he seized her other shoulder.

''No. Really. My father was Wilton Chase Lange of Langtree Plantation, north of Baton Rouge.''

''You're a Lange?''

''Let me finish. My mother was his mistress, not his wife. When I was young I had no idea I was illegitimate. I thought my father's long absences were due to business. Then, when I was six, his wife, a daughter of the powerful Moreau family, found out about my mother. To protect me, or himself, my father sent me away to school in Pennsylvania, as I told you. I hated it. Hated being away from my mother. An older boy took pity on me and would write letters to her for me. But she would never let me come home. Said I'd understand, thank her someday. I understood, all right, that day ten years later. The headmaster called me to his office to inform me my father was dead and that his name had not been Kingston after all, but Lange. And his wife, Simone, would no longer pay my expenses.''

''A lot of men have overcome such a start in life, and risen to prominence, for heaven's sake. Surely my father's well-being is worth a few snubs from some prigs.''

Pierce released her, and his eyes became as unreadable as they were the day she met him.

Her hands turned clammy.

Pierce's gaze drifted away. ''There's more.'' The words had an ominous sound. ''I've kept something from you that's far more damaging than anything you've done. Let me finish. When I returned home, I found my mother—this gentle, elegant lady—living in a bordello. She had been there for years, since Simone Lange first learned of her, and that she was . . .'' His words died away.

His mother was a prostitute? How awful for him. ''I'm sure that must have hurt terribly.'' She reached for his hand.

At her touch he drew away. ''I don't blame my mother. In the caste system of the South, it was either that or starve. Even though she was no longer a slave, a beautiful young octoroon is given no other choice.''

''Did you say 'octoroon'?'' Georgie felt the blood drain from her face. Knowing how shocked she must look, she was grateful he didn't turn back to see it.

Instead he continued to stare at the wall as if he expected it to move. ''My father's wife made sure everyone knew that I, too, had Negro blood—no matter how minute the amount. It mattered not that I had the best education and impeccable manners or that my school friends were from the most prestigious eastern families. I was shunned. Forced to take a job dealing cards where my mother worked.''

He chuckled, but there was no humor in the grating sound. ''How the mighty have fallen.''

As his gaze shifted back to Georgie, she did her best to erase her own disturbed expression.

''I tried to get my mother to quit, let me support her. She refused. She said it didn't matter anymore. Didn't matter . . .''

As his voice died away, his skin became so ashen, his suffering so unmistakable, Georgie could hardly bear to witness it.

He sighed and looked away again. ''When I couldn't stand to watch my mother debase herself any longer, I left and started working on the riverboats. At first it was better. The people I met didn't look at me as if they thought I was filth. But then Simone Lange's spies caught up with me and spread the word, made sure I was put back in my place. Any young lady who'd taken an interest in me would, of course, be forbidden to speak to me. And no matter how far north I went, some hireling of hers would eventually find me, make certain I didn't contaminate any unsuspecting souls. Yesterday I was clean. Today I'm filth . . . something to be wiped off the feet of polite society.

''But despite all Simone Lange's efforts, a few enterprising businessmen felt it was worth the risk to let me invest with them. You see, I'd garnered a lot of valuable knowledge about eastern business practices during my years in Philadelphia. When I'd finally accumulated enough capital to leave all the vindictiveness and mendacity behind, I vowed never to return.''

As he turned back to her, the lines of bitterness marring his aristocratic features smoothed. ''And with my child's future at stake, my pledge, if anything, is doubled. My only regret is that my mother refused to come with me.'' He exhaled heavily. ''So now you know. After the baby's born, you're free to return to Louisiana and all it stands for. I won't stop you. But you will not take my child. I won't take a chance on having it subjected to such cruelty.''

She was married to the son of a freed slave. A man with Negro blood. Georgie knew that as a daughter of the South she should be appalled. Yet how different was he, really, from the man he'd been five minutes ago? He was still the same person with whom she'd fallen in love. He had the same body, mind, and spirit. And didn't her heart do flip-flops at the mere thought of him making love to her?

Was that how her mother had felt when she, the

daughter of a staunch Presbyterian New Englander, ran away with a Catholic French swamp rat? Grandfather Winston had never forgiven her, never accepted her union with one he considered a heathen, dirt beneath their feet. But had Papa been any less lovable because he was a Catholic Cajun instead of a Protestant Scot? Mommy couldn't have loved him any more, even with all his failings. And he'd absolutely worshiped her, in spite of her straightlaced ways till the day she died. There'd been no recriminations, no regrets.

Finding the courage now to look Pierce in the eye, she found him staring at a shirt button as he aimlessly fiddled with it. His features were slack, and he looked painfully defeated. He obviously expected to be rejected.

After all they'd been through together, how could he think her incapable of looking beyond ugly prejudices? Did he really believe her love for him was that puny? That fickle?

Well, she would let that question pass. For now. ''Hurry up and get undressed. The attendant gave us only one hour, you know.'' Georgie removed her chemise. Then, after tossing the last of her clothing onto the bench, she noticed that Pierce was just standing there staring at her.

''That's all you have to say?'' he asked. '''Hurry up and get undressed'? After what I just told you?''

''If you had told me yesterday—or better yet, last week—we would already be in the tub. Now, take your danged boots off.'' She reached up and tugged his shirt from his arms and shoved him toward the bench.

As he dropped down on it with the dumbest expression, Georgie stepped onto a stool next to the giant half-barrel and dived over the rim into heavenlike liquid silk. As it drew the fatiguing heat from her body, she also felt any niggling doubts float away as she remembered his kindness to the jockey. She also now knew why he'd offered to buy the "virgin" in San Francisco.

The deepest compassion for Pierce poured into her, filling her whole being. She fully understood why he would never go back to Louisiana. He couldn't return there. And she would never dream of exposing their child to the strangling prejudices of that old world. Not with the freedom of the West awaiting them. Out here Pierce would be judged by his deeds rather than his heritage. And as far as she was concerned, his mother's sacrificial courage far outweighed his cowardly father's betrayal.

Yes, from this second on, she would make up for all the sorrow and shame he'd endured. She would love it all away.

Smiling at her last thought, Georgie swam back to the edge of the barrel and peeked over the rim.

He had removed his boots and socks, so she watched him shuck the remainder of his attire and rise, displaying every lean, masculine inch.

"Did I ever mention," she said, snapping his attention to her, "that I think you're even more handsome without your clothes?"

He didn't smile, but his eyes told her he was pleased as he came toward her. "No, I don't believe we've ever discussed my looks."

She came to her feet, and water sheeted from her own endowments. "What a dreadful oversight. Come join me, and I'll tell you all about it."

He still didn't smile as he climbed in, and his expression hardened—definitely not the reaction she'd expected. "First, I have to know. Can you stay married to me? Can you love the bastard son of a betraying adulterer and a . . . and my mother?"

Georgie moved through the water to him. Stopping within inches, she ran her cool wet fingers along his much warmer jaw. "Of course. Absolutely. Till death do us part. And besides, if anyone's getting the worst of the bargain, it's you. Your so-called flaw is not even of your making. But you, you've got Louie Pacquing's smart-mouthed tomboy to keep up with. Now, if you think you can handle that, kiss me, fool, till I faint."

Pierce complied with astonishing swiftness, his mouth plundering hers, ravaging her as his arms captured her and held her against his hot chest. His hands rode her curves as he wrapped a leg around hers and hugged her to his growing arousal. His heart pounded hard and fast against her breast.

Her own heart raced even faster, sending a sweet agonizing hunger rushing to every inch of skin touching his. The pulse in her throat sent throb after throb down to her nether region as she raked her fingers through his hair.

The kiss deepened, his lips, his tongue finding new ways to excite her senses until she knew if she didn't slow her breathing, she truly would faint.

Panting shamelessly, she broke away and warded him off with a straight arm. "I think . . . maybe we should . . . slow down a bit."

"I'm sorry. I was too rough. I'm just so happy." He opened his arms. "Come here. We'll just swim around. Cool off."

As she moved to him, he lay back, taking her over him. Then, with one of his feet bracing them, they floated around the barrel.

"Oh, yes, this is so wonderful," he crooned as he brought her cheek to rest on his chest.

One of her legs fell between his and rubbed against his

hardened manhood. Just the thought of where she intended it to soon be sent a tremor through her body, and
her breathing picked up pace again.

She really needed to think of something else until she
calmed down a bit. She had no intention of fainting on
him now of all times. . . . Think about floating like a
boat. Think about boats. . . . Oh, my goodness, yes.
Boats!

She reached out and caught the barrel rim to stop
them, then dropped to her feet. "Pierce, I have the
greatest idea."

"So do I." With a lazy grin on his face, he lightly ran
the back of one finger down her arm.

"No. Listen. Steamboats. We'll race Pegasus a few
more times. And with the money you've already got, we
should be able to send for plenty of steamboat parts. At
the going rate of passage here in California we'll make a
fortune. We could get more boats. If what we've seen so
far is any indication, cities will be springing up all
around the bays and up the rivers. We could build a
ferrying empire. The Kingston Ferry Company, Limited.
And your mother—it would make her so proud that I
know she'd come. Especially if I sent Papa to talk to her.
Mommy always said he could talk the birds out of the
trees. He's such a charmer. I'll get him to bring her with
him. We *have* to have him of course. When it comes to
steamboats, no one's more capable than Papa."

Pierce's eyes widened, then slammed shut, and he fell
back into the water and sank to the bottom.

Alarmed, Georgie yanked on his arm. "Sweetheart?"

He came up, wagging his head, a slack grin on his
face. "Did you just call me sweetheart?"

"I don't know. I think so, but that's beside the point.
How many races do you think it'll take to get all the

money we need? I want to write Papa as soon as possible.''

Pierce drew her to him. ''I guess there's only one way to shut you up.'' He descended toward her mouth.

She blocked him. ''But what about my plan?''

''My horse farm and steamboats?''

Taking his face in her hands, she nodded eagerly. ''Yes. Let's do it.''

He groaned. ''Tomorrow. We'll write your father tomorrow. Now, come here.'' He cupped her bottom with both hands and lifted her up to him. ''I've got some plans of my own you're really going to like.''

Her passion was instantly rekindled at just the idea of where his plans might take them in this cool, caressing water. She wrapped her legs around him and, eyeing that tender spot just above his collarbone, circled it with her tongue.

With a moan coming from deep within his chest, he reached for her mouth, and she had no doubt he would make good on this promise, too.

After all, her Pierce never lied.

Dear Reader,

As a fledgling author, I'd be most grateful for any of your comments expressing your opinion of *River Temptress*. You may send your note directly to me at: 66-365 W. 5th Street, Desert Hot Springs, CA 92240.

I'll do my best to answer each and every letter. A self-addressed, stamped envelope would be appreciated.

Thank you so much,

Elaine Crawford

Diamond Wildflower Romance

A breathtaking new line of spectacular novels set in the untamed frontier of the American West. Every month, Diamond Wildflower brings you new adventures where passionate men and women dare to embrace their boldest dreams. Finally, romances that capture the very spirit and passion of the wild frontier.

__**COLORADO TEMPEST** *by Mary Lou Rich*
  1-55773-799-1/$4.99

__**GOLDEN FURY** *by Deborah James*
  1-55773-811-4/$4.99

__**DESERT FLAME** *by Anne Harmon*
  1-55773-824-6/$4.99

__**BANDIT'S KISS** *by Mary Lou Rich*
  1-55773-842-4/$4.99

__**AUTUMN BLAZE** *by Samantha Harte*
  1-55773-853-X/$4.99

__**RIVER TEMPTRESS** *by Elaine Crawford*
  ¹ 55773-867-X/$4.99

__**WYOMING WILDFIRE** *by Anne Harmon*
  1-55773-883-1/$4.99 (April 1993)

__**GUNMAN'S LADY** *by Catherine Palmer*
  1-55773-893-9/$4.99 (May 1993)

For Visa, MasterCard and American Express orders ($15 minimum) call: 1-800-631-8571

FOR MAIL ORDERS: CHECK BOOK(S). FILL OUT COUPON. SEND TO:

BERKLEY PUBLISHING GROUP
390 Murray Hill Pkwy., Dept. B
East Rutherford, NJ 07073

NAME_____

ADDRESS _____

CITY_____

STATE_____ ZIP_____

PLEASE ALLOW 6 WEEKS FOR DELIVERY.
PRICES ARE SUBJECT TO CHANGE WITHOUT NOTICE.

POSTAGE AND HANDLING:
$1.75 for one book, 75¢ for each additional. Do not exceed $5.50.

BOOK TOTAL $ ____

POSTAGE & HANDLING $ ____

APPLICABLE SALES TAX $ ____
(CA, NJ, NY, PA)

TOTAL AMOUNT DUE $ ____

PAYABLE IN US FUNDS.
(No cash orders accepted.)

If you enjoyed this book, take advantage of this special offer. Subscribe now and...

Get a Historical

No Obligation

If you enjoy reading the very best in historical romantic fiction...romances that set back the hands of time to those by-gone days with strong virile heros and passionate heroines ...then you'll want to subscribe to the True Value Historical Romance Home Subscription Service. Now that you have read one of the best historical romances around today, we're sure you'll want more of the same fiery passion, intimate romance and historical settings that set these books apart from all others.

Each month the editors of True Value select the four *very best* novels from America's leading publishers of romantic fiction. We have made arrangements for you to preview them in your home *Free* for 10 days. And with the first four books you receive, we'll send you a FREE book as our introductory gift. No Obligation!

FREE HOME DELIVERY

We will send you the four best and newest historical romances as soon as they are published to preview FREE for 10 days (in many cases you may even get them before they arrive in the book stores). If for any reason you decide not to keep them, just return them and owe nothing. But if you like them as much as we think you will, you'll pay just $4.00 each and save at *least* $.50 each off the cover price. (Your savings are *guaranteed* to be at least $2.00 each month.) There is NO postage and handling—or other hidden charges. There are no minimum number of books to buy and you may cancel at any time.

FREE

Romance
(a $4.50 value)

Send in the Coupon Below

To get your FREE historical romance and start saving, fill out the coupon below and mail it today. As soon as we receive it we'll send you your FREE Book along with your first month's selections.

Mail To: **True Value Home Subscription Services, Inc. P.O. Box 5235**
120 Brighton Road, Clifton, New Jersey 07015-5235

YES! I want to start previewing the very best historical romances being published today. Send me my FREE book along with the first month's selections. I understand that I may look them over FREE for 10 days. If I'm not absolutely delighted I may return them and owe nothing. Otherwise I will pay the low price of just $4.00 each: a total $16.00 (at *least* an $18.00 value) and save at least $2.00. Then each month I will receive four brand new novels to preview as soon as they are published for the same low price. I can always return a shipment and I may cancel this subscription at any time with no obligation to buy even a single book. In any event the FREE book is mine to keep regardless.

Name _____

Street Address _____ Apt. No. _____

City _____ State _____ Zip Code _____

Telephone _____

Signature _____
(if under 18 parent or guardian must sign)

Terms and prices subject to change Orders subject
to acceptance by True Value Home Subscription
Services, Inc.

867

AWARD-WINNING AND NATIONAL BESTSELLING AUTHOR

JODI THOMAS

__CHERISH THE DREAM 1-55773-881-5/$4.99
From childhood through nursing school, Katherine and Sarah
were best friends. Now they set out to take all that life had to
offer—and were swept up in the rugged, positively breathtaking
world of two young pilots, men who took to the skies with a bold
spirit. And who dared them to love. (On Sale April 1993)

__THE TENDER TEXAN 1-55773-546-8/$4.95
Anna Meyer dared to walk into a campsite full of Texan cattlemen
and offer one hundred dollars to the man who'd help her forge a
frontier homestead. Chance Wyatt accepted her offer and they
vowed to live together for one year only...until the challenges of the
savage land drew them closer together.

__PRAIRIE SONG 1-55773-657-X/$4.99
Maggie was Texas born and bred. The beautiful Confederate
widow inherited a sprawling house of scandalous secrets. But
more shocking was her newfound desire for a Union Army soldier.

__NORTHERN STAR 1-55773-396-1/$4.50
Hauntingly beautiful Perry McLain was desperate to escape the
cruel, powerful Union Army captain who pursued her, seeking
vengeance for her rebellion. Yet, her vow to save Hunter
Kirkland plunged her deep into enemy territory...and into the
torturous flames of desire.

For Visa, MasterCard and American Express orders ($15 minimum) call: 1-800-631-8571

FOR MAIL ORDERS: CHECK BOOK(S). FILL
OUT COUPON. SEND TO:

BERKLEY PUBLISHING GROUP
390 Murray Hill Pkwy., Dept. B
East Rutherford, NJ 07073

NAME_____

ADDRESS_____

CITY_____

STATE_____ZIP_____

PLEASE ALLOW 6 WEEKS FOR DELIVERY.
PRICES ARE SUBJECT TO CHANGE

POSTAGE AND HANDLING:
$1.75 for one book, 75¢ for each ad-
ditional. Do not exceed $5.50.

BOOK TOTAL	$ ____
POSTAGE & HANDLING	$ ____
APPLICABLE SALES TAX	$ ____
(CA, NJ, NY, PA)	
TOTAL AMOUNT DUE	$ ____

PAYABLE IN US FUNDS.
(No cash orders accepted.)

361